RISING
WOMEN
RISING
TIDES

Here's to Women rising! All the best, Kathleen

RISING WOMEN RISING TIDES

Stories
of
Women,
Water,
and
Wisdom

Kathleen L. Martens

Kathleen L Martens

BYZANTIUM
Sky Press

Byzantium Sky Press
Ellendale, DE, 19941

ISBN 978-1-955872-03-4 (paperback)
ISBN 978-1-955872-04-1 (ebook)

Library of Congress Control Number: 2021919552

First Byzantium Sky Press paperback edition, October 2021

Interior design by Crystal Heidel, Byzantium Sky Press

Manufactured in the United States of America

Body of book is typeset in Adobe Jenson Pro
Decorative Story Title is typeset in Rumba

RISING WOMEN RISING TIDES

Dedication

I'm eternally grateful to Maribeth Fischer, my teacher and Executive Director of the Rehoboth Beach Writers Guild, for ushering me into the world of fiction. The joy that writing brings me has its roots in her challenging lessons and experiments in plot, character, and voice.

Thank you, Maribeth, for my beautiful escape.

Acknowledgments

My thanks to the people who supported my writing process and helped bring my words to print.

Judy Catterton, my teacher and story editor, dedicated endless hours to sharing her incisive insights, and uncanny ability to find my hidden inconsistencies and timeline issues.

Maribeth Fischer, my teacher, brought to life the skills and thrills of experimenting with style and voice in my short stories.

Nancy Powichroski Sherman, my eagle-eyed copyeditor, provided her invaluable feedback and guidance to polish this work.

Kristen Janine Sollée, my daughter and brilliant author, shared her perceptive feedback for my short story endeavors.

My friends and readers, delivered meaningful advice and inspiration as I wrote these diverse works:

Jean Aziz
Sarah Barnett
Christy Briedis
Jane Klein
Kristen Janine Sollée
Judy Jones
Judy Wood

Rehoboth Beach Writers Guild—provided unparalleled support, encouragement, and writing opportunities to me as a member.

Seaside Scribes, the sisterhood of women writers who have been so generous and caring as I pursued my later-in-life venture into writing.

The Publishers, who gave me my start in short stories:

Terry Plowman, Editor, and Publisher, *Delaware Beach Life* magazine, Rehoboth Beach, Delaware

Nancy Day Sakaduski, Founder and Top Cat of *Cat & Mouse Press*, Lewes, Delaware

Rehoboth Beach Writers Guild, publications, *Rehoboth Reimagined* anthology, and member reading events, Rehoboth Beach, Delaware

Steuart Martens, my husband, for his loving support as I pursue my writing projects.

Crystal Heidel, Publisher and Founder of Byzantium Sky Press, delivered her professionalism, personal touch, and outstanding creativity in designing the cover and interior to represent this diverse collection of stories. Being in the hands of a dedicated publisher who is also a gifted designer and writer is an asset to any author.

The Women, Water, and Wisdom Stories

Streaming Memories

Water. The word alone lures a liquid stream of memories. It seems to flow in and out of all my recollections, murmurs through every crevice of my mind, washes over so many meaningful moments in my life. A constant current. A river of reverie. Am I a water woman? Yes. Always have been.

I can lead you through my passages from childhood to graying gal with that fluid, essential element. Is it the Pisces in me? Although the stories in this volume are fiction, my experiences with water are the threads of truth. If you look carefully, other strands tie these diverse stories together—a common image, word, expression, visual, or voice—but the most powerful theme that connects them is water.

The stories don't reflect my life on land; these tales are not my true memories, but they float on the waters I've known, that bubble up, become real. Just add water.

Water, water, everywhere. Enjoy.

In My World

DEE SWAM AWAY from me. She arched her sleek body and dove down. Rising again, she slapped a goodbye twice with her flukes, washing me in her wake. After three years of pure joy, my aching loss had begun.

I treaded water near the boat where my colleagues had slipped Dee from a canvas sling. This was the way it should be, wasn't it? It was what I'd worked for—to release her into the ocean where she would migrate up and down the East Coast waters and live naturally in the wild with her adopted pod? I could see the dolphin group she would join, circling just a few hundred yards offshore.

Determined not to turn her into a pet, dedicated to protecting her from too much human influence, I'd succeeded in preparing Dee for her new life. But that hadn't stopped the heaviness in my chest. I would never know what had happened to her mother. What tragedy had brought her newborn calf into my life that day? My time with Dee had changed me, made me realize why

I'd spent years studying, just for a chance to make a difference. It was no longer about grades, research, and a graduate degree in marine biology; it was about one tiny orphan dolphin that had stolen my heart.

Exactly three years before that May release day, I'd found the bottlenose calf, gritty yet alive, on the St. Augustine beach, rolling and flapping in the foam with her little pulsing blowhole, and no mother in sight. She couldn't have been more than few hours old. Measuring about four feet, she was an average-size calf, with a visible vestige of her umbilical cord.

Think, think. This isn't a lab pool; this is real, Deborah, I'd told myself. "It's all right little one . . . it's all right."

I'd left my phone in the car to go for my run, was alone on the beach, couldn't call for help. Talking to comfort her, I'd entered the water with my running shoes on. Once I had washed the sand from her body and from around her fearful eyes, she was smooth again with that sleek feel of those special cetacean creatures. Realizing she was too heavy to pick up and not wanting to jeopardize losing her, I'd immediately put one foot on either side of her, bent over, scooted my hands beneath her, and guided her forty-pound body a few feet deeper into the water. Her only chance was for me to walk her two miles along the shore through the calm surf to the rehabilitation center. I'd learned about the challenges of rehabilitating and releasing captive dolphins. Still, I couldn't have known what was ahead—for me, for the calf.

Walking her out a bit deeper, I'd stroked her glossy, rubber-like hide, put my face near the water, and created a signature whistle—a call she would associate with me and eventually try to imitate, a call I hoped would comfort her. It would serve as an essential vocalization we would use to communicate while I rehabilitated her before reintroducing her into the wild again off the Florida coast. *Click click whistle whistle click ah-ah-ah-ah-ah.* I'd made up the inspired and awkward, vocal pattern hoping it would replace her mother's call. So many recorded versions of dolphin-speak from my lab work were fresh in my memory.

Petting her and repeating my signature whistle over and over—as her mother would have done—we'd made progress down the coast. Too young to vocalize, she'd opened and closed her mouth as though telling me about the tragedy that had befallen her.

The sex of the newborn dolphin would be determined at the center, but I somehow knew the calf was female. "I'll call you, Dee." That delightful, perpetual smile on her upturned beak enchanted me. The flattened, lateral crease on her forehead made her look as if she were thinking about her uncertain future. She'd nodded her head in agreement, opened and closed her mouth, at first silently, days later, talking to me, releasing chatters, chirps, and a laugh—I swear. Was this really happening the first week of my internship at the St. Augustine Marine Life Rehabilitation Center?

Floating on my back, I'd kicked with one arm wrapped under her belly, the other stroking her pliable, soon to become firm, dorsal fin as she pushed us along with her flukes. I held her to my chest and, I confess, I fell in love.

Arriving at the center, soaking wet in my running shorts and T-shirt, I called and waved for help with one arm around the dolphin calf. My boss Jim, was amazed that I'd been able to bring the little aquatic mammal so far. The dozen team members opened the nets to the protected, open-water training lagoon, dropped them to prevent her escape, and went into overdrive to save the calf. The adult female dolphins immediately encircled her, vocalizing support.

"She's in good shape. Nice work, Ms. Sheridan."

"Can I work with her, Jim, please?"

"Not our policy with interns, Deborah. You'll be gone in a month, then what?"

I was already so attached, and she was imprinted on me too—an attachment that happens to newborn animals, even to humans if their mothers are not there. I couldn't imagine not helping her survive and find her way back to the tides and tastes of the ocean to join a group of her own. It was a marine biologist's dream challenge.

"What if I stayed and worked for free until she's ready?" I'd blurted out the words before I'd considered the consequences—my fiancé Rob's feelings, our still unsettled wedding plans, and my new job commitment to MERR, the Marine Education Research and Rehabilitation Institute in Lewes, Delaware. I'd forgotten all of that in an instant, but I'd remembered that in the wild, nearly forty percent of newborn dolphins die. And I couldn't forget the look in those flickering, frightened calf's eyes.

My look must have melted Jim's seasoned heart. I could tell by his spreading smile. "New calves nurse for over a year. Five or six times an hour at first. You remember that, right?"

I must have been crazy. I wasn't hearing anything; I was only seeing the calf, thriving in the ocean, leading a natural life.

It just felt so right to me. I was in for the long haul.

"We're talking two, maybe three years of twenty-four-seven until release. Sure you've got this?"

"I can be professional, Jim. I know cetacean cow habits, calves too. I can do this." Honestly, the realities didn't really register at the time, just my instincts.

"OK, Deborah, you've got your chance, but no falling in love with the calf. Could break your heart, you know."

Too late, I should have said. I knew he was right. I'd already learned firsthand what we'd studied in school—it was human instinct to romanticize a relationship with a dolphin, especially a little calf with a permanent smiling face.

I would ensure Dee remained a wild dolphin with her natural instincts intact.

I got started right away. I wore a waterproof, continuous-loop recording device to broadcast my constant signature whistle, mimicking the repetition a dolphin mother would use to bond with her calf. After five days, Dee had imitated my call, pushing the sounds from her complex nasal passages through her blowhole. After one month, she'd created a unique acoustic signal all her own. Dee's imitation of my call was missing a whistle, a click, and an ah-ah. I smiled. So much to understand about the soundings, those acoustic signals that dolphins use to communicate. Or was it an actual language that those bottlenose beauties were speaking? Research had shown a dolphin's whistles may actually be words and sentences. If only I understood them.

If she was to have any chance of being released into her natural

world, I would need to avoid reinforcing behaviors that were enter-
taining to humans or any behaviors unnatural to her. Behaviors
she learned from me that weren't true to dolphins would only have
to be extinguished later. It was a disciplined, fine line for marine
biologists to ride. Stay close, observe, nurture, yet stay detached,
blend in.

I stayed with Dee all day, through that night, and for the next
for six nights. While camping out at the center on a cot, the veteri-
narians checked her and taught me how to feed her. When I offered
her the bottle, her tongue curled around a rubber nipple designed
to replicate her mother's teat. Little finger-like projections on her
tongue locked in like a zipper to keep the milk shake-thick nutrition
from spilling into the water.

I fed her underwater, just as she would have suckled from her
mother, short bursts, as dolphin calves do. Only five-second stints
of voracious nursing and we were off parallel swimming, her body
tucked in close to mine. Then ten minutes later, she'd be back
nursing again. It made me happy to see her begin to swim and toss
seaweed with the other young dolphins. The thought of suckling
her for two to three years kept ticking in the back of my mind.

I couldn't wait to go home to our apartment on the seventh
day to tell my fiancé Rob in person about this miracle in my life.
Dee was feeding well; I had a colleague fill in, but I couldn't leave
her for long.

Rob had just returned from a week away on business. He'd seemed
less than excited on our phone calls, listening politely. I knew once
I explained, he'd be amazed.

He wasn't.

"I know it's a financial sacrifice for us, and we hadn't made our wedding plans." Wasn't Rob the one who'd been delaying our wedding due to his work, saying as long as we're together that's what mattered? "The experience I'll gain could mean a big step up in my career." I tried to find the practical reasons, the justification for my crazy, spontaneous decision.

Rob wasn't buying it. "Deb, do you realize how much money you're turning down not taking the Delaware job? Working for *free*? For God's sake." He turned away from me and looked out our apartment window with his hands on his hips.

"I have some savings and the time will fly. We have our whole lives . . . and you're always on the road anyway, Rob. If we stay here for a few years, you can still keep your sales job. Airports are even closer for you here than they are in Delaware. You complained about that when I got the MERR offer. Didn't you say, being together is what counts?"

He spun around and spat his words at me. "Two to three *years*? You'd jeopardize everything for . . . a *damn* fish?"

"Dolphins are mammals. In my world, Dee's not a damn fish, she's . . ."

"Not in my world, Deb. It's a damn fish." He grabbed my shoulders. "What about *me*? Our wedding, your job? Have you lost your mind?"

"Rob, I thought you understood my work. I thought you said you could do your sales job from anywhere in your region on the East Coast. I thought you would—"

"You thought I would what? No, Deb, you *didn't* think."

The sound of the door slamming after two weeks of unending arguments stunned me. The morning of our breakup, I was shaking, questioning what I'd done. But *a damn fish*—those words made me realize that Rob understood nothing about me at all. Three years together, hearing me talk about my work, my passion, and he knew nothing. Why I'd thrown everything up in the air sky-high like confetti for a *damn fish*, I didn't know. But I was learning things about myself—what I needed.

The day Rob left me, Dee bumped up against my side all day long. Was she sensing my misery? Jim must have too. He went to bat for me and made a call to MERR. They'd have a job for me when I was free, Jim said. I was grateful.

I moved my things into a small apartment near the center and set up my cot in a screened tent by the water's edge. Now I could focus on Dee's rehabilitation.

For the first few months, when I swam, Dee folded in body-to-body beside me and drafted in my slipstream, a behavior essential for a calf to keep up with the pod. Barely eighteen inches longer than her and sixty pounds heavier, I wasn't much help. I laughed. My human speed was slowing Dee down. Even as a baby, her burst speed was five miles per hour. A year into our rehabilitation, she'd accelerated to ten miles per hour. *I* ended up drafting on *her*.

As she grew more powerful, Dee swam with a mature female dolphin who'd been injured by a boat and had lost her calf. While the mother dolphin was being treated for her minor wounds at the Center she'd bonded with Dee. But Dee always circled back to me. How could I stay detached?

I never felt lonely after Rob left. He'd rarely been there for me anyway, I realized. I had so many like-minded colleagues for company, and I'd made a good friend who understood my dilemma. Olivia, a thirty-year-old, experienced marine biologist from England had also found it hard to balance love and her dedication to her work—enough to make her take a job to start over here in Florida. It was good to have a kindred spirit to share ideas about work.

"Deb, I can't believe how well you are doing with Dee." Olivia walked along the edge of the training tank giving me pointers about how to teach Dee to hunt for fish, navigate, and communicate—skills every dolphin would need to survive in the wild.

"Thanks. I wake up every morning so ready to work with her. Is that strange?"

"Who can resist unconditional love and a constant smile?" Olivia laughed.

At the Dolphin Center, we were all philosophically aligned, similarly dedicated marine biologists. We weren't trainers. Dee was never a toy, never on display to visitors—no hoops, no entertainment, no tossing dead fish in the air. There were only dolphins—and humans who tried to be part of the dolphins' natural scene. To be intimate, yet detached, to avoid applying your human instincts became a Zen-like challenge for me. Stay patient, stay calm, clear your mind of expectations and let her thrive.

At three months old she was ready to try to eat fish as a supplement to her milk. First, I hid behind a blind so Dee wouldn't associate me, *the feeder*, with the fish. Starting with dead fish, I fed her underwater through a submerged plastic tube. She ate voraciously. Then I served a combination of dead fish and live. One day, I released a live, shimmering fish from behind the blind. Dee dove, lunged, and caught it. Victory.

I found ways to use Dee's sonar capability to teach her echolocation, as her mother would have—bouncing sounds off objects to identify distance and size was a skill she needed to avoid the deadly propellers of boats and to socialize with other dolphins. I followed all the protocols; she learned fast. Dee did so well during the three years of feeding and training. She was eating fish often and taking milk infrequently. I knew she had the skills to join a pod and survive in the ocean.

"Great work, Deborah." Jim stood by the edge of the lagoon.

"Three years. Unreal, right?" Dee popped up next to me. "I figure another year or two and—" I could see his face said otherwise.

"It's time, Deborah."

"But I still haven't—"

"I'll arrange the release boat next week." He turned to leave. "It's to your credit, you know. Record time."

"Yeah, I know." Dee slipped in front of me and turned over, floating, showing off ribs with a healthy layer of blubber. My throat closed. I ran my hand over her silky belly and looked up at Jim. He understood. Dee flipped over, nudged me, and gave that open-mouthed smile.

It killed me.

A week later, as Dee's glistening body disappeared into the horizon with her new group, she was a mere shadow against the kaleidoscopic early evening sky—the kind of sky that looks like a child's painting, broad brush strokes of rainbow colors. I felt a deep satisfaction and a profound loss. Dragging my feet through the sand, I went home to pack for my job in Lewes, Delaware.

Olivia had painlessly freeze-marked the letter "D" on Dee's dorsal fin. "I'll track her for you, Deb, and keep you advised as to her location. The fisherman along the coast are great at reporting sightings." Olivia handed me a map. "You did a great job. You should be proud. Here, put a pin wherever she's spotted, just so you feel connected."

"Oh, Olivia what a great idea."

Tears were gathering, and my throat was tightening as I got in the cab to the airport. No surprise at the depth of my connection with that little creature. It was like another breakup—in some ways harder than my separation from Rob. Like losing a child. I'd worked hard not to jeopardize Dee's release. I felt good about that and sad about my departure from Florida.

I rented a weathered cedar cottage, silver gray like Dee's gleaming back, in Rehoboth Beach, just a short ride from my job in Lewes rescuing sea turtles and the occasional injured seal or dolphin at MERR. Running the mile-long boardwalk daily after work, I always searched the horizon for dolphins. It was common to see them swimming and emerging amid the swells offshore in the late afternoons.

After two years, no matter how hard or far I ran, whether my feet pounded the boardwalk that paralleled the shore or the wet sand beside the ocean, I couldn't outrun the loss. An unexpected pressure pushed against my eyes now and then when I scanned the water's surface.

Then I received a call from Olivia while I was running one morning. "Dee was spotted just south of Ocean City, Maryland, twenty-three miles down the coast from Rehoboth Beach."

"Oh my God, Olivia, really?"

"Good luck, Deb. So amazing. I hope you spot her. But so great to know she's well and part of a pod again. That was your goal. Congratulations."

"Thanks, I'm overwhelmed." Hugging myself, I could see her wide-open smile in my mind. Those early years with Dee all rushed back. I paced back and forth, but no dolphin sighting. At home, I pushed a pin into my map and slept restlessly that night and the next.

On a blazing, sunny, late afternoon two days later, I saw a pod of dolphins unusually close to shore. They were feeding in the cool water on a bait ball—a school of frenzied fish—the dolphins bobbing, circling, and bursting through the surface, excited by their find. I ran with shivers through the cool June waves and began to swim with the tide. I was a skilled swimmer; I could reach them and get back to shore easily, I thought.

Checking every few strokes, I could see they were still in sight. As I neared them, an unseen current pulled me toward the pod. I was so close, and my instinct took hold at the sight of them. I called out over the water, bubbles tickling my face as I made my signature whistle, *click click whistle whistle click ah-ah-ah-ah-ah*, hoping it would cause some curiosity and draw a few nearer to me. Then it took hold—the rip current I'd ignored.

I swam parallel to the shoreline toward the dolphins to release myself, but the tide pulled me farther out to sea. I was tiring. I knew what to do. I gulped a breath, let go, and let pull of the tide take me. On my back, eyes to the sky, I prayed I would have the strength to swim to shore once outside the rip current.

I dove down to check the movement of the water below. An undercurrent took me fast, tumbled me. I released my breath in spurts of bubbles that rose toward the glittering surface above. The constriction in my chest became unbearable, tighter, threatening an explosive discharge of what little oxygen I had left. I was in trouble. It wasn't the first time I'd lost all judgment when it came to those beautiful creatures.

A powerful thrust. A rogue wave? My head hit a solid object and things went murky. I was disoriented. What could it possibly be? My hands grasped the edge of something unstable—rocking. A wave dunked me under again and I rose up, gasping to fill my lungs with a swallow of briny air. Then I was eye-level with a pair of large feet attached to tanned, muscled legs, connected to a tall, fit body with strong arms, who fought to balance his paddleboard. Looking up at his shocked face, I tried to stop gasping. I couldn't speak.

"Hey, you OK?"

Chest still heaving, I sputtered, "I'm . . . fine."

"*That* was amazing." His square jaw hung open, a swath of dark, wet hair draped across his face. He struggled to level out his board.

"What, me trying to outswim a rip current?" I choked out a laugh.

"Damn, I've never seen anything like it. I'm here, day after day, trying to get close to them like that." He reached out his hand, helped me slide up onto the board, and sat facing me, cross-legged. "Hi. I'm Brian."

Before I could introduce myself, he bolted upright. "He's *back!* Behind you, quick, look."

By the time I looked behind me, there wasn't anything to see, but I felt a slithering under the board and it lifted, like a swell was passing beneath us. Then I heard it, *click whistle click ah-ah-ah.* The sound shot down my spine, electrified me, and Dee lunged up over the board, wanting to be part of the fun.

She circled around us and came to my side, nudging my hand. I burst into tears and laughter at the same time. Dee opened and closed her beak, rapid fire, and gossiped in squeals and whistles through her blowhole, as though telling me everything that had happened since we'd parted.

"Is this for real?" My new paddle boarding friend leaned over. "This is my dream, seriously." Brian ran his hand down Dee's uplifted beak. "Hi, Buddy." Then he looked at me. "What are you, a dolphin whisperer? I'm blown away. Who *are* you?"

I laughed and hugged Dee's head. "Me? Deb. She's named Dee, a female dolphin I worked with in Florida."

"Florida? Hi, Dee. You're too pretty to be called 'Buddy,' right?" Brian stroked Dee's head again. "You've come a long way, pretty dolphin." He smiled at me. "Feel this—she's so smooth."

I laughed. "Yes, I know." I looked into Dee's eyes—so many memories, so much emotion. I wanted to be selfish, cherish a few more moments, but I was filled with my original determined dream—I wanted her to be what she was, a dolphin, in her own world, accepted and thriving in the wild. Had emitting my spontaneous signature whistle ruined my years of hard work?

Nearby, I could see Dee's group dispersing, one by one, two by two, moving northward, leaving the stirring waters as the bait ball was depleted. She backed away, clicking and whistling, half her body suspended above the water. Then Dee submerged, rose up, turned, and dove again.

The last thing I saw was the tracking mark, the letter "D," as she made her second plunge and disappeared. The last thing I heard was her clicking, whistling signature call that had captivated me years before. I tightened my jaw, stopped my instinct—not daring to repeat my own patterned whistle. I couldn't risk her returning to my call, couldn't jeopardize the delicate transition she'd made to bond with her adopted family.

Brian and I both stared in silence, breathing in the balmy salt air, watching the flashes of the slick backs of the dolphins in Dee's pod as they stitched their way up the coast against the vibrant late sky. Facing each other, we straddled the paddleboard and stretched our necks searching for Dee, our bodies rocking left and right with the rolling waves.

We didn't speak until the houses blocked the sinking sun behind us, the shafts of late daylight disappeared, and night had nearly drawn a shade down across the navy-blue chop.

Shifting to his knees, Brian lifted his paddle, then stopped in midair, staring out toward the horizon. "Isn't it the most beautiful thing in the world?"

"It is in my world."

"Mine, too."

And I knew he understood.

The End

First published by Cat & Mouse Press, Lewes DE 19958 in *Beach Life*, Rehoboth Beach Reads series, 2017.
Winner Second Place

Second Place, Delaware Press Association Communications Contest, 2017.

Flight of the Songbird

CORA JEAN JOHNSON had experienced plenty of *firsts* throughout her childhood. Not many of them good. Cramped with her momma in their one-room, third floor walk-up on Columbia Avenue in North Philly, Cora remembered the first time she looked into dead eyes, the first time her cousin got whooped on his way to school, the first time she felt the ache of her empty stomach before Momma got her maid's job at the Nelson's.

There was at least one great *first* in Cora's young life. At twelve-years-old, stretched out on the gleaming hardwood floor doing homework in Momma's small maid's room, Cora had first heard that recording of Billie Holiday crooning through Mrs. Nelson's parlor door. Her mother's employer loved jazz singers, all the greats.

Cora's momma only liked her singing hymns for the Lord with the Zion Baptist Church choir. But, from that day on, Cora didn't mind studying after school at the Nelson's while her momma finished up her workday. That's when Cora would listen to that jazz. Something different happened inside Cora when she sang those tunes. Jazz made her woozy, tingly; it swirled inside and sent chills down her arms. More moving, more stirring than the feeling she had singing anything else. Except, maybe, "Amazing Grace," she thought.

By eighteen, Cora had memorized every line, captured every vocal nuance, for every song that was delivered to her through that crack in those double mahogany doors—Sarah Vaughan, Ella Fitzgerald, Dinah Washington, and her favorite, born right in Philly too, Billie Holiday. Cora loved the spirited church choir harmonies, but when she heard her own smoky, velvet, lone voice, she felt freedom living right inside those jazzy notes—the most beautiful thing she ever felt, with just a little edge of wrong.

Cora had different kinds of *firsts* in the summer of 1959, as the first high school graduate in her entire family—the first time on a long-distance bus, first time out of Philly, first time to the ocean.

Her momma wanted her out of the steaming sweat of the city. Wanted her breathing soft air. Somewhere clean and happy. Like where she was headed by bus for the summer, Rehoboth Beach, Delaware.

With a coy smile and her chin tucked into one raised shoulder, Cora sang Billie Holiday's hit, "I'll Be Seeing You," to her mother at the bus stop in North Philly. It would be Cora's first time away from her. Cora imagined seeing her mother's sweet moon face in every lovely summer day while she was away at her Aunt Edna's, like the lyrics said. She sang the words about all the light and new things she would see that would lift her up from her life in the swelter and relentless threat of the city. Cora swayed with one arm around her mother, the other holding her small satchel of clothes. "Thank you. Thank you. I love you, Momma."

The most surprising graduation gift she could imagine—a bus ticket to a summer with her mother's favorite sister, Edna, who owned a café in Rehoboth Beach. Cost her mother nearly all her savings. Cora would clean rooms at the Henlopen Hotel to earn her keep. The hotel sat right on the boardwalk next to the beach. The thought of putting her feet in the Atlantic Ocean—that *first* alone made Cora smile. She'd go home with a fist full of dollars, too, Aunt Edna had said.

"Don't you be singing that around Sister Edna, Cora. You hear? That jazz music, it's got sin in it. Not the way to use your God-given gift. You ever look at where those women like Billie Holiday end up?" her mother said after Cora let the soothing farewell notes float from her mouth.

She felt the weight of her mother's words on her heart. At her Aunt Edna's hometown, Cora was hoping for another *first*. There was a jazz supper club at the Henlopen Hotel where she would be working. Cora's older cousin had heard them rehearsing through the walls. Hearing those songs *live*, well, that would be beyond any *first*.

And Cora was grateful for some *lasts* too. The last time she would see fear in her mother's eyes as Cora left for school. The last time she would climb the brick steps to do her homework at the Nelson's, to hear her mother's aching sighs, and smell the scent of bleach and that new Lemon Pledge.

A job cleaning for the Nelson's next door neighbor was offered to Cora on graduation day. They were good people. That would make Cora a third-generation maid. It was respectable work, but honestly, Cora wanted more. She knew that's why Momma helped her go away. To buy Cora some time, a chance to see the world outside of Philly.

Cora had no idea where her life would take her. Possibilities had always felt impossible—but she was moving. That was a good feeling; just moving somewhere felt like those elusive possibilities were indeed coming her way. But *what* to dream?

"Behave yourself. Make me proud." Her mother's face ran tears as she waved her handkerchief.

Cora knew where to go. She stepped up onto the bus, and with her head lowered, she walked down the long narrow aisle, passing the rows of white people. Glancing sideways through scratched window after window, Cora memorized her mother's face until she reached her proper seat in the last row.

Fingering the yellow foam through a long slash in the seat, Cora watched the reflection of her own face floating in the glass as the bus traveled along the highway. The sun kept winking at her from between crumbling buildings, then came out full as the towns gave way to highways and onward to endless farm fields with scarred redwood barns. After nearly two hours, Cora knew she must be getting close to Rehoboth. Aunt Edna said she would see lots of cornfields. But they weren't growing too high on that June day. More like fields of green tufts.

How wonderful it would be to sing right out there in those fields in the open air just to let her voice go as loud as she could. To hear her soulful lyrics, carried by the wind to somewhere far off—not like holding back in her little bathroom running the tub water to cover up the sinful tunes, or in the back hallway of her school.

Keeping her eyes cast down as she rode, Cora found herself singing, "God Bless the Child That's Got His Own." Another favorite by Lady Day, Billie's nickname. She sang about the haves and have-nots. Cora wanted to *have*, but what? The space out the window let her breathe, let her thoughts go out a long distance away, about a handsome young man, maybe. A job where she didn't use her hands till they ached or feel the pain in her back like her mother did at the end of each day. Cora respected her mother's hard work that kept them afloat after her Daddy left with her two older brothers. She remembered when Cora's grandmother got her mother a job cleaning beside her at the Nelson's. What else had Cora ever known? Did her momma have any dreams when she was young?

The late afternoon sun flashed through the trees bordering the cornfields like a celebration of her adventure. Cora kept on singing. As the sweet notes floated from her mouth, she felt eyes on her—sky eyes, green eyes, some brown, staring from white faces. A child gripped the back of the seat, frozen, with his blue eyes peeping at her. Keeping her chin down, Cora glanced up again for just a flash. Their looks mostly seemed curious, but a few were unkind. Cora stopped singing. She didn't want trouble.

Cora was the last one to descend the ridged bus stairs onto the main street just a few blocks shy of the boardwalk. Uncrumpling the walking map her auntie had sent, Cora put her back to the scribbled, wavy lines that represented the ocean. She headed in the opposite direction toward the sunset that was dropping fast at the west end of the small beach town. Aunt Edna had said if Cora kept going straight down the main street heading west, where the paved road turned to crushed clam and oyster shells, she would find the Negro section. Her aunt lived in the small white house just beside the church.

Feeling the pull of adventure behind her, Cora stopped. She turned around and walked east toward the water. She just had to see the ocean for the first time—*the* Atlantic Ocean. Aunt Edna wouldn't worry if she was a little late; Cora would walk fast.

She got a few strange looks from white people who were shopping in the rows of stores, waiting in line for ice cream, or sitting in restaurant windows eating along the busy main street, so she hugged the outside of the sidewalk tight-rope-walking the curb. Jim Crow flew far, she thought.

Still, the town seemed gentler than Philly, for sure. People smiling, relaxing.

Reflected in Snyder's candy store window, tall and slender as she was and stylish in her one Sunday blue dress, Cora thought she looked fine. *Older than your years and so pretty*, Momma had said. Well, that was her momma talking, she thought. A sweet aroma was coming from the candy shop door, and Cora took a deep breath of the alluring, sugary scent.

A group of four women who looked a lot like her momma, dressed in bright white and gray maid's uniforms, walked by her toward the boardwalk. Just a few blocks away, according to the map. To be safe, Cora folded in behind them. Something was changing. Maybe her hopes. Hopes that seemed to rise with the salty breeze that lifted the hem of her dress, just as the sidewalk turned into rough wooden boards.

At the end corner was Dolle's saltwater taffy that Aunt Edna said she loved. Cora wanted to buy her aunt's favorite maple walnut, but she didn't know the rules for Negros in the town.

Was there segregation in the stores? Sometimes there were no signs but plenty of rules in Philly. Best not try.

When the women stopped at the edge of the elevated boardwalk to admire the ocean, Cora quickly made her way down the wooden steps to touch the warm sand. She remembered the smell of her mother's ironing while watching TV at Mrs. Nelson's. She was kind to let them watch, Cora thought.

One of the white-uniformed ladies called down to her, "Chile, you alone? Lookin' for the colored's beach? Crow's Nest, they call it." She pointed. "By the big drainage pipe. 'Tween those two rotten ole jetties. See? Just past the big, white Henlopen Hotel up there, where we work. Never mind, you best walk with us."

"Yes, chaperone us to our night shift," another woman joked.

"Thank you, ma'am. Excuse me, but I'm going to be working there, too. Starting tomorrow, I think." Cora came up the stairs and joined the women.

"You'll do just fine if you mind your work and mind your manners."

"Funny, that's what my Momma said when I left home."

"Must be a wise woman, then." The women all shared a laugh.

"Be especially careful with that pretty face and fine figure of yours, young miss."

"That's for sure. Uh-huh."

Cora walked along, listening to the women talk about how easy it was to get a summer job with all the tourists around. "There you go, missy. Just stay in that small beach section, and you'll be fine. You be careful going home, you hear? You have a place to stay, don't you?"

"Yes, ma'am. I'm staying with my Aunt Edna."

"Edna of Edna's Café?"

"Yes, ma'am."

"Love her food. You'll be eating well *and* have a good job. Lucky summer, I'd say."

"Thank you for the help." Everything was so exciting, Cora thought.

Waving goodbye, she walked beside the big drainage pipe in between the jetties to the water's edge, put down her satchel, and took off her shoes. There were just a few people on the beach, and the sun was low, scattering diamonds of light on the ink-blue water. The milky meringue of seafoam sizzled over her feet. It was so hard to leave the rolling sound, the waves arching, then collapsing in a sigh, the calling gulls drifting and dipping overhead. Heaven. Cora breathed in the balmy salt air, leaned back, put her face to the sky, and whispered, "Thank you, Jesus."

Strolling, with shoes and satchel in hand, she walked the boardwalk barefoot to see the Henlopen Hotel where she would work with her cousins. It looked fine. And then the beautiful sounds, faint but familiar, caught up in the summer air and passed on as a gift to her ears. Jazz.

Following the tempting lilt to the hotel's side door, that familiar feeling filled Cora, captivating her, like the seaside rhythmic waves. She knew the song, every word, every note. Leaning her back against the wall around the corner from the door that was leaking the melodic sounds into the evening air, Cora swayed her head.

A warm male voice delivered Sarah Vaughan's melody from inside the hotel. He sang "Misty." Funny to hear a man singing about being a helpless kitten up a tree. Cora looked up at the darkening sky streaked with white fluff. She too, was clinging to a cloud, as the lyrics went.

She didn't know how long she'd stood there enraptured, but the shadows descended around her, and the sun was hanging over the horizon. Still daylight, yet the lights of the hotel blinked on above. Cora sang along; her voice rang out in the alley and echoed back to her. The music stopped, and she heard a door open and close around the corner from her. Then, no sounds. After waiting a few minutes, she resumed her medley, serenading the early evening sky. No stopping, eyes closed, Cora freed her favorite songs stored in her heart, freed them like a fluttering of birds from an opened cage.

"You've got *pipes*, miss." The liquid tenor of a man's voice startled her.

Cora turned to leave.

"Wait, slow down. Excuse me. Hello? I'm just a songbird like you. No harm here. Sammy Farrow, from DC."

"Cora Jean Johnson, Philly." She cautiously shook his hand.

"That's my band in there, Sammy Farrow Quartet. Where'd you learn to let go like that?"

She sized up the gentleman. Kind eyes. Looked like Reverend James in her first church. "Choir at church, I suppose," she said.

He smiled at Cora. "I meant, your *style*? Dead ringer for Sarah Vaughan, *and* Billie *and* Ella . . . Where do you sing *now*?"

"Here. Just started here, Mr. Farrow. Oh, and in school hallways and our small bathroom."

"So we had the same start, huh?" His laugh had a relaxed tone. No sass. He lit a cigarette, drew in, leaving a long, raging, red ash, and blew out slowly from the side of his mouth with one eye half-closed. Pushing his white coattails back, he slipped his left hand in his pocket and leaned against the wall. "So, you play the Henlopen? I've never heard of a Cora . . . oh, I get it. You must use a stage name, huh?"

She smiled and looked out to the ocean, trying to seem older, confident, mature.

"Listen, Miss Cora, there's a full house in there, all decked out for dining, and I'm missing my lead female singer tonight. Getting by with my inferior male vocals, as you heard."

She said nothing.

"Miss Sarah Vaughan sings 'Misty' better than me, don't you think?" He smiled and tilted his head, and his warm laugh escaped again. "Am I too bold to ask? Do you want to sit in? Pay's good."

"*Pays?*"

"Well, maybe not what you're used to in Philly. But it's a supper club so it won't be a very late night."

Cora nodded. It wasn't in her control, that nod. A kind of lie, she knew. Another *first*. She would let herself have this dream. A dream she hadn't known enough to want. Then her mother's words made her stomach twist. "There's sin in that jazz." Cora promised herself she could be good. Would avoid the sin in it. She'd kept herself pure and never got into drugs like her Philly cousins, hadn't she? Momma never gave her much time to get in trouble. But she'd had a drink or two. Cora could handle the challenge, she thought. *I'll let the end justify the means—money and a dream beyond dreams— Momma would be happy in the end*, she thought.

Examining Sammy's formal tails, Cora swiped her hands down her Sunday best dress. Was it nice enough for this fancy place? She stepped back and wrapped her arms around herself.

She just knew the joke would end. Sammy would see her for the young girl she was. She'd be a fool to think . . . And singing in front of all those fancy people?

"By the way, meant to say, you look fine in that blue dress, Miss Cora, just fine for the stage." He seemed sincere.

Another moment of hesitation. This chance would never happen again, she thought. Not in a million years. Cora saw her momma climbing the brick steps to her cleaning job with an aching back, and Cora doing the same. "I happen to be free. When shall we start?"

How did the time get away from her? The sun was setting, and Aunt Edna had expected her for dinner. The walking map was melting in her sweaty hand. Cora was about to turn.

A lean young man, cocoa-skinned like her, but maybe mid-twenties, with the same kind eyes as Mr. Farrow, came out of the heavy metal door. "Hey, man, we're on."

"Jackson, meet Miss Cora." Then his words made it all real. "She's fronting our band for the next set. Why don't you two make a song list that suits her? I'll be right in." He took another long drag.

"Sure, Sammy. Please, this way, Miss." She saw Jackson glance back at Sammy and lift his shoulders.

"Ladies and gentlemen, please welcome to Jazz Night at the Henlopen, all the way from Philly, *Miss Cora*." Sammy gestured for her to move to the big silver microphone. Her name rang out and was swallowed by the applause.

She stared through the nearly blinding spotlight into the ballroom, filled with tables, set with silver, white tablecloths, white faces—men in jackets and ties, ladies in dresses. The scent of luscious food wrapped around her. The fancy and curious audience was smiling at her, politely clapping their hands together. For *her*.

Being on the stage seemed to chase *Jim Crow* away, she thought. Amazing grace.

The room went silent. A few stray voices were hushed by the attentive audience, some leaning forward, setting chins on fists, elbows on the table.

Cora heard the lead-in, closed her eyes, put her moist hand around the silver mic stand, and whispered the opening notes. Her voice was trapped. How could she do it? Maybe it was her lying stealing her voice, like her Momma said. Was that the sin she'd talked about? Lying and sex, drugs and drinking? Cora just wanted to sing.

She'd never sung to a big audience before. Wait, that wasn't true. She imagined being in the front of the choir singing her solo, "O Holy Night," to the congregation on Christmas Eve. Closing her eyes, Cora turned that fancy white club into the Zion Baptist Church—stained glass and all. Then her tight throat opened. It freed. She held onto the notes of an impossibly long time, letting the words *breeeeze* and *treeees* wrap like loving arms around each listener as she sang the soulful tune "Tenderly."

She kept her mind on the soft, salty evening breeze that had sent its quivering breath through the trees that lined the town's main street. Then she was in the open fields. Her voice was going out far into the air as she warbled through a half dozen songs. Again the roar of appreciation.

Cora hung her head in gratitude and tried to breathe.

"Miss Cora, there are no words for you." Jackson was beaming, and she felt a shiver from his warm smile from across the stage. Such sweet, kind eyes.

Indeed, she had no words for the vibration of the thundering applause, the whistles, the hoots, and woo-hoos. The standing ovation at the end of the set was overwhelming, filled her soul, made her hold her breath. The possibility that had seemed an impossibility. The most beautiful thing she ever felt with no edge of wrong.

At the intermission, Jackson handed Cora a Coke and a little plate of tiny sandwiches. "Thought you might be hungry—got you a few finger sandwiches from the kitchen. Miss Cora, you were just smashing out there tonight."

The look in his eyes wasn't something Cora had ever experienced, a tender seriousness she would call it. "Thank you. These are so cute and tiny." She took the plate and searched his eyes again to understand that look.

Smiling, he slid his free hand in his pocket and took a sip of his drink, sending that same look over the rim of the glass right at her. "You are something else, Miss Songbird."

She'd seen teasing eyes, evil eyes, angry eyes, sly eyes, and holy eyes, but never this. She liked it. Dipping her shoulder, she tilted her head and fluttered her lashes in response, like she'd seen in the movies. Something so sweet about this young man. Not like the boys she'd known at home.

"Excuse me, I hate to interrupt—" A woman holding a glass of champagne with blonde hair and the bluest eyes handed Cora her program. "Would you mind signing this? You were just enchanting.

I'll have to come to see you in Philadelphia sometime. Where do you sing?"

"Um . . ." There could be no lying; isn't this where the sins begin? Cora flashed a desperate look at Jackson as she signed the program. An autograph? From me? Holding back a giggle wasn't easy, but now Jackson would see her for who she really was—just a poor girl from Philly.

And she'd never really had a conversation with a white lady before. Not like this. "Ma-am, I'm not performing in Philly at this moment. I—"

"Really? That's so wonderful. I mean, sorry, I wondered if I could introduce you to my husband. We're here on vacation, but . . . well, he's over at the bar . . . I don't usually interfere with his business but in this case—"

Her husband? His business? Cora was confused. Did she do something wrong? The heat in Cora's face raged, and moisture gathered on her top lip. She wiped it quickly with the back of her hand when the woman went on her toes to signal her husband.

A man in a pinstripe suit came to the edge of the stage where Cora and Jackson stood. Jackson swiftly took her plate and glass and stepped aside as Sammy swept in and stood beside Cora. "Mr. Miller, good to see you."

"Sammy, good to see *you*." He shook Sammy's hand, but spoke to Cora. "Phil Miller. Pleasure. I'm sorry, Miss Songbird of the Sea, your name is?"

"Cora Jean Johnson."

"So you've met my wife, Margie? She has good taste when it comes to talent. Look, we're here on vacation, but I would never miss the chance to meet a pro like you."

"Pleasure to meet you. Sir." What was happening?

"Please call me when you're home." He handed her a business card. "I've got a jazz band who needs you in Philly, Miss Cora. Maybe you would consider the opportunity. Do you have an agent?"

"Uh, not at the moment." Cora clenched her jaw to politely keep her laugh inside.

"Then I'd like to discuss representing you."

"Thank you, I'd be interested in discussing it with you." Cora took on the same formality she'd heard in his words. She scanned the crowd clinking their glasses and enjoying their elegant meal. Instead of being bent over housecleaning, the thought of "singing for her supper" sent a feeling through her like the fizz of the champagne in Mrs. Miller's glass.

"Well, we don't want to keep you. Looking forward to your second set, Miss Johnson."

Sammy nodded his approval and pointed his chin at the departing man. "He's *the* man in Philadelphia. Hard to get, Cora. OK, let's knock 'em out, Miss Songbird."

Cora was numb. The second set flashed by as though someone else had taken over her body.

"They want an encore. You up for it, Miss Songbird of the Sea?" Sammy stepped beside her.

Cora whispered her favorite Billie Holiday in his ear.

Sammy winked and tilted the mic. "Ladies and gentlemen, our one and only Songbird of the Sea, Miss Cora Johnson."

Cora stepped up to the mic again. "Thank you . . . so much."

Her voice trembled. Her head lowered. Talking was different from singing. But this time, she wasn't in the church; the audience wasn't the congregation. Cora would sing to the sparkling crowd in the beautifully decorated room.

"Shh! Shh!" A few customers chastised the talkers, and the crowd settled.

The band started poppin' the beat, and Jackson called out, "*Yes, Miss Sister Sea!*" He lifted his horn to his lips.

Looking out at the crowd, Cora had a new feeling inside. A knowing. Singing was her gift; she'd give it. "This is dedicated to Sammy and his trio . . ." Her words were soft like a breeze at first. She looked at Jackson, and then the audience, and caught the eyes of Margie Miller, who rocked her hand in a quick wave. Cora's shyness took flight. "And every one of you fine ladies and gentlemen." *And for you, Momma,* she thought.

Applause encircled her. Then a call came from the audience, "Miss Songbird of the Sea, let's hear it."

She moved the mood from mellow to upbeat and let it out, singing Billie's "T'Aint Nobody's Business If I Do."

The perfect lyrics almost made her laugh out loud. Cora closed her eyes, rocked her shoulders left and right, rolling her happy head side to side. Yes, if she went to church on Sunday, and then sang jazz all Monday . . . "T'Aint Nobody's Business If I Do."

The End

First Published by Cat & Mouse Press, Lewes DE 19958 in *Beach Nights,* Rehoboth Beach Reads series, 2016.
Winner First Place

First Place, Delaware Press Association Communications Contest, 2017.

Second Place, National Federation of Press Women Communications Contest, 2017.

Outrageous Exhibitionist

EDWARD TOOK MY gloved hand and helped me down from our carriage as I gathered my layers of flounces and petticoats. The groom settled our horses, snapped the reins, and took off to leave room for the next arrivals. Sounds of whinnying horses blended with the buzz of excited voices as art-lovers and those wishing to see and be seen gathered on that lovely, summer opening night.

We stood before the Burlington House on Piccadilly, the home of the Royal Academy of Arts. I'd eagerly anticipated this night out in London with my husband to see the latest exhibit. Was there anything I adored more than art—and was there any gallery more prestigious than the Royal Academy? Eighteen fifty-eight, a year to remember. I smiled; I was newly married, and despite the practical aspect of my arranged marriage, I was in love.

"You must feel at home at exhibitions, my dear Frances, coming from such a well-established family of artists. I look forward to seeing portraits by your grandfather, *the* Sir William Beechey."

"It's a family gift it seems. Mother is an impressive miniaturist.

And my aunt—" Well, women's art counted for nothing but a hobby in the London art world, I thought.

"Your father is quite the artist like his own father. He showed me some of his watercolors last Saturday after dinner. They were superb."

Such a proper gentleman, my new husband, secretary to the governor-general of the Hudson's Bay Company. His broad shoulders and tall stature made an average woman like me feel petite and especially feminine. Even my father, an arctic explorer, Royal Navy officer, and respected watercolorist, couldn't help but approve. Coincidentally, Edward's father was also a watercolorist, so my husband understood my passion for painting.

At twenty, I was proud to have a mature and dedicated husband— one who appreciated the arts. Maintaining my upper-class status had always been my mother's dream for me. My friends had no expectation of being in love with their arranged husbands. Still, as a romantic woman, the love of a man like Edward Hopkins was my fantasy.

What was it that caused Edward's perpetual smile—a permanent fixture on his handsome face for the entire two weeks since our wedding? Was it his joy at finding love after the tragic loss of his wife Anne? I harbored no jealousy for his past wife. According to my mother, it seemed I'd cast quite a spell over the charismatic man. He'd entirely fallen for my youthful charms, my beauty, and my art, he'd said to my father when he'd asked for my hand. My new husband vowed he would deny me nothing; I pledged I'd give him everything.

Tonight, something was different. Suited in his Sunday best, his top hat perched jauntily on his head, he stopped and took both my hands. His fading smile caused me concern. "Frances, I have news." He stared off at the mingling crowd awaiting the exhibition's opening. It wasn't like him to avoid my gaze.

"Am I wrong to assume from your expression that I won't welcome this news?"

"Something that might take some adjusting to, darling." He took off his top hat, raked his fingers through his wavy, dark hair, and replaced it. Still, no smile.

I clutched my hands in his. Hadn't I adjusted enough, having willingly taken on three sons from his previous marriage? Of course, I would, those poor children, losing their mother to cholera. And I would give him even more heirs to build a family around him to soothe his heart and give him a loving homelife again.

"The governor-general has assigned me to Hudson's Bay Company office in Lachine, Quebec to save the fading fur trade." His blue eyes again drifted from my scrutiny.

"The fur trade is in *jeopardy?*" I was confused.

"It's essential we have the best local Canadian voyageurs to make better connections with the aboriginals in the wilds who hunt our furs. Our competition with the French and the style change from beaver felt to silk in fashionable hats today are serious threats to our business."

I'd never seen him so serious. Edward went on about the beautiful natural scenery and the canoe trips down the rivers to the spectacular, remote outposts where the aborigines came to trade animal skins. Of course, with the plans to construct the transcontinental railroad, so much would change, he'd said. Edward was at heart, an environmentalist. Contrary to the commercialism that had established his family for generations, he had an affinity for the indigenous peoples and their lives spent so intimately in nature.

I withdrew my hands and straightened the cage crinoline under my skirts to buy time. But Canada? Living in British North America? I could hear my grandmother's words of advice, *Think before you speak, Frances.* Tilting my head down, I adjusted my hat, praying its sweeping brim, ostrich feathers, and blooming silk flower would distract him from noticing my displeasure. Leaving London, our friends, my family? I'd overheard Edward's colleagues describing Canada's canal construction on the wild waters that powered sawmills and flour mills in Lachine. What life would I find there? Had it been Montreal with its arts and culture, that would be change enough, but a lesser town nearly fifteen kilometers away from society?

Edward explained that trains would soon all but eliminate traveling by hand-crafted canoes with French Canadian voyageur guides steering down the treacherous, rugged rivers to access furs. The untouched landscape and the fascinating aboriginal ways would be invaded by modern man as cities grew along the railroad routes. Wildlife would be impacted, as well, I thought. An entire way of life would disappear into the annals of history. I knew that distressed Edward to his core.

"Did you hear what I said, dear?" He rolled his shoulders as if to release tension in his neck.

The gesture made me pause. My good fortune, Edward was a patient man. "Edward, I—" I paused my response as my imagination engaged. Wouldn't I find fascinating subjects for my paintings there, like no other British woman had ever seen? Such a dream— capturing the last days of the Canadian canoe voyageur life in sketches out in the wilds and then to paint them in watercolor and oils at home in my studio. I *would* have a studio in our new home wouldn't I?

"Frances?"

Smiling, I gazed into his eyes. Had I inherited my father's explorer spirit? I fantasized about painting aboriginal hunters—feathers, beads, textures of animal skins, the foamy curls of the rapids gurgling around the canoes. I imagined sketching the rugged Canadian voyageurs who were the link between the aboriginal hunters and the Hudson's Bay Company. All these were compelling and intriguing images for a privileged woman from London.

As a British lady artist in London, my life would be lived in a boring, isolated studio, I thought. Why hadn't I seen that before? Ironic, who would have thought the arrival of the railroad in Canada would bring me such an opportunity? Yes, I would capture scenes of the outdoors in the wilds. A joyous feeling sizzled and swirled throughout my entire body. I determined to happily join my husband on his adventure. Audacity suited me somehow. "Edward, that's *wonderful*. I'm so pleased."

His eyes grew wide. "I'm relieved, darling. Frankly, I . . . I thought you would be disappointed. You realize we'd be gone for the better part of two years . . . maybe longer. So, Frances, you're happy? Despite leaving your family and the arts in London?"

"As long as I'm with you, Edward. And the chance to paint such scenery no British woman artist had seen, let alone exhibited. Isn't it time a woman had equal opportunity in the arts? Isn't that what you always said to me in our most intimate moments?" I nudged his silk cravat, a subtle reminder of my arranging it earlier in the evening—a kindness that had led us to an intimacy that had almost delayed our evening's departure.

"Well, yes, but dear one, the world of British North America, the Canadian wilds and savages is not for a delicate woman— talented with a pencil and paintbrush or not. I hadn't meant to imply . . . but perhaps . . ." He furrowed his brow in thought and pressed my hands tighter between his. "Perhaps I can write descriptions upon my return from visiting the trading outposts for you to sketch or paint. And we wouldn't return to London often, dear, but Canada is a command performance, so to speak." He took my face in his hands. "I admire your adventuresome nature."

"*Or* I can exhibit scenes from our new adventure that I observe *first-hand?* From a canoe?"

My husband smiled faintly but did not respond.

I imagined I would have to employ a simpler medium on such adventures. I would pencil sketch to preserve the memories and do watercolors in Lachine until I could create large oils when we returned to our home country. Yes, only immense oils would capture the drama of the wilds. Something no woman I knew of had ever done, I thought.

As we walked across the courtyard, I worked to get his seal of approval. "Edward, having first viewed my works, you said the restrictions against women in the arts were absurd." I stopped him and looked into his eyes, conveying promises I hoped he couldn't resist.

"Maybe we should join the others. We're missing the exhibit. We'll talk later."

"I love that we support each other, Edward." It was my intention to plant one solitary seed before his withdrawal behind his proverbial wall. Mother had warned me that avoidance was a man's tactic in a marriage—going silent amidst conflict. I was seeing it for the first time. He would let my newly-steamed engine cool down at the station, so to speak.

I let him guide me into the gallery as the last angles of sunlight escaped into the night in the courtyard.

We wandered past the paintings. So many works of women subjects painted by men, but none by women. Tiresome portraits of countryside themes and women seated in chairs, burdened by brocade and bustles. I squirmed in the constriction of my own encasements—a tightly laced corset over a bodice—a seeming metaphor for my social limitations to exhibit as a female artist. My grandfather was a respected portrait artist and member of the Royal Academy. My father is an exhibited watercolorist; my mother a yet unveiled miniaturist; my aunt an unknown, talented miniaturist; my cousin paints exquisite landscapes, yet she is also unknown. Still, after generations of artists, no English woman had been exhibited.

I complained to Edward, touched his arm, and pleaded, "Do we not have the same eyes, the same hands, the same pigments, and brushes. Do women not see colors? Have the capacity for expression? Feel passion? Perhaps there's even more nuance in our feminine viewpoints, it's been said."

Patting my hand, he nodded and whispered, "Of course, my darling. Your words are not only convincing but so Shake-spearean." His eyes flickered toward a couple who stood nearby, eaves-dropping no doubt.

"Although admittedly I'm not formally trained, you graciously said my work was as good as any painting in this room." I went on with my spontaneous soliloquy.

My husband dipped down a bit to press his sincerity into my hidden eyes, shaded by my new hat. Pacing the words one at a time, he proclaimed, "You-are-a-true-talent-and-a-natural, Frances."

For a moment, I was wordless. Edward's sentiment was touching. I'd married a gem, a man of profound kindness. His suffering over the loss of his first wife was undoubtedly not the liability my mother had feared. It had tenderized him, made him see the importance of living with passion in each moment. He saw me, not just a young woman to care for his children and to walk down the street on his prideful arm.

"Thank you, my love. I'm touched." I read aloud from the inscription on the wall, placing my hand on my chest to regain my focus. "'The Academy's purpose is to promote the creation, enjoyment and appreciation of the visual arts through exhibitions, education and debate,' according to their own declared mission. Yet the Royal Academy is closed to us 'inferior' female artists—not ladylike unless we work in fabrics and textiles. Phooey!" Derision dripped from my words. "I'm grateful you share my perspective, Edward. This is something I admire about you . . . love about you." I was only slightly ashamed of my well-timed, wifely tactics—sharing my loving words with Edward to take behind his wall with him. I wanted my desires in his mind as he contemplated my words for I knew in my soul this adventure to Canada was meant to be.

The lingering gentleman and his wife passed us, exchanging looks of disdain, clearly having overheard my conversation with Edward. The lady stretched her neck up toward her husband. With a flirtatious, compliant tone, she exclaimed, "Outrageous for women to dabble in men's arts, and . . . *exhibiting?* Scandalous! Isn't it, dear?" They departed—the woman curling her shoulder and lifting her chin, the gentleman shaking his head with contempt for my pluck.

Taking my arm, Edward quickly diverted my attention to the front of the room, where the young Royal Highness, Albert Edward, Prince of Wales stood staring at the featured painting of the night. He seemed self-assured beyond his years.

Looking into Edward's eyes, I could almost see my husband's thoughts churning. His smile, which I feared had escaped me for the night, returned. I couldn't read my enigmatic spouse, known to me for too short a time. I seized the moment to reconnect us, with a curling of the corner of my mouth and a tilt of my head, pursing my lips ever so slightly into a promised kiss.

Edward escorted me toward the prince and introduced us. "Your Royal Highness."

I remained demure, curtsied properly, lowered my gaze.

Edward explained his role in the fur trade and the railroad's impact on modernization and the vanishing voyageurs' life. The young prince was clearly relieved to speak of something of interest that was of the times—the indigenous peoples of British North America, the wilds of Canada, and the fur trade. Then, my husband's final words almost made me swoon—romantic words for this lady. "Sir, perhaps in the future, you would accept a gift of those rare and exotic images captured in sketches to astound you."

I drew in a quick breath of surprise, knowing Edward's intent.

"Thank you, I would indeed." The Prince smiled and flashed his eyes around the room. "I admit a bit of the outdoors would be so welcome." His look and words reflected his boredom with the evening.

"Should there be a purpose in the future for you to visit Canada, we would be honored to host you, Sir." Edward suggested.

The young prince's face lit up. "That would please me. But I've not been entrusted with any assignments from the Her Majesty the Queen, as yet. Soon, perhaps, when I've completed my education."

"We will be stationed some fourteen kilometers from Montreal . . . a fascinating terrain. Until then, perhaps I can arrange for a talented young artist to capture those scenes for you. One who is soon to be on-site with me. Unique and incomparable sketches for your rooms in Windsor Castle?"

"Would you truly, Sir? Thank you."

Edward tucked my hand in the crook of his strong arm, smiled, and addressed His Majesty the Royal Prince. "I know just the artist, Sir."

The children enjoyed the extended journey by ship to Lachine, as did we. We settled into our new home in Lower Canada. Our three boys were so content with their outdoor lives, and our Canadian governess was quite willing to picnic by the Lachine canal with them and explore the countryside. Our shared stories at the dinner table of the boys' adventures and my daily sketching pleased Edward.

Fulfilling my wifely roles, I hosted many formal dinners for visiting dignitaries and guests to honor Edward's position and reflect well on him.

I kept my opinions about women artists and my aspirations

for my time in Canada to myself, knowing in time Edward would fulfill my desires.

I painted our family's house and garden on the shore of the St. Lawrence River, the neighbors' house next door, the Lachine pier, and nearby Dorval Island. I compiled my sketches into what I called the "Lachine Sketchbook, 1858 to 1860." Watercolor paintings I'd created during our two-year tenure were similarly stored away unframed in a folder. Nowhere else for them to go. Still there was no river voyage for me as a result of a constant flow of British government officials and Hudson's Bay Company executives visiting.

The more I'd heard Edward's colleagues' tales about the savages and wild Canada terrain, and the trading outposts, the more intrigued I'd become. Finally, there was a lull in the long string of visitors. Perched on the gold silk chair in my boudoir one morning, I saw that look of his again. "You are about to fulfill my dream aren't you. Which outpost will I see, darling?"

Edward stood across from me, splashed in the sunlight from the window through the open brocade curtains. "Darling, I know your dreams have been postponed as you dedicated yourself to our family and my career. I so regret . . . well, my work demands have meant I've been quite occupied."

"I understand the delay, dear." True, I'd been crestfallen—patient for over a year and still no time and no invitations to join his adventures. "I'd hoped by now—"

"I have some news that might require some adjustment."

"Yes?" I drew in a quick breath.

"We're being transferred."

"*What?* Tell me quickly. Let the pain be a flash, not a slow burn."

"I've been given a post in Montreal, just a bit away, Superintendent of the Montreal Department. Does my promotion disappoint you? We leave next week."

I discharged a very un-ladylike laugh. Edward's look of shock made me throw my head back and release a second burst. "In Montreal, I would at least enjoy the arts society events and meet other artists, and many of the river trips to the outposts depart from Montreal on the St. Lawrence River, don't they?"

"They do, dear."

With the move to Montreal behind us, I settled into more hosting and caring for the children again with no opportunity to see the wild countryside. I spent time teaching the children to sketch, and tried to be patient a little longer. Meanwhile, I studied the aborigines and read about canoeing techniques. I expressed my love for my husband passionately in our most intimate moments in hopes he would warm to the idea of our first outing. Still no invitations to join him in a canoe trip to the alluring outposts. Then the most delightful delay—the birth of our first son together. A blessing but with four boys to carry on the line and my social obligations, would there be any time for voyageur adventures? I would have been even less hopeful had I known we would grow our family over the coming years to six children with another son and our little girl, Olive. Ironically, it was then, my chances improved.

I made my forever disappointment apparent in my conversations with Edward. He acquiesced. It happened in stages—from his hiring additional help to assist me with the children and my obligations to allaying his concerns about my safety by engaging a guide for a canoe day trip to assess my genuine interest and capability.

To my surprise, one night, while sitting in our parlor, Edward lit up his pipe and looked at me, the smoke curling around his dark wavy hair. "I've heard from your canoe guide." On the third puff, he paused and shared that certain gaze that meant he'd made another decision. "I've been thinking, Frances. If I entrust you with our children—and as the love of my life—should I not trust you to know your own heart? To accept your own fate? I don't want fear to rule my life. Though I confess, I fear any harm to such a treasure. You may join me and the voyageurs to do your sketches. We will see if it's a workable plan."

"I've been asking much of you, Edward. Perhaps too much." I thought of the loss of his beloved Anne. He would naturally fear a second tragedy and this one on his conscience. "Are you certain?"

"My love, I don't want to be the reason your artistic passion for capturing the wilds lays dormant, or your smile leaves your beautiful face."

I'd waited so long for his approval. Was I thrilled or petrified of the chance to fulfill my ambitions?

For weeks I made plans, studied maps, gathered my supplies, and partook in one other activity. With a less-than-willing voyageur as my teacher, I practiced paddling on the river in one of the company canoes. I knew it was Edward's understanding that I would only ride along for the adventure and sketch the scenery. I believe I might have misspoken to the voyageur when I implied my husband wanted me to learn to paddle a canoe.

Casting off my encumbering clothes for frontier gear, I'd felt quite peculiar, yet liberated. Trading my layers of silk brocades, ribbons, colors, lace, and fuss, I purchased a simple, pale blue, cotton full-length dress that buttoned up to my neck. I'd be able to move with ease, I'd thought. A friend brought me a blue calico cotton shirt and plain pantalets, should I have the occasion or the courage to wear them. How had I ever carried the weight of my gorgeous clothing and pendulous jewels? Of course, I maintained my corset beneath the thin cotton dress, shamefully loosening it, I admit.

The first time I viewed my made-over self in the mirror, I gasped and laughed out loud. *So there you are, Frances Anne Hopkins. The real you.* No hourglass silhouette, no bustle. Just my natural shape. In some ways I felt free and sensual; in other ways I felt unattractive and not the least bit feminine. So many new thoughts about how we lived, as I pondered how others did.

The day came—my first river voyage with Edward. Our nannies and the children perched on the bank of the river and saluted our departure. Was it fear or amazement I saw in their eyes? Perhaps they shared the same question I had: Why was I so comfortable casting off in a canoe with my husband and seven strangers, the *voyageurs?* Yet wasn't I the strange one after all? A woman in a simple cotton dress with no bustle, leaving my indulged life behind to sketch the scenery of the wilds.

These men who accompanied us were legal fur traders hired by the Hudson's Bay Company. A bold lot of French Canadians, the voyageurs provided the connections and communications with the aboriginal trappers and hunters, who provided access to furs, I'd learned. Our translator, one of the voyageurs hired by the Hudson's Bay Company who'd lived among the aboriginals for years and spoke Iroquois and other native languages, would help make our communications clear.

We pushed off in the canoe into the calm canal with no way to imagine our destiny. Sitting toward the rear of the canoe behind Edward, I made sure to have a spare paddle beside me. Having seen the dense calluses on the voyageur teacher's hands, I wore my thickest gloves. It was quite pleasant with sounds of unfamiliar birds and the many species of trees along the banks—at first. The sun's glare blinded me to the threatening obstacles ahead. I was grateful I couldn't see beneath the reflecting, inky blue.

When we turned into the rocky river, I needed no other signal than the quick straightening of the voyageurs' backs as we approached the first stretch of raging, white water. I grabbed the paddle. Edward sat in front of me unaware.

Our voyageurs spines bent forward in unison as they dug into the foaming water with their paddles. Mimicking their gestures and timing my pulls in concert with them, I laughed with pure joy edged with more than a bit of apprehension.

Edward turned around. His face turned a pale color. "Dear God, *Frances!*"

Heart pounding, I worked my oar along with the men to navigate the rocks and fallen trees. Praying the curved spines of the canoe wouldn't splinter in the thundering chutes, we swept through swirling water between steep banks. I questioned my sanity, ached for the safety and calm of my boudoir, but then there was something in the challenge that spoke to me.

I'd longed for this since Edward had first mentioned the Canadian wilds. Did he see my delight in the perfect rhythm of my strokes? Yes, he did. But his proud smile evaporated instantly when a wave hit the side of the canoe, tilting us and dousing us with foam. I powered my paddle with the others to prevent a disaster.

Edward's gasp turned to laughter and a loud whooping sound as the canoe settled into a calm, wide open turn in the river. I'd never heard an utterance like that from my dignified husband's mouth. We shared a feeling of freedom.

When we exited our canoe in the shallow waters to set up camp for the night, I again felt the weight of my womanly clothes. Assisting in dragging the canoe ashore, my gathered, long skirt, soaked with river water, impeded my progress, pulling me back into the soul of the river. But I managed to keep up. The men had given up trying to stop the lady from participating in the required work. It delighted me that I'd earned their respect or at least some modicum of acceptance.

"Frances, I don't know whether to laugh or apologize." Edward scanned my unkempt condition.

Looking down at my muddy boots, the rusty stain that encircled my dress thigh-high, my straw hat askew on my head, I was aware of a change in Edward and me. "You may apologize . . ."

My mannerly husband put his hand to his chest; a concerned look crossed his wet face.

"Yes, Edward Martin Hopkins, you should apologize . . ." I paused for effect. "For not inviting me sooner."

He let out a breath of relief, smiled, took my hands and kissed them.

The voyageurs busied themselves setting up camp, glancing at us, clearly enjoying the rare chance to see their serious superior in a romantic moment.

A bond had been forged between Edward and me that could not have been formed by any other means—the freedom, the outrageousness, the elation for having shared this wild adventure. "I would pay the price of losing my ladylike pride to have seen your face as we maneuvered through those rapids."

He looked at me. "It's as if I am seeing you for the first time. Yet not."

The tough and weathered Canadian voyageurs had spent days with us, camping by the shoreline in canvas tents, sitting by the fire talking of the sights from the canoe that day. After a time, a few of them seemed quite comfortable having a woman amidst them; a few did not. The men shared stories of the "naked savages" we would meet, obviously to challenge my limits.

I resisted being shocked, denying them the joy of frightening a lady, but I was a bit unnerved by their descriptions of the aborigines—their dark hair twisted around feathers, wearing little more than a woven waistband that held their knives close at hand, and a flap of cloth that scarcely covered their most private aspects, particularly in the wind. Was my blushing face upon hearing their descriptions as crimson as it felt? Or did the flames of the campfire obscure the rush of red on my complexion?

Sleeping in my clothes in a tent with Edward was another new experience—no boudoir, no primping or perfuming, no lady's maid to dress me. The absurdity of not having the capacity to dress oneself as a wife and mother struck me more than once. Did I feel free without all our fancy ways, or deprived without our luxuries? I wasn't sure. The lack of daily personal preparations certainly left me with more time to sketch.

Two days before our arrival at the first outpost, we pulled ashore, and all eyes were on me. "Edward, why is everyone staring at me?" I stood soaking on the shore, wringing out my skirt and waiting, confused. It was nothing they hadn't seen before.

Turning around, I faced three muscled aboriginal men standing behind me. I hadn't heard a sound as they'd approached—a skill that was indeed an asset for hunters in the wilds but disconcerting to me. Beside them were large bundles of animal skins they'd portaged in to trade at the outpost. One native had some kind of fishnet fastened to a branch slung over his bare shoulder with twine. Not naked natives, as I'd been told, they were mostly clothed in shirts and pants and skins. Despite their simple attire, they had a strength, a dignity, a look of pride that impressed me. The superiority I'd heard in the voices and words of people back in "civilization" in England suddenly seemed quite misplaced when it came to these so called "savages." I thought of the line in Hamlet, "The apparel oft proclaims the man."

My mind moved so fast trying to assess my feelings, trying to see my own life through the aborigines' eyes. I watched my husband bite his lip to prevent his tell-tale smile. The other men in our party struggled to do the same. I understood the humor—from fashion and social sophistication, laced up to our chins, in contrast to the primal, unadorned life of a savage, naked or not. Which was wiser, more dignified? Did the clothes really proclaim the man? In that moment, I understood they did not.

I swallowed my uneasiness and walked up to the natives keeping my eyes on theirs. There would be no backing away after having been denied this opportunity for so long. I refused to give the voyageurs the pleasure of seeing me so much as flinch.

I would provide no excuse for Edward to preclude any future excursions.

Assuming they'd experienced our way of greeting after their many encounters with the Hudson's staff, I smiled at our surprised interpreter, and extended my hand to the first native. Repeating the sounds I'd learned from my paddling instructor, I said, "*Nyah-weh-sgeh-noh*." I added, "Pleased to meet you. I'm Lady Hopkins."

Each native shook my hand, clearly pleased that I had spoken their language. I made eye contact easily with the hunters who seemed to lack self-consciousness about their differences or my differences—an endearing trait I didn't share.

"Well done, Frances," Edward said.

The voyageurs followed suit, their inclination toward laughter having dissipated.

"Frances, as I've always said, you are a natural." Edward looked at me with such admiration, I confess I nearly cried.

"The natives are intrigued with having a woman artist among them," my translator said while sitting by the fire on that first night the aborigines had joined our party.

In the evening, with the canoes tied along the shoreline, I took out my sketch pad and began to capture each native's wide, dark eyes and muscular chests against the backdrop of the lush trees.

Over the next few days on our canoe trip to the trading post, my pencil caught each detail, the aborigines' glistening dark skin, high cheekbones . . . every fluttering feather. Their fascination with *me likewise* fascinated me. My comfort with their state of dress unfolded slowly; finally, my own self-consciousness dissipated at the sight of buttons opened to reveal a powerful chest.

I'd become a kind of good spirit among them with my magical talent, the interpreter said. They'd cradled their portraits I'd sketched and exclaimed, "Ahhh!" To see themselves captured on the woven paper gave them such a sense of what? Power? Joy? Holding my sketches next to each other's faces, they smiled and nodded, acknowledging the accuracy of the portraits, no doubt. I couldn't begin to know the world inside them. I'm sure any interpretations about their culture and their thoughts were naïve on my part.

It was my first experience with another culture, except the French or other modern-day people who came to London to visit. But these men were part of nature, an unspoiled human experience. I soon preferred the words, natives, or aborigines, or indigenous people, or friends, for they were quite lovely people and not the least bit *savage*. No pretense possible, no complications or demands of society, it seemed. So straightforward and uncomplicated, not constrained by a thousand rules and expectations, unlike my own culture.

I would never forget Edward's words as I handed him my set of sketches and watercolors from our first adventure as he sat at home in his library. "Frances, these are remarkable, *stunning*. Your timing is perfect—we will soon be hosting someone special."

"Who would that be? Her Majesty the Queen." I laughed.

"Close." He winked. "His Royal Highness, the Prince of Wales. His first assignment as hoped for—a visit to British North America, and specifically Montreal as a special stop . . . perhaps to see a certain artist?" Nodding, Edward grinned as if to say, I did this for you.

"Edward, what? Please clarify. Are you jesting?" I sat on the edge of the velvet chair, squirming a bit in my tightened corset.

Shuffling the sketches in his hands, he laughed. "No indeed. I'm only delivering sketches of the aborigines in the wilds to him, as promised." Edward paused, took a deep breath, tilted his head, and rounded one shoulder—such a feminine gesture. I was confused. Was he about to mimic me? That would be a first. "Outrageous for women to dabble in men's arts, and . . . *exhibiting?* And at Windsor Castle? Scandalous! Isn't it, dear?" He spoke with a high voice and the gestures of the judgmental woman. Could I ever forget Edward's hearty laugh and his words quoted from that critical woman at our first visit to the Royal Academy of Arts two years ago?

I rushed across the room and kissed him then and there. "Don't tell His Royal Highness they were done by a woman. I'd love to hear they were framed and hung in Windsor Castle only to learn they were done by an unknown artist, an audacious lady."

With a puff of his pipe, Edward smiled.

I perched on the arm of his chair and kissed him again.

"Had I known your sketches would have launched you across the room into my arms, well, I wouldn't have taken so long to approve your voyages with me."

Hosting the Prince of Wales was both an honor and a daunting task. The guest list arrived from Edward's office—men, all men, except me, my sister who was visiting, and a woman traveling with the Prince. All of my previous efforts at pampering the traveling British guests of honor in the past, as well as the Montreal art set, were paying off. The sketches were swirling in the background of my mind as I orchestrated the reception and dinner.

Somehow, when the Royal carriage arrived, all was ready, and I was weak-kneed. If not for Edward's promises to His Royal Highness, my sketches would have likely remained in the portfolio in my studio until they yellowed and curled. Wasn't this what I'd always wanted? Then why did I suddenly want to cast off in our canoe into the wilds and the safety of the "savages," a much safer feeling than exposing my inferior art to the world. I took a deep breath and held up my hand. *Stop, Frances. Take a lesson*, I chastised myself. *The natives have no fear of revealing themselves near-naked to the world. You can do the same with your art. You are worthy, despite being a so called inferior woman artist*, I told myself. My own words made me stand up straighter. I smiled, amused by my analogy and sarcastic thoughts.

The evening was a blur except for the moment alone in our library after dinner when Edward presented the sketches to the Royal Prince.

"These sketches are superb. The detail, the scenery. I've never seen anything like them. They're almost photographic. So much more interesting than those butter-on-bacon, excessively over-wrought works that hang in Windsor now." His Royal Highness paused and look over his shoulder. "Apologies. I shouldn't have said that, I suppose."

"Yes, Your Royal Highness, these scenes of the voyageurs' river trips to the outposts preserve what is soon to be a lost way of life. We can only imagine what natural beauty will disappear with the coming of the railroad and modern society to the region." Edward smoothly brought the Prince back to the subject at hand.

"So impressive. It's only that—"

"Yes? What is your apprehension, Sir, if I might ask?" Edward flashed a look of concern my way.

"This sketching artist, would he also be a painter?"

"She, Sir."

"Excuse me?"

"The artist is a woman, Sir." Edward shifted from one foot to another. I'd never seen him nervous, ever.

"All the more amazing. Would she possibly be a painter, as well? I would like to commission her to make these sketches into large watercolors or even oil paintings. Is that possible? Is she—"

Edward's sigh of relief was audible. "Yes, Your Royal Highness."

Hadn't we failed to look beyond his title to his age, we'd later discussed. A young and new generation with a fresh outlook, it seemed. Or at least not yet fully inculcated with the prejudices of the past.

"Let me allow you to ask her yourself, Sir. You've actually met her." Edward turned toward me, took my arm, and guided me in front of His Royal Highness the Prince. "The artist, Sir, is my wife, Lady Frances Anne Hopkins."

I worked day and night. When ready, the works were shipped to Windsor. I had no opportunity to see them in their places of honor. It was a win that wasn't witnessed. The young prince sent word that he was enormously pleased. That message did boost my determination to paint more of my sketches into large oil paintings.

I pictured my works decorating the walls of his private quarters. That same afternoon, I cast off in our small canoe by myself and traveled up the St. Laurence River to be alone with the natural world to celebrate. People passing in boats stared at me, looking once, then twice, to confirm they were seeing a lady in a canoe paddling up a mighty river—her hair scandalously let down, flowing in the breeze.

Pulling the canoe onto land, I sat on the riverbank, and sketched for a few hours to capture scenes fresh in my memory. There was an ache inside me when I arrived home that afternoon—a profound responsibility to share the world of the natives and the fur trading voyageurs before the train replaced the river trips and the cities grew up around the railroad stations spoiling the culture. I sighed each time that thought came to mind; it emboldened my resolve to finish my work, trip after trip, over six years.

From 1864 to 1869, time and again, I left our six children in the care of our loving governess and staff to accompany Edward on his work tours of the fur trading routes. We visited the Upper Great Lakes—Manitoulin Island in Lake Huron, and Kakabeka Falls near Lake Superior—and the Mattawa and Ottawa rivers. For convenience and ease of transporting materials, I worked in pencil and watercolors, typical of the times. Still, I yearned to complete my work in oil when I returned back home to England.

After returning from an invigorating tour to the farthest outpost down the Ottawa River with Edward, I entered our library. I'd changed into my nighttime blue velvet dress with a display of cleavage and clean, styled hair. Which version of me was authentic now? In my proper lady's clothes, I often felt as if I were constricted in a costume. It was amusing to change from my rugged, muddy, exhausted look after a treacherous canoe trip into the poised, pristine hostess, Lady Hopkins. The transformation had quite an arousing effect on my husband. I liked that. How lovely after years of marriage to still have the passion we shared.

Standing in front of one of my watercolors, his hands in his suit pockets, Edward wore a wistful look. It was his favorite painting, showing him among the aborigines in the Ottawa Valley against the background of a lush, primeval forest of deciduous and coniferous trees formed over thousands of years. We'd made passage down the spectacular river, its banks dominated by birch, maple, beech, oak, ash, and pine. I couldn't pause my pencil for a moment when we'd arrived at the outpost; I was so anxious to sketch and later paint my loving husband into the scene. And in the background, a woman—me.

"Frances." He turned toward me and had that look.

Where are we off to now, I thought. "Darling husband, please, no. Will I be doing more adjusting?"

"We will be returning to Hampstead permanently next month."

"I see." I turned to stare out the window at my exquisite gardens. How did I feel about our return to my home country never to ride the rivers again? Still, how would the London art society receive me now that my paintings might be hanging on the walls of Windsor Castle?

Grandmother's advice still held. Think before you speak. I'd become quite the prominent hostess over the years with a reputation for my boldness in my work here in the Montreal art scene.

Would I be received in the same way in my own country, the more formal London society? Within seconds, I realized I didn't care. How lovely that I didn't care. Charging down raging rivers in hand-made canoes with my "savage" friends and the voyageur guides had changed me. Very little frightened me anymore, especially *change*, for I had changed, like transforming a sketch into a full color painting. But would I find yet another adventure for my life? Yes, I would. Didn't the surging waters shift with every turn?

After nearly twelve years, I'd seen enough and captured enough in my sketches that I could paint forever and not want for ideas. I would gladly return to my home country to paint and paint to my heart's content. No one could ever erase my profound memories of this experience.

"I am ready, Edward. Let's go home. Would you take the responsibility of telling the children?" I wanted to run to the river to bid my farewell.

"Of course, but truly I thought you . . . well do I ever know what you'll think?" He wrapped his arm around me, and we gazed at the watercolor. "Time for your oils now?"

To have the acrid scent of oils in my life again was a pleasure. Working diligently, I made the transition from watercolor back to my favorite medium, and from paper to oversized canvases. I'd loved working large and laboriously, standing back to see my memories come alive on a massive canvas. Bold scenes live better on big canvases, I'd found.

How else could I have captured the emotion, the drama of the Canadian wilderness, but to have *lived* it? One after another, I painted the scenes that had captivated me as I traveled to each outpost—Me, Frances Anne Hopkins—*Audacious woman from salon to savage lands.* That might be the title of my memoir should I ever find the time to write it. It rolls off the tongue with its alliterative aspect, but I still preferred to say aboriginal or native lands. I laughed; I'd done it, I thought, as I cleaned my brushes of paint. I'd followed my passion with the loving support of Edward.

Adjusting to my old life brought peculiar feelings and perspectives. Everything seemed so formal, our British customs so absurd in some cases. Why were we women all tied up like prisoners in our corsets and clothes that restricted movement and weighed a ton— as if the weight exemplified our worth. Ah, thus the expression "worth her weight in gold." I supposed I'd never feel as free again as I did in the wilds with my lightweight cotton dress and secretly loosened corset wading into the pristine water.

We hadn't settled in at home for more than a few weeks when I received a grand surprise. British society had become enamored with my works—far more than the North American collectors of my art. I was overwhelmed with commissions and purchases that filled my personal coffers. With all my proceeds, I surpassed my dear husband's ability to support us in style. I'd never thought of the financial impact of my paintings' popularity.

Living in Hampstead at thirty-one, I completed a painting of one of my favorite sketches from my life overseas. I wiped off my hands on my painting rag and stood back. Capturing the vapor that hugged the canoes as they blindly made their way across the lake was my most rewarding achievement yet. I stood in front of the canvas admiring the oversized work. I could almost feel the moist haze and the strain on my muscles as my paddle fought with the power of the swelling water. I relived the sense of freedom and the drama of the experience. I named it for what it was—*Canoes in a Fog, Lake Superior*—and added my signature to the corner of the painting.

Edward came into my studio. He wrapped his arm around my waist and examined the romantic landscape. "Exquisitely powerful, darling. I have news."

I knew this man by now; he was hiding something. "Oh, Edward, not again, please; I'm so very content with my life right now."

He laughed. "You know me too well. But not this time. Sit down, dear."

I sat, holding my breath.

"Yesterday, I had a visitor, and I confess I allowed him a quick view of this painting. He would like to purchase it. For an obscene number of pounds, Frances."

"Splendid. Who is the buyer, so I can imagine where it might hang? This is all too exciting, Edward—barely finished and it's already sold."

"Oh, it was to be a gift; not anyone from here, dear."

The next day, the oil barely dry, I watched my painting exit my studio door, carried away by the shippers. Why did selling my art feel like giving away one of our children? My representative, Edward, had a certain knack for pricing my work. I was not involved in these negotiations except to watch my worth grow beyond my expectations.

As more of my creations found homes with notable art collectors, I still hadn't seen my way into an exhibition in my own country.

My only showing was in Montreal where a few of my watercolors were put on display at the Art Association.

Taking my gloved hand, Edward helped me down from the carriage. We stood outside the Royal Academy in London, again, where it had all begun. Where had twelve years gone? Surrounded by women wearing hats and gloves, bell-shaped dresses with draping and ruffles, and wide pagoda sleeves, I thought of my nights sleeping in my practical pantalets and calico shirt and smiled. I'd had the adventure of a lifetime, painting the most extraordinary scenes of natives and nature in the wilds of Canada. Still, with all the interest in my voyageur oversized oil paintings, not one was considered worthy of the Royal Academy of Arts. That fact ground like gravel in my shoe and didn't bode well for my art hanging in any gallery soon.

Wrong gender, as always. I wanted to boycott the Academy. "Edward, you know how I feel about coming here. Still no women."

"Let's call it sentimental, celebrating our wedding anniversary."

I would be gracious. Things would change, I prayed. I wouldn't have traded my experiences in the wilds for a hanging in a gallery anyway, but still . . .

He led me inside.

Can I ever put into words my reaction when I first saw it? Edward pulled me close to keep me from slipping to the floor. Looming over the central exhibition hall was my painting in all its drama. My work, exhibited, being celebrated by art lovers, hundreds of art lovers, and London society. A buzz of chatter filled the room. Words of admiration reached my ears: How did she capture the fog? You can almost feel the moisture, the movement of the canoe. How is it the clouds seem to move? Wait, is that a woman in the canoe?

I stood in disbelief when I read the sign—*Canoes in a Fog, Lake Superior* by Frances Anne Hopkins. Romantic landscape. 1869.

"For the first time in England's long gender-discriminating history, a woman has exhibited at the Royal Academy of Arts. And it's me," I whispered to Edward through a voice tight with emotion.

He reached in his pocket and showed me the two photos of the artist Edward had provided for the catalogue. They made me smile. My two lives, side-by-side: Me in my voyageur gear, hair pulled back, muddy boots, tilted straw hat tied under my chin with a cotton sash—rugged artist. Me corseted and bustled in my favorite silk ball gown, glistening jewels, hair swept up—proper lady. Together, a full portrait of myself.

A fashionable woman and her husband stepped beside us and commiserated. "Impressive, no doubt, but a *woman* artist exhibiting? What will be next? Who is this brazen *woman?*" He looked at Edward, assuming agreement.

Edward stepped forward and proclaimed in his best baritone, "Outrageous exhibitionist! A woman dabbling in men's arts, and . . . *exhibiting?* At Windsor Castle and the *Royal?* Scandalous! Isn't it, dear?"

I smiled as he took my hand and drew the couple in.

"Might I introduce the artist, my wife, Lady Frances Anne Hopkins?"

Their words sputtered from their mouths. "Oh . . . so pleased to . . . We didn't mean . . . Oh dear, we . . . Well, the painting is quite impressive . . ." They glanced up at the massive painting, then down at me. The couple's shocked expressions were reward enough for this mere woman artist.

Audacious Woman from Salon to Savage Lands

I rested my pen on my writing desk and smiled at the memory of my first major exhibition at the Royal Academy. I was thirty-one then. And who was more audacious, me or Edward?

Soon after that thrilling breakthrough, I visited Windsor Castle at the Prince's invitation, only to discover my paintings had made their way into the main receiving room. Who knew my romantic, realistic painting style would *appeal* at home in England? Who would have guessed by my fifty-third birthday, I would have exhibited eleven times at the Royal Academy in London?

I often turn the pages of my album to relive those surreal Canadian adventures. How else could an upper-class lady have accurately painted works like *Canoes in a Fog, Lake Superior; Canoe-Party Around a Campfire; Voyageurs at Dawn; Canoe Travelling in the Backwoods of Canada, Shooting the Rapids; Canoe Manned by Voyageurs Passing a Waterfall.*

Some say I'd employed my feminine wiles with Edward to launch my career, but wasn't it *I* who ran the rapids? Wasn't it *I*, who dabbed my brush into nature's hues to capture clear images of my *own* treacherous, voyageur adventures? Can you blame brazen me for daring to insert just one woman in each of my wild canoeing scenes, hidden among those amiable aboriginal and voyageur paddlers? After all, I was there, paddle in hand. How had I developed such pluck as a young woman? To this day that is a mystery to me.

Outrageous exhibitionist! Remembering Edward's words made me smile. A *woman* paddling a canoe in the wilds of Canada? Sketching *near-naked natives?* And *landscape painting?*

Too rigorous for a proper lady.

The End

Uncommon Connection

I ADMIRED HER style, her champagne Chanel suit, the way she held her spine straight and sent her soft smile my way when our gazes met.

I observed her at the buffet table—the way she inspected and selected every tidbit she put on her plate, turning each shrimp to embrace the other. So graceful and creative—placing raspberries, strawberries, and slices of kiwi in a circle like a holiday wreath around three seared scallops wrapped in bacon. Classy, I'd say—everything so perfect, so tasteful, refined, and fashionable. Wait—except for her worn-out shoes. Her scuffed black flats baffled me—the color, the condition. Strange.

While stealing glances at the rolling ocean outside, I was setting up for a fundraiser for the Special Olympics at the Boardwalk Plaza Hotel that summer evening. I finished arranging the last place settings and started filling the glasses with ice water. Shifting toward the window, I lingered. That view. Such a sweet bonus to my meager paycheck. I sighed. Can anyone resist taking in that glinting glory just as the sun sets, the shards of light skittering across the water's surface?

The manager came out of the kitchen and flashed his eyes at me. "We have a hundred and fifty people streaming through those double doors in the next ten minutes, Lorena."

"Of course, sorry." I drew my eyes back into the room, moved to the next table and resumed pouring. Not even that spectacular Rehoboth Beach view was worth the loss of one of my two waitressing jobs. I couldn't afford to get fired; not after what I'd been through.

The elegant woman cruised along the bountiful buffet table again, taking seconds.

I assumed she was a big donor. So confident.

Another waitress I'd worked with on occasion swept by me with a tray and nodded toward the woman. "Weird, I've seen her at three other events this week. Same outfit. What's that about?"

"Really?" I became even more intrigued.

In the din of the friendly chatter, the elegant lady sat alone at a table in the back, sipping her white wine.

I moved closer and watched as I refilled the water glasses at the next table.

A group of four approached her. "Are these seats free? Do you mind if we sit here?"

She nodded but shared no conversation with her new tablemates.

I couldn't tell if she was nervous or condescending. Why was I so fascinated? It didn't make sense—three events wearing the same clothes and those *shoes*.

Three other guests filled in the seats at the eight-top. Still, no exchanges. Wouldn't she know someone at a local event like this?

As I circled her table with water, a wave of unease surged over me. Something was wrong. Was it that her plate was a little too full or that she'd eaten a little too fast? Or the way she'd panicked while digging through her purse for the all-too-familiar amber prescription bottle? Or that she'd glanced over her shoulder before she took one pill and then another, with a long swallow of water, resuming her perfect posture? Was it her unpolished shoes I swear I'd seen at the thrift shop just yesterday? I wasn't educated about much, but I knew those pills and that look, and I knew a hungry, on-the-edge pill addict when I saw one, no matter the clothes.

I wiped my hands down my uniform, stood back against the wall, and studied the forty-something woman as the speeches began. I wish I could have eaten like that back then. Some of the women in rehab were like her, the opposite of me; I couldn't keep anything down. But maybe I was jumping to conclusions.

Young heroes, athletes with disabilities, stood at the mic telling inspiring tales of their journeys and receiving medals. I understood the joy they'd found in their wins.

At twice my age, the woman was everything I wasn't: Her tall and shapely body, my short, boyish body; her long, chestnut, styled hair, my scrunched, brown nest. Another surprise, her unpainted chewed-down nails; my work-worn stubs; otherwise, worlds apart. How could I have known how much more we'd had in common then?

I was both grateful and sad, thinking back to my addicted days in rehab and then the women's shelter. There was no way I'd go back there, although they'd been good to me. Not me. Never again. Not with my sweet daughter Jenny back in my life now.

Amid the clatter of conversation and applause, the woman stood and walked toward the Ladies Room. The tilt in her gait compelled me to follow her inside.

Slow-motion, she rocked left, then right. I recognized that same bleary-eyed look I used to see in the mirror. The clink of her diamond bracelet like a bell announced her imminent collapse as she lost her grasp of the slick sink.

Slipping my shoulder under her arm, I prevented her fall to the hard tile floor. "Are you OK?" Such an awkward intimacy, the beautiful, classy woman so close I could smell her winey breath and feel the heat of her body leaning against me. "Let me call someone for you."

"There's no one. I'm OK."

I remembered that feeling of "there's no one." No one to help me through the pain; no one to stop his fist, no one to stop him from walking out on me and my little girl, no one to care for my daughter when I had my surgery; no one to stop the gavel from slamming down on my life. No one.

Would I ever forget the pleading look in my Jenny's eyes or her seven-year-old scream as they took her away? Or the joy on her eight-year-old face, running down the courthouse hallway toward me? The dark and light of my recent life.

The woman tried to shuffle toward the door. I couldn't afford to lose this job for some rich, fancy stranger, right? I had no time and no way to let my boss know I was leaving. Maybe he wouldn't miss me. Why me?

"I'm fine, I'm fine." She tried to stand alone, then slumped back into my arms.

I remembered the quote from *Narcotics Anonymous, Living Clean: The Journey Continues: . . . The desperation that drives us to our* knees fuels the passion that carries us forward. When hope manifests into reality, our lives change. Mine had. Against all odds, mine had. Maybe the woman needed hope too. My mother's critical eyes as she closed the door on me flashed through my mind. Wasn't that the biggest *no one* of all? "Please, let me help you."

"I'll be fine." The woman sat down on the floor and leaned against the wall. "I just need a minute to find my car keys."

I couldn't let her drive herself. No job was worth her getting killed or killing someone else. And hadn't I made a commitment to my recovery, including my pledge to *help the next suffering addict?* I thought of my Russian roommates, summer waitresses looking for an adventure in a foreign country. I'd given them an adventure they hadn't expected when they'd seen me with my sign on the side street. *Please help me.* Their kindness had bridged our cultures and halting language. It was the moment when I'd first felt hope.

Outside the door, I heard the emcee's magnified voice asking for donations. Her voice echoed into the Ladies Room. She spoke of the Special Olympics of Delaware commitments. "Our core values embody our culture, spirit, and commitment to do our best at all times—Excellence, Inclusion, Integrity, Respect, Trust the Team."

Trust the team, I thought. There are always messages if you want to hear them. I knew what to do. I wasn't going to call the cops or take her to the hospital; she was high, but she wasn't in a medical crisis. I'd been trained to look for that in Narcotics Anonymous. I didn't want any trouble—for me, for her. I recognized that Gucci gold double-G logo on the front of the woman's purse from my mother's exquisitely outfitted closet. I took the car keys out of her purse and helped her navigate the back stairs.

The Governor's voice echoed down the stairwell as the heavy gray door clicked shut on the closing keynote address. No turning back.

"I'm Lorena, and I'm going to take you home, OK? Where's your car?"

"Here, somewhere." She swiped her arm across the parking lot.

"Actually, what's your name?" If I were going to risk losing my job, I better well know her name.

"Elaine."

I didn't catch the last name; it melted in a slur. Who was this woman? She's a woman who needed help, I told myself; that's all I needed to know. I clicked the fob, the car chirped, and the lights flashed. *Oh my God, a Mercedes.* I helped her into the passenger seat and clipped her seatbelt. Sliding into the driver's seat, I scrambled to find the controls to raise the seat. The gas gauge was on empty. *Dear God, help me.* Watching the security guard come out of the exit in the rearview mirror, I carefully drove away. Don't draw attention. "Where do you live?"

She straightened her jacket as if that would straighten her out too. Turning and dropping her gaze to the floor, she shared a look of what? Shame? "Somebody stole my good shoes," she slurred, then wilted down with her face in her hands. "My pills. I need my pills."

I could feel a stream of sweat run down my chest as I studied her striking profile. Pulling over, I opened the glove box and found the registration. Elaine L. Harrison, New York, NY. Not a local. "Are you staying near here? A hotel? A friend's house?"

"No. I . . ." Her face went slack. Elaine was in no condition to say.

Now what? No choice. I'd take her home with me. Would the car make it the five miles home? I couldn't risk it. I pictured myself accused of car theft. First, I'd have to buy gas with my tips from my lunchtime waitressing job today. Why me, Lord? Remember your recovery pledge, I told myself and pulled into the gas station.

When I arrived at the trailer I'd rented, Elaine was passed out in the seat next to me. No way I wanted my daughter to witness Elaine's condition. Inside, Natasha and Angelina were watching the movie *Frozen* with my daughter. I nodded my head toward the door, then Natasha and whispered, "Someone needs our help. Can you two please help get her out of the car? Her name's Elaine."

No questions asked, they left. Teamwork. My two loyal friends took over while I got Jenny off to our bedroom.

"Mom, you're early." She threw her arms around me—no sweeter greeting than my daughter's hug.

I kissed her curly hair. "Nine o'clock, sweetheart, time for bed. Brush your teeth." I kissed and hugged her and tucked her in, remembering the aching void in my life when she was with Child Protective Services for that long year.

I prayed helping Elaine wouldn't cause trouble for me. Who was she? What was her story? I confess, she reminded me of my mother, which chiseled at my compassion.

My roommates had helped get her from the car to the sofa. The spare pillow and blanket were waiting for just such guests. We undressed her. I couldn't let that Chanel suit get crumpled under the covers.

Natasha nodded toward my bedroom door and then whispered, "I take Jenny early church breakfast then drop at school for you."

"Thank you, Nat." What would I have done without these two young, foreign summer workers who'd shared my home with me to help me stabilize financially so that I could get my daughter back? The cramped but secure trailer had felt like a dream come true all summer. But winter was coming—fewer tourists, less work, less money, roommates departing for Russia. *Please, God, let me make it.* I'd saved a bit, and I had a new extra job working the lunch shift at Café Azafran, and I couldn't be late. It had worked out fine with my catering company jobs at night. My roommates worked the day shifts and covered for me with Jenny, alternating on their days off. When schedules didn't work and I could afford it, there was a day camp at the church.

"Elaine? Good morning."

She moaned, then opened her red eyes. "Where am I?"

"You needed a little help. I, uh . . . took you to my place to rest. Get dressed. I know where we can get a nice hot breakfast."

"I need to get home. Please?" She held the blanket to her chest, her eyes wide with fear.

"Of course. Don't worry. You're OK." I handed over her blouse and suit.

She searched around for her purse, and when she found it beside the sofa, she released a deep breath.

Did she think I would rob her? That ticked me off.

"I'm sorry, I should thank you, but I, well, I don't seem to have

73

any cash." She dug around for the pills in her purse and gripped them in her hand.

A *tip?* That stung. I guessed she needed her pride.

She stood and wavered. "May I have a glass of water?"

It wouldn't be long, I wanted to warn her, as I gave her the water. No pride possible with *those* drugs. But it was no time to get into it; I hardly knew her, and she'd had a tough night.

"I'll drive you. Where are you staying?" I helped her up.

"My beach house in North Shores."

I was confused. We got into the car, and I followed her directions. In minutes, we arrived in front of an ocean-front mansion. Stabbed into the sand by the front driveway was a sign, *For Sale.*

"Would you like to come in? I want to thank you properly. Uh . . . I'm sorry." She held her head. "I'm afraid you got a terrible first impression." She sighed and smiled.

"Lorena. It's Lorena."

"Right. Lorena." Inside the door, she flipped on the switch, no lights.

"No utilities?"

"Oh." She sighed. "They turned them off yesterday."

It was a familiar routine. One I didn't want to repeat.

Elaine invited me to sit. "Honestly, the house and the car are all I have, but once I sell the house, I'll start over somewhere." She sighed, dropped down in a leather chair, and rotated toward the gorgeous summer ocean view.

I gaped at the six-foot-high seascape paintings and the white leather furniture against the lovely blue walls. Elaine's story came out. Her accident, the opioids, her husband leaving her, no children, losing her interior design company. "I'm broke, everything's gone . . . because of these damn things . . ." She shook the prescription bottle. "But then, I need them, you understand."

Only too well, I thought. I knew the struggle, but this was not the time for a sermon. "You hungry?"

"Very."

Dammit. She needed help. I couldn't just leave her at the house with no food, no lights, no water. I called in sick to my job and took her to the free breakfast at the church.

Her paper plate bent under the weight of her choices. "Thank you. For last night, and this." She touched her fork to her scrambled eggs, then ran her fingers back through her hair. "I must look a mess."

Obviously, she'd read my look.

"Bigger problems than messy hair, I know." Elaine scanned the room. "Lorena, who are all these people needing breakfast? Right here in this affluent vacation town?"

I watched her eyes fill. "It's a reality check, right?"

"Why hadn't I ever noticed? And so many children. And how did I ever get here?"

I took a deep breath. "You have to get off those pills, Elaine. They'll derail your life."

"I think I've already gotten off track."

I could see it was an effort for her to concentrate, but her well-practiced manners couldn't be denied.

"Tell me about *you*, Lorena."

The truth was something I'd evaded for so long until my rehab. It all came out: my affluent upbringing on Long Island, my partying, my pregnancy, the abuse, and the resulting surgery and the drugs and losing my daughter, my mother's devastating gift of shame and rejection. And me an only child. It wasn't enough my dad had abandoned Mother, but she'd repeated the crime with me. "No regrets about leaving my former life for this charming beach town." I wrapped up my saga.

Elaine touched my arm. "I'm so sorry you went through all that. But your story is so inspiring. When you mention Jenny's name, your face lights up, Lorena. I only wish I'd had a daughter."

"I only wished I'd had a mother . . . who cared."

I spent the next day giving Elaine a tour of the local organizations that helped the indigent. *Indigent* always sounded so sophisticated, to me—more fitting of a drugged-out woman with a mansion and a Mercedes.

For months, I stuck by Elaine's side. A strange duo. I helped her navigate the system to get help as fall flowed into winter. While visiting her in detox, I empathized with every withdrawal symptom—her muscle aches, the chills, the sweats, the haunted look in her eyes. Missing one shift after another, I risked getting fired. I wiped her brow and held her hand when she thought she couldn't make it through. It was like looking after a fragile, injured bird while reliving my past.

"I'm so grateful, Lorena," she murmured one night when I brought her soup.

"Just a sinner's search for redemption, Elaine. We're all in this together."

She squeezed my hand.

Elaine was a fighter. After waves of symptoms, by early spring, she was recovering surprisingly well. My circumstances got worse as Elaine's got better. No way I would burden her with my current situation. My shifts got canceled as the town slipped into sleepy winter hibernation. I missed my rent twice, and then that dreaded eviction notice arrived. I had ten days before my life would fall apart again.

Working through my panic, Jenny was my hope. My well-being always reflected the seasons—off-season in winter, I was off balance trying to make it financially. In-season during tourist time, my world was bright. I job hunted and managed to find work cleaning a coffee shop in town while the usual cleaners were on vacation. I made it through another winter month. The church kept us fed through the cold winter.

My ear was always to the ground. The blustery March day Elaine was released from rehab, I planned a surprise. I'd arranged with the Resource Center to turn Elaine's utilities on using some new grant money I'd heard they had available from the state for such needs. I smiled, imagining Elaine standing on the second floor of her toasty house, celebrating with arms spread above her, gazing out the glowing wall of windows at the ocean. A new beginning.

Why didn't I hear from Elaine for weeks after my special utility surprise? She knew where I was; she knew my schedule. It wasn't as if we were close friends, but I thought at least she cared after all we'd been through together. No, she'd become more than a friend, I realized. She was so much like my mother, concerned and understanding. That was before I'd embarrassed my mother and disappointed her by becoming a pill addict then pregnant. Before my father had abandoned her. I'd confided my most intimate stories during Elaine's stint in rehab. Her silence and sudden disconnect hurt and worried me. Was she OK? Would *I be?*

Meanwhile, I worked to make up for the lost time. One lunch shift, my co-worker handed me a note. "Your friend, Elaine, wants to see you. She called here last night. I told her I'd let you know. "

"Really? Thanks." I hoped she hadn't relapsed. With no room-mates to stay with Jenny and the off-season after-school care not affordable now, I walked to Elaine's house with my daughter. Winter in a closed-up tourist town had been my enemy, but spring was coming and none too soon. "You cold, honey?" I tucked my scarf around Jenny. I'd find a way. There'd be no losing my precious girl again.

"Thanks, Mommy. Is Elaine's house like a real house?"

I thought of our trailer, the two small, brown bushes by the front door, the rusted-out car next door. "Yes, honey, it's like a real house." As we approached Elaine's beautifully landscaped home, Jenny couldn't contain herself.

"Wow! It's beautiful."

The *For Sale* sign was down. I rang the bell. When the door opened, I was thrilled. Elaine looked like a new woman, coiffed, refreshed, and clear-eyed.

"You sold your house! I'm so happy for you. A fresh start. I guess you'll be leaving now?" My chest tightened. Trying to sound upbeat, I wrapped my arm around Jenny's shoulder. Was I supporting my daughter or me? I didn't address Elaine's weeks of silence. She didn't owe me anything. But then there was this erup-tion of emotion that surprised me. I held it back with a clenched jaw and a deep breath. Trust had been a fragile thread in my life. With my work schedule, I had people I knew from my jobs but no friends. No, that was an excuse. Was that why I'd stayed at a distance from people since my troubles? A fear of trusting? Is that why I never let friends into my life? Abandonment. You see what happens? I let myself get close and now . . . hurt again, I thought.

Elaine had a strange look I couldn't read. "Lorena, remember the recovery slogan, *Not Alone?*" She guided us into the living room.

"Of course." Unforgettable, since I'd often felt alone. Yes, I was feeling sorry for myself.

"Welcome home, roommates." She hugged Jenny. "Would you consider . . . I hope . . ."

"I don't understand."

"I'm staying."

"Staying? *Here?*"

"Yes. Sorry I've been out of touch. I was busy getting my life together. I wanted to be ready for you . . ."

"Ready for *me?*" Now I was totally confused.

"I have a new job. An old friend helped—I'll be opening a new branch of her company nearby in Milton. So, will you? Please?"

"Seriously? Be roommates?" I was still confused.

"We can help each other. You've been such a good friend, I thought—" Elaine let out a puff of a laugh. "Probably the only person who truly knows me."

"I can't afford to—" Not just financially, I thought; I was short on trust, yet I wanted it.

"Lorena, we're kind of like family now. After all, we've been through together." She ruffled Jenny's hair and gave her shoulders a squeeze, drawing a wide smile from my daughter. "You've been so good to me, Lorena. You're like, well, to be honest, I feel like you're the daughter I never had." Elaine walked to the window and gazed out at the ocean, then turned back to us. "And who charges rent to family?" Elaine smiled, raised her hands palms-up, and shrugged. "And what would I do with six bedrooms?"

I put my arm around Jenny. I needed to protect her. From what—having a home and a support system that didn't change with the seasons?

"*Really*, Miss Elaine? We could live here?" Jenny twirled in front of the panoramic view. "Mommy, *please?*"

I couldn't answer, but I could picture the eviction notice on my desk. Elaine was right; we could try. *Not alone* sounded so good right now. I had to trust for my daughter's sake, as well as for mine. But I still had that cautious gripping in my stomach.

"Please, Mommy?" Jenny waited with a hopeful look.

When hope manifests into reality, our lives change. The NA quote weakened my case to say no.

Elaine shrugged. "Come on. We have so much in common."

I looked down at my gray and white waitress uniform and Elaine's blue cashmere sweater, then down at her thrift shop shoes.

We both laughed.

"Yes, Elaine, so much in common. I knew that from the first time I saw you."

The End

Think Small

"HEY, CJ, ARE you sitting down?"

"Candace, I'm driving on the Schuylkill Turnpike."

"Oh right. I just got the DNA report on your ancestry you ordered."

I hadn't told anyone about my heritage search since I'd lost both of my adoptive parents this year, except Candace. I wondered what my young, diligent staff researcher had found? "Irish and Italian, I assume?"

"Not at all. Get this. Apparently, you're a descendant of a Delaware Nanticoke Indian tribe."

"*What?*" I swerved to avoid a car changing lanes.

"There's more, listen. I did some more digging."

"Wait, Native American? What percent?"

"One hundred percent."

I pictured the single-color of the pie-chart of my past she was holding in her hands. My warm skin tone and the strong structure of my face now made sense. It had been a tough year losing both of my parents to sudden illness one after the other. I was divorced, alone—orphaned *again* at fifty-five, and now my surprising lineage.

"Check this out, Miss Chairman and CEO—you are the great-great-granddaughter of a Nanticoke tribal chief. And you have a *living* relative."

Chills. I gripped the steering wheel. "I'm listening."

"I traced him to an assisted living place in a town called Milford, near the Delaware beaches."

"*Seriously?* What's his name?"

"James Gilbert Wright. He's your uncle, your mother's only sibling."

"My *mother's* brother?"

"And get this, he's freakin' ninety-years-old.

"Wait, slow down. You found my *birth mother?*" The thought ricocheted through my brain. As a child, I longed to uncover the mystery of my origins. When I'd first asked my adoptive mother, she'd stopped brushing my thick, dark, waterfall of locks in mid-stroke and said, "You're Irish and Italian like us, dear." Her sad expression had convinced me never to inquire further. And I hadn't. Mom and Dad had given me the perfect life, full of love. I owed them so much. But now that they were gone . . .

"CJ, you there?"

"I'm here." The traffic was getting dense as I approached downtown Philly. I needed to drive carefully, I told myself. With a shaking hand I adjusted the rearview mirror.

"I'm sorry. She's, well, she *was* eighty-seven, and she's gone."

"How long ago?" My throat tightened.

"A year ago last week. It says September fifth, twenty-seventeen."

"What was her name?" I squeezed the words out. Had I secretly hoped the reports would lead me to some romantic, emotional, open-armed reunion with my biological mother?

"Adrienne Wright. One offspring, a daughter, deceased . . . with your birthdate."

Deceased? Would I ever unravel *that* mystery? "Candace, please cancel my meeting; I'm coming back to the office. Sorry . . . I've got to hang up now." I took the next exit and turned around. Can you grieve for someone you've never known? I'd always longed to know something, anything, and now I knew my mother's name. But she was gone.

I was numb for most of the hour drive home. Taking the short-cut through the farms, I pulled over, hung onto the steering wheel and stared off into a blurry field of tan dry stubs of corn. With no family now, I ached to belong somewhere.

To *someone.*

When I reached the corporate offices, I parked my car and took the elevator to the top floor. Everyone on the executive office floor was in a conference. I sat in my leather office chair and took my old Nikon out of my desk drawer. Giving up my photography to attend Wharton, and becoming a corporate executive had all been for my dad, I realized. Now that he was gone, I found no joy in my work; it wasn't really *me.*

How had I become instant heir to my father's technology company and alone? I had business associates, but no friends. Decades of analyzing profit and loss statements with my high heels kicked off under my rosewood desk had exhausted me—my laptop on fire twenty-four-seven, constant international travel, contentious board meetings, and managing the nineteen-hundred brilliant techies in my employ. Never mind time for a social life—insomnia was my unrelenting companion since my divorce.

I buzzed Candace. My assistant and researcher was loyal and sharp, the closest personal relationship I had now. "I'm here, but I need to go now. I can't resist."

"I knew you would. CJ, there's a Nanticoke Indian Museum in Delaware—I'll text you the address. They're open on Saturday. You sure you want to face the Friday beach traffic? What am I thinking, of course you do. Grab a sandwich from the coffee room. Leftovers—we had an event earlier. I'll make you a hotel reservation near Milton. Good luck. I'll text."

With a dull ache inside, I called the number for my uncle's assisted living residence in Delaware.

"A *visitor?* How *nice,*" the administrator said.

I explained I was a long lost relative. "It should take me two to three hours. I hope to be there by three o'clock."

"I'm sure he will look forward to meeting you. How lovely."

Re-routing my GPS, I prepared myself to meet the lone leaf clinging to my family tree. Friday traffic was heavy—cars loaded with kids and cargo, creeping to their last weekend beach vacations of the season. Families. I could hardly breathe. Did I have a family somewhere out there? I rocked my head to release the tension in my neck.

Sipping the French Vanilla coffee I'd bought at a roadside Royal Farms, I wondered why my Nanticoke mother had given me away; who were my people? The whole thing was surreal. Did I really want to shine this light on my life like the glaring shards of fall sun were slashing through the trees along the highway? Could I take another loss or disappointment?

As I walked up to the converted old Victorian home, I saw a tall figure of a man in the window above. I waved. Surrounded by the musty scent of the past, I walked through a recreation room where a muted TV flickered, pairs of people played checkers, and lone souls rocked in creaking chairs.

"Hi. I'm Charlotte Jenkins. I called about visiting my uncle?"

The woman in charge directed me upstairs. "He knows you are coming. I didn't want him to be caught off-guard. Such a surprise and his first visitor."

"Mr. Wright?" I called, knocking. I smiled at that—*Mr. Right*.

"Come in." He stood by the window in the dusty sunlight, a few remaining strands of black hair peppered his long silver pony tail. Despite his aging, it was clear he'd been a muscled man. "I never thought I'd ever . . . oh, you look just like my dear sister Adrienne." He pointed to the single wood-framed photo of my mother on his nightstand.

My mother! In the aging photo, she stood in front of a small white house with a confident look, thick dark hair, light coffee and cream skin tone, straight spine—a posture I recognized as my own. My legs threatened to collapse. "May I sit?"

He signaled to the wicker chair, then lowered himself into his rocker beside me.

"I'm Charlotte."

"You're really Adrienne's baby?"

I showed him the report.

He clutched his fists over his heart and looked into my eyes. "Oh, I didn't need a report—the proof is in your lovely face. So much like my sister."

Strangely, his warm smile made me feel at ease. Without thinking, I reached over and covered his hands with mine.

"You have her kind spirit too," he whispered, and his eyes edged with tears. "I miss her."

I reached over, picked up the photo and cradled it in my lap. We both gazed at my mother's face, the key to my mystery. The ticks of his bedside clock suspended us there, strangers connected only by blood.

I looked around the simple room. "Are you happy here, Uncle?" The words just came out.

"I accept what is. I need a little help now and then since Adrienne passed." Staring straight ahead, his weathered hands gripping the arms of his rocker, he shared tales of my mother and our Tidewater people, our Nanticoke tribe.

With every story he told, I came to know myself. I'd come by my leadership skills, naturally as the progeny of a past chief, Uncle James said. Searching, as though I could find her there, I ran my eyes over my mother's series of small watercolor paintings of marshland and waterfowl that hung crooked on my uncle's light green walls. He told me of my mother's garden and the flowers she'd grown and sold to local florists.

"Your mother took me in when my wife and children were taken by a dreadful fire years ago."

"I'm so sorry." My *mother*. Just the word made my chest squeeze tight. A picture of her spirit came together—strong, kind, creative, nature-lover. "Do you know who my biological father is?"

My Uncle went silent. His pause was painful. "Not his name, no. It's a story we try to forget."

"Please, Uncle James? I've waited for so long to know . . . why she gave me up."

He closed his eyes. "Had I only been there." He rose and stood looking out the window. "A Nanticoke passing through. He . . . well, Adrienne was shamed. Not a man worth knowing, Charlotte. And not a man to have as a father." His pained look was too familiar, like my parents' faces when I'd questioned my ancestry. He went on. "Not all stories have endings worth telling."

"Uncle, my ancestry reports say that I'm . . . *deceased.*"

His head dropped. "I'm sorry. Adrienne wanted to protect you. She sacrificed her only child to keep your father from ever finding you. She wanted you to be free of fear and the burden of shame. The agency required anonymity. She was never the same."

Free. I imagined my mother fearful for my well-being. In that thought, I inferred her love for me. I'd always wondered. I was touched by her sacrifice.

My uncle pulled a yellowed deed from his dresser drawer. "There's just you and me now. With your mother's passing, the family land is yours."

"*Land?* I couldn't . . ."

He ignored my protest. "It's all that's left that shows we *were.* Promise me you'll go by water, like our ancestors did, not by car."

My uncle's quivering hand drew a crude but detailed map. Taking his ancient story-telling hands in mine, and searching his liquid, dark eyes, gave me the final nudge I needed to lure me down the path to my mother's past.

Encouraged by my many college photography trips by kayak, I cast off in my yellow rental boat, wearing my yoga pants, a blue T-shirt, and rubber water sandals I'd bought to replace my linen suit and heels. I relaxed my vice grip on the paddle and the crude map settled into my lap, held in place by my neglected Nikon and my iPhone.

Washed in the morning sunlight, I maneuvered around each curve, protected from the fall breeze by a waving wall of emerald and amber grasses. I felt so alive, so connected to everything around me, as my kayak made an artful incision through the opaque water. Weighty things like budgets, stock buy-backs and mergers seemed to ride the slip stream beside me and were swept away in my V-shaped wake.

What would I do with the land, sell it? I couldn't; it held my tribal history. My uncle wouldn't be able to use it. In a way, the gift seemed like a burden.

Snowy egrets swished and stirred-up the muddy shallows with toothpick legs. Plucking the occasional fish or frog, flicking it sky high, they swallowed it down their long gullets. I jumped at a thick snake that slid beside my kayak, nearly capsizing myself. I laughed—that's years of living in concrete and steel, I thought.

Even here on the hidden marshy inlet of the Rehoboth Bay, there was that scent of salt in the balmy fall air. Screeching birds and the gurgle of my boat's progress were the only sounds.

Following the winding passages, through the marsh, I watched crabs skitter left and right in the shallows along the sandy banks without a human in sight. Could I cast off my outer shell so easily? How had I lived my life without the daily guidance of the moon, the tides, the aching of the Earth as she changes her seasons?

My biological mother's boat must have slithered through these very grasses. She must have paddled by these gnarly trees, bare now, like old bones. Their branches, like witches' fingers reaching to the sky, provided the perfect perch for large nests of twigs. Recognizing the scene from the painting on my uncle's wall, I imagined my mother setting up her easel on that craggy point at sunrise to create. I shuddered, knowing her somehow, missing her.

Zooming in my camera lens on an empty nest in the tree above me, I felt a profound loss. Then a large snowy egret landed on the sloping bank just yards away. Plucking a flapping, iridescent fish from the water, the bird turned its bright yellow eyes my way, and posed for me. I held my breath. My long-neglected love of nature and my creative passion turned the prism of my life's perspective around. From that very first click of my camera on the path to finding my mother's home, I knew just what I wanted—to be present for a hundred thousand more intimate moments just like this.

At the end of the channel, following the wrinkled map, I slid up onto the sandy edge of a point of land. The plop-plop-plop of a fleet of frogs diving into the quiet water seemed to applaud my arrival. Exploring beyond the overgrown banks, I spotted a rough path leading from a cottage to a main road in the distance.

Securing the kayak on shore, I sat under a tree to think. I couldn't regret my privileged life with my loving parents. Still, I regretted the life I'd missed with my artistic mother, a woman of the land. There, fifty feet from shore, were the remains of a cottage where Adrienne had lived out her days. The richness of her land, her modest cottage and wilted gardens were now, mine. The roof was about to collapse-in; the outside walls were tinted green from the damp weather. Two rocking chairs with peeling white paint were silent on the front porch, holding a wealth of memories I would never have.

I pushed opened the door and lit up the emptiness inside. It pierced my heart—my mother was a Nanticoke Indian of simple means, living only hours from my parents' palatial home in Pennsylvania? *I'm so sorry Adrienne . . . for what you suffered and sacrificed.* I didn't want to call her Adrienne; I wanted to call her Mother. To tell her what a privileged life I'd led thanks to her sacrifice. There was no blame; there was only sorrow and a deep sigh as my awareness blossomed.

I made the phone call on pure instinct. The best call of my life. "How are you, Robert? I have a building project for you . . . a new home." I paced in front of the cottage and imagined it renewed. "No, no, Robert, think simple, think *small*—for a family of two. I'll send photos so you can replicate the three-bedroom cottage exactly like the original . . . No, my ex-husband and I are not getting back together. It's for my uncle and me."

I hoped I was right. "And please put my houses on the market. Yes, the New York apartment too. And the bid on my company . . . please tell the board to accept it. No, I haven't *lost* it . . . I've actually *found* it. We'll talk."

I felt at home in my own skin for the first time. A rebirth— as the hard shell of my former corporate life cracked away and released me to a new life. I'd hatched into *me*, surrounded by the simplicity and glory of nature. Who could ever have imagined this spiral of fate—the escape hatch from my deeply entrenched corporate city-life to the hidden life of my own past? I danced in circles celebrating with my arms above me, thanking my loving parents, my natural mother, my ancestry, my DNA, and hoping my uncle would return home into my care.

A long-repressed emotion surged. Pulling back my arm like a string on a bow, I closed my eyes, breathed in, and flung my iPhone, watching it arc high through the salt-scented fall air, glinting as it turned, spinning, as though unwinding me, unraveling the lifelong knot inside me.

That afternoon, I returned to my office. Candace was already busy packing up my things.

"CJ, *really?* I've been trying to reach your cell all day. You're selling everything? I'd received the news about the business, but your homes?"

"Candace, none of those places felt like home. And I'm going by my real name now, *Charlotte*."

"But CJ . . . sorry, Charlotte, you told me never to call you that, it sounded too *country*, too *old-fashioned* for a corporate executive."

"Do you know what that name means? I looked it up. Ironic. It's the female version of *Charlot*, meaning, 'free man.' So I guess I was meant to be a free woman."

"Yes, and now I'm free too, maybe with no job or at the mercy of the new owner." My slender, overworked, young blonde-haired assistant shrugged with her pleading hands in the air. "What the hell happened to you in Delaware?"

"I found my sanity. Candace, remember you said you always wanted to work in London?"

"Well, yes, but—"

"I don't want you to miss out on your dream. We all should follow our dreams."

"Is this Charlotte Jenkins who's talking to me? Workaholic of the universe?" Candace shook her head.

I would add to her total confusion. "Candace you've been working day and night. I owe you. I snagged a great management position for you with a British associate of mine."

"What?"

"Executive Assistant to the CEO for a reputable research company." I handed her an envelope with a printout of the offer. "At a rather significant salary increase, and a two-bedroom flat in the coolest part of London included. Only if you want to . . ."

"Seriously? Oh my God. This is crazy. It's contagious. *Yes!*"

"Crazy good." I shared my story of my trip by kayak with Candace, as she helped me finish packing up my office. Hearing my own words made me realize there was no turning back. What if my uncle didn't want to live in our new family home with me? I would cross that bridge, later. Living on my mother's land was where I belonged. I didn't know what I would do; I didn't need to. I was over goals and planning and annual reports. I didn't need stats; I'd use my instincts.

Now I had to meet with the board, refuse a going-away bash, and say goodbye to my loyal staff. I'd already ensured the new owners would take care of the people who had always been there for my father and me.

I arranged to put everything from my homes in storage until I could sort it out. I would only keep the sentimental and essential things. With my three houses up for sale, and my father's company's sale in the works, I needed a purpose, a way to carry on my mother's legacy. Something to paint on my clean canvas, the *tabula rasa* of my new life.

Shivers danced down my arms as I pulled up in front of my uncle's home. Would he come to live with me? Was I crazy? I didn't even know the man. But his kindness had shone in our first conversation. My connection with my only living relative had saved me from a work life that didn't suit me, never had—and now knowing the real me, I knew why. I owed him somehow. No, it wasn't guilt or charity or indebtedness; I *needed* him. I needed family.

But what would I do with the rest of the twenty acres along the marsh that now belonged to me? He'd simply handed the deed over to me because I was blood; I would take care of him for the same reason—blood—my bloodline, my family.

I pictured my uncle in the window two stories up as I had the first time I'd visited him. He had no idea how wealthy his niece was now—thanks to his gift—not the land's value, but his request for me to travel by water to find my past, as my ancestors had. That kayak ride with my camera and the beauty of the natural scenery had led me to cast off the cumbersome possessions and responsibilities that had weighed me down. The same wildlife scenes that had captivated my mother had captivated me too.

I could still feel my uncle's warm hand holding mine as we both studied my mother's painting that hung across from us in his small room. The connection we seemed to feel, as we stared into my mother's eyes in the framed photo I'd cradled in my hands, had been palpable.

I would listen to my elder for the answer, I thought, as I checked in at the desk and climbed the stairs. Wouldn't that be the tribal way, to listen to my elder? There was so much to learn. I rehearsed what I would say. Would he agree?

I knocked.

His baritone voice, with an edge of rust, invited me in. He had an approachable look about him, standing in his simple quarters, wearing his pressed jeans, soft, cotton collared shirt with a bandana tied at his neck and weathered leather vest. "Charlotte, so good to see you."

"Uncle, I need your advice, and I have a question." I was aware that I was shifting from one foot to the other like a child.

"I suggest a question should be answered first. I have one as well." His smile took down my nervousness.

"Then I suggest your question should be answered first, Uncle, out of respect for my elder."

We laughed together.

"Charlotte, I can tell you one thing about your mother."

"Oh, tell me everything you can remember."

"She shared your laugh. When I hear the joy in your voice as I tell a story, I hear her joy. But telling you everything would take a longer time than I have."

Somehow the story of my past no longer mattered, only the story of my path forward. "What is your question, Uncle?"

"My question is . . . *Did you see the scene from your mother's painting? On your water journey to our family home?* I forgot to ask you on your phone call."

"Yes. In fact that leads me to *my* question. But why do you ask?"

"I look at that scene every day, right there on my wall, and know

Adrienne is with me." He pointed to the artwork. "Still, I regret I will never again see those waters that are a lifeline to our past."

The way he engaged my eyes made me realize how little intimacy I had in my life right now. No parents, no husband, no friends, just business associates who had no time in the blur of succeeding. At least not any that looked at me with such . . . what was it, a depth of feeling? The connection Uncle must have felt with my mother, he now seemed to be transferring to me. I held my breath as he finished.

"I was hoping the love of that place would be passed on to you. This why I asked you to take the water route."

I found my courage. "Uncle James, what do you wish your legacy to be? The thing you . . ." I hesitated for a moment, uncomfortable being so familiar. "The thing you wish to have left behind to say to the world, James Wright *lived?*"

He met my eyes in a way perhaps no one ever had. "Community, the legacy all people strive for, and live for . . . yes, I would say, to have left behind *community*. But regretfully . . ." He stared up at the painting again, pulled back a stray strand of hair into his silver pony tail, and tucked his hand in the pocket of his well-worn brown leather vest.

I wasn't sure how to respond. How could I fulfill a legacy of community that couldn't be—him without family, me a lone orphan. Ideas exploded in my mind. I envisioned building a large community center where children could learn about Nanticoke tribal traditions, where the deep voice of Uncle James telling stories could bring their ancestors to life, an annual Pow Wow, a place where we could build community . . . connections.

Uncle James didn't speak; he stood with his spine straight, like my mother had in the photo on his night stand—just as I had, when important things needed to be said. My emotions were still pushing against the dam of my inhibitions.

His lips began to move. "I . . . wish—" He stopped.

I looked out the window, to save him from the discomfort of my eye contact—afraid to ask, afraid he would refuse. In the weighty silence, I turned from the wall of paintings and faced him. Doesn't connection have its root in *two?* Doesn't community have to start somewhere, I thought. With me?

A stream of tears ran down my uncle's cheeks. He smiled—a smile that made a flash of hope pierce through me. His voice rose another octave. "We are blood. We are family. And I hope you will return to visit when you can."

I moved closer, and shoulder to shoulder we lost ourselves in the vivid scene on the wall—the young lime-green waving grass of spring, the cluster of Great Blue Herons on the shoreline, the water and sky, every hue of blue, and the gnarly trees arched over the winding edge of the stream. At the top of the painting, a single, hunched owl was perched high on a sun-bleached tree trunk that had lost all of its greenery to aging.

My uncle pointed to the bird. "A metaphor for me—alone. We birds were meant to flock together like our people did not so long ago."

Think small, I told myself, and I took a breath. No grand plans right now. No distractions from this precious, intimate moment between two people who were . . . family. "Uncle?"

He looked deep into my eyes and tilted his head waiting for me to continue.

I pointed to the lone owl on the ancient tree in the painting.

"How would you like . . . a bird of the same feather to land on that branch with you?"

The End

First published by *Delaware Beach Life* magazine, Holiday issue, 2018.

Honorable Mention, Delaware Press Association
Communications Contest, 2019.

Relevé

HER MEMORY WAS everywhere. The buckle on my purse clunked against the coffee table and echoed in the thirty-foot ceiling . . . *Juliette, don't leave your backpack there!* It was strange to be in my mother's house after all our silent years, especially without her knowing.

My Aunt Cynthia put her arm around me. "Juliette, are you alright?"

"Oh, sorry, it's just . . . being here puts me back in time . . . Mother's voice . . . it's everywhere. Are you sure this is OK?"

"It's fine, Juliette. Anywhere she's been always feels . . . well, a bit haunted. If you'll forgive the term."

It was my Aunt Cynthia's idea for me to see my childhood home again after my mother went into an assisted-living residence.

Had she hoped it would make me sentimental, or compassionate enough to attempt to see my mother again? Cynthia understood how I'd suffered my mother's relentless rejection over the decades; she'd endured her older sister's continuous crime of alienation of affection too.

"Just think how you'll feel if you never go to see her, Juliette. Do it for you and Sam and the kids, if nothing else." She kissed my cheek. "We have to be who *we* are. You understand? I have to run. The alarm is off, the code is five-two-eight-five-five. Just set it when you leave."

"My *birthday?* Her code is my birthday?"

"Oh, honey, who could ever understand Genevieve? She hasn't spoken to me in decades, and then she makes me her executrix— through her lawyer, no discussion." Aunt Cynthia sighed and gave a smile of understanding. "In any case, take your time, dear."

Aunt Cynthia was right, it was best that I try to reconnect with my mother once more—for my own sake. It couldn't hurt any more than it already had, I thought, as I entered the library. The familiar altar that paid homage to her career took up an entire wall. I touched the glass dome that held her ballet shoes, preserved with the starched ribbons spiraling up inside like climbing vines that ended in the shape of a heart. There was not a speck of dust. Mother's lifelong household staff clearly still came to clean, out of loyalty, or fear, or both, I thought. Still, a musty scent had crept into the house in mother's six-month absence, not something you could avoid in a closed-up mansion of this age.

The program for George Balanchine's first full-length work with New York City Ballet in 1954, *The Nutcracker,* sat in a hinged, double-framed glass box. One side held the program, the other, his personal letter. Mother was at the height of her career at thirty when she'd become pregnant with me. A difficult pregnancy, she'd always declared.

I read the regretful note to Genevieve from Balanchine himself. She'd hung the precious memento over the table above the six-inch-thick album of her previous performance programs as proof for everyone to see. The letter testified to her promising future, a possible *Prima Ballerina Assoluta, the absolute first ballerina,* he'd written. It was the ultimate praise, although an outdated term. She was happy to remind me of her *misfortune*—because of *you,* Juliette. *Of course you couldn't help it,* she'd say from time to time.

Like a visitor to a Paris museum, I scanned the walls as I entered the formal *receiving room,* as Mother liked to call it. The view of the Hudson River made me sigh. I could see myself taking in the water scene as a little girl, waiting for the Circle Line tour boat to pass by. *Please, Mother.* How many times did I beg her? At ten, I knew the boat's schedule. Breaking Mother's rules, as I had back then, I drew back the heavy brocade curtains and pressed my hands to the window, remembering her words, *Juliette get away from that window; we are not going on that filthy river cruise.*

I pushed away my regrets and continued the tour of my childhood home. Expecting the usual elegant décor, I was stunned that my mother's Victorian home was filled with unexpected items and desecrated art. I'd anticipated change, forty years after all, but not like *this.* Our home was never cluttered. Always so precise. There was almost a line of demarcation when she'd started to lose her faculties, reflected in the things she'd collected that were scattered around. Like she'd made a switch from Sotheby's and her interior designer to yard sales or picking through trash—like looking inside her private thoughts, the degradation of her mind painfully exposed. A doctor could have done an early prognosis by just walking through this place over time, I thought.

Sounds of clinking toasts and sophisticated voices with Mid-Atlantic, American-British accents and French words sprinkled in smart conversation still lived there in the silence. The room was filled with morning sunlight that lit up the bizarre décor in rainbow colors from the stained glass window on the far side of the room.

Rainbow, it's meaning had evolved, I thought. I couldn't help but feel a pang of pity. I could see my mother holding court like a queen, magnetizing the room filled with luminaries. Genevieve always delivered clever but refined commentary on subjects of the day, served laughter and charm along with the passed hors d'oeuvres and champagne. Mother made everyone feel special, engaging their eyes just a little longer than was the norm.

Along with everyone else, I'd adored her when I was a child.

A picture of my younger brother Gregory holding on to Mother's studio practice bar was the only family photo in the room. I had no talent or inclination for the dance, and she'd been devastated, wanting to live through me, I assume. I owed her at least that much; after all, wasn't I the one who'd destroyed her career, as she'd once said in anger when I quit ballet.

Mother had *"don't touch it dear"* exquisite taste and the family money to support it. In my childhood, we had rooms like library, parlor and receiving room; Sam and I had a family room and a playroom for the kids in a loft apartment. There was never anything that wasn't purposeful and perfect in my mother's home, except for my father. Oh, and me.

Here and there through the *tacky* emerged the *tasteful*, like exquisite orchids popping up among abandoned junkyard castaways. An original impressionist painting by Monet was juxtaposed with a plastic-framed Keane-Eyes clown and a McDonald's

Happy Meal toy—and not the retro collector's kind. It seemed she had absorbed common culture in spots after her illness began, like batik dyes soaking in on the cloth wherever there wasn't wax—her childhood showed through.

My old doll house had been resurrected and was set up on the Persian rug. Only the mother figure was inside, resting on the four poster bed with a puppy at the foot. Mother always hated pets in the house. Dirty, smelly, classless. *How many centuries had humans worked to get the animals out of our homes?* she would ask me whenever I begged for a puppy. *"And now we take them back in? Ironic,"* she'd said.

A geologist excavating her life over the decades could explore her through the layers of decoration in the rooms, revealing story under story—the history of her tragic fall. The finest, the best the world had to give—an ancient Greek urn, a rare Chinese ivory ball with delicate dragons intricately carved—ball within a ball, within a ball six times. The treasures sat side-by-side with random sentimental objects—a scraped hula hoop, an old broken Polaroid camera, a stack of used coloring books.

I could see how the balance had shifted over the past years since she'd begun to fail—tackier, more childlike as she'd lost her constructed, worldly self. I imagined how her ability to be flawlessly organized waned, how she found herself attached to random things from her own childhood, excavated from the basement, no doubt. Was she failing as seriously as I was imagining?

I recognized my Popeye Pez dispenser propped against a Louis Quatorze white marble and bronze mantel clock with two horses holding up the fragile mechanism. Priceless charcoal sketches of ballet dancers by Edgar Degas, given to my mother after her performance in Paris by some admirer, lay on the table out of their frames. Someone had colored in crayon across the precious art—a primitive scribble of a spinning ballet dancer on perfect point. The box of crayons stood nearby with the black one sticking out, worn down to a stub. I understood; she had returned herself to her rightful place. I could picture Mother's maid Marie watching her deface the priceless art. No one ever questioned Mother.

My phone rang; it startled me.

"Honey? You OK over there?"

"I'm in shock, I guess. You know, my mother was always such a perfectionist, so classy, so—"

"What's changed?"

"I can't even begin . . . can't you just come with me to the Ovation Residences, Sam? I don't want to go there alone to see my mother. It's too hard. She's never even accepted my birthday calls, not a single contact in forty years."

"I'll come with you next time, but you have to go first. Go see your mother today, Jules. Promise me OK? Then we can put this whole thing behind us. If your mother can come, she comes. If not . . . you'll know you did the right thing in offering."

"OK, I promise. I'll go today. I hope Di and Steven appreciate this."

"It's a good thing, having your mother at our wedding. It's a good thing, honey. The kids are right. She won't be with us long."

"Oh, Sam, she never *was*."

"I know, sorry. Love you, sweetheart."

"Bye. Wish me luck. I love you too . . . oh, Samantha?"

"Yes, I'm still here."

"Should we just tell her your name is Sam and then Photoshop the wedding pictures?"

"Funny, Jules."

It was a crazy thing the way the law had changed. Four years ago in 2011, New York legalized same-sex marriage. At sixty-one, we had two thirty-something children and a grandchild, and after forty years together, we were finally getting married.

I stared up at the enormous oil portrait of my mother over the fireplace, painted for her fiftieth birthday, a present from my father. I don't imagine it made up for the gift I'd given her after the guests left that night. I was twenty when I came out to her. Mother's Juliette would have no Romeo. Happy half-century birthday, Mother!

"You'll get over it," she'd said, as though I had the flu. "You should talk to the priest."

I've heard lots of people say that's what they heard from a parent, word for word. It was temporary, you'll get over it, you can fix it. The implication was you're sick or broken.

I'd crushed mother's picture-perfect dreams. It had been the final blow. She'd divorced my father. My "illness" had to be *his* fault, and *his* support for my lesbian love affair was the ultimate affront to my perfect mother. She hated the idea of me being gay; I hated the idea of her hating the idea. You would think being in the performing arts and having gay friends in the ballet that it wouldn't be so offensive to her. How could she stop loving me just because I'd found love? How could she cut me off so easily? We'd been estranged ever since. She'd made no effort, nor did I at first. Her rejection was too painful.

When I moved out to college and met Samantha, our love was

immediate. Powerful chemistry. Spontaneous combustion that has lit us up ever since. We had two *in vitro* babies, one pregnancy each—a boy and a girl. We'd shared everything, and my partner worked hard to help me get past the loss of a loving mother in my life. Sam was grounded, dedicated and affectionate enough to make me almost forget.

My father was my rock during the forty-year estrangement from my mother. She'd never seen him again either. He'd never once pushed me until he was dying. "Maybe you should try once more with your mother." His words pierced deep. We understood we'd shared one thing—a sudden broken heart. I felt such guilt that she'd divorced him because of me.

For the past several years since he'd died, I tried harder to bridge the gap with my father's wish in my mind—even showing up at her door. Marie had tears in her eyes when she'd opened the door to say my mother wasn't taking visitors. I could see Mother at an angle sipping wine in her library, staring up at her shrine of memorabilia, her tribute to herself.

Mother had a stubborn streak. My calls and letters were unreturned. I'd finally given up.

Walking around the receiving room, I stopped my usual hurt from rising. Counseling and four decades of being loved by Sam had given me a certain skill to deal with the pain. Still, being in my childhood home again had resurrected the echoes of those regrets. And I never could bring myself to take that Hudson River tour—the memories of Mother would steal the joy. I drew the heavy drapes shut tight on the memory. With the alarm set to the absurd code, I closed the door and sat in the car thinking, preparing myself to see her again.

I was nervous beyond anything I'd ever felt. Knowing she could still scare the hell out of me felt strange for a woman my age. A lesbian getting married was strange for a woman my age—although becoming more common among our friends. I thought I would turn the car radio on and they would admit the whole same-sex marriage legal thing was a hoax.

I was very much alone in my vote to leave my mother out of the wedding. The kids ganged up on me. *She's going to be ninety-one. She has dementia.*

They'd done their homework, calling the assisted-living residence. The nurse had said my mother was doing well on a new medication. She was able to socialize and attend the wedding. On and on. I was out-numbered. They had no way to imagine what my mother was like. I wanted to share the story of the "filthy" Hudson River, my childhood dream to cruise around Manhattan but I couldn't tell them the negative stories—it felt wrong to pass on that legacy of hurt to our children. Rejecting me was like *suddenly moving from a lifetime in sunny San Diego to Seattle gray*, I'd told the kids one day.

I found my way to the nursing home an hour outside of Manhattan and parked my Prius. Not surprising, it was palatial, like a fine French hotel. The entryway had an atrium with a stained-glass dome in which tiny geometric pieces of colored glass formed magnificent designs of trees, flowers, and sky. Even a few small birds had mistaken the place for a beautiful park and had found their way inside.

The Director Mrs. Gleason and Mother's private nurse Angela

met me at the reception room. "Good morning. I'm so glad you came. I'm so sorry that I didn't realize Mrs. Dupont *had* a daughter until *your* daughter called. Six months now, she hasn't mentioned—"

"Yes, well, my mother and I . . . well if she's been here six months, you must understand."

"Understand? She's so lovely. Well in any case, do you have some identification?"

Identification? As though a stranger would pose as a daughter and break in to kidnap a ninety-one-year-old woman with dementia and a mean streak, I thought.

I proceeded down the hall, "dead woman walking," came to mind, and I had to laugh at how petrified I was like a recalcitrant child. After all this time, my confidence melted at the thought of confronting her. I can't say I had a clue as to what would transpire. I didn't hate her anymore—too much love in my life for that since our kids were born. But, still, would the pain erupt? Would I scream out everything I'd ever felt? Would all those years of therapy evaporate? Would the scab rip off and start me bleeding all over again? Did she still blame me? Was she resentful, all these years? Or did she even care? Would she leap across the room and slap me—thoughtless daughter? Or would she say she was sorry—thoughtless mother?

My hair. She's never seen me in short hair. She hates short hair, so unfeminine. Ridiculous things your mind does to you, I thought. Parents can have such a hold. What do I care what she likes. Her judgments haven't mattered in decades.

"Here we are," Mrs. Gleason said. "Enjoy your visit. Angela will stay with you in case you need anything."

Mother sat in a brocade chair next to a lovely view of a garden in full-June-bloom. She was my wizened look-alike. I never thought about looking like her in my later years. She was a well-kept, gracious, elderly lady with coiffed, chin-length, snow white hair, decked out in a handsome coral couture suit with a pleated skirt. She was wearing earrings I remembered my father had given her in celebration of one of her many ballet successes.

"Juliette is here to see you," Angela said, setting two glasses of water with lemon and mint on the little side table.

"*Juliette!* Oh my, you look so beautiful today. Come hold my hand."

I couldn't move.

"Come," she said and reached out her hand.

My throat squeezed and the pressure and heat behind my eyes was unbearable. I was incredulous after forty years of angst, that the heavy weight that sat just outside my life waiting for me to let it go, could dissipate with one sentence. At first I was relieved, then angry. What the hell? All these years and you just say, *Come, hold my hand.*

I sat in the guest chair and held her hand. Her eyes, although deeper set and surrounded by wrinkles were still so blue and beautiful. I was shaking.

"It's so wonderful to see you. You've been well? Oh, you're shaking, *mon amie.*"

I was astounded. This was not at all one of the expected options. I confess, I wanted to fall into her chest and have her hold me, and tell me she was so sorry, and say she was devastated by her career loss, *but it had nothing to do with you, precious child.*

She must have seen the emotion on my face.

"Tell Genevieve what's been happening in your life?" She engaged my eyes, her specialty.

"I . . . where shall I start, what do you know?" I wasn't sure if my brother had ever discussed me with her on his rare visits.

"Very little, I'm afraid." Her eyes stayed kindly riveted on mine. There was no hint of blame.

I shared my life stories about college, meeting Sam, having the children, my art gallery.

She asked lovely questions. It was just that, lovely.

I lifted a book from her table when there was a lull. It was familiar. All of the ballet positions explained and a history of the dance. I opened it and she began to tell me the rigors of learning those stances. Her face was blushed and happy.

"What's this one?" I asked.

"Oh, dear, oh yes, *relevé*. That's French for *rise*. When a dancer rises up, up, up to the tip of her toes."

I felt I was rising—rising up out of my lifetime of hurt on the tips of my toes, at sixty-one no less. I needed to cry with her. *Too much, too soon*, I said to myself. I took a breath and asked her. "Well, Sam and I would like you to come to our wedding next Saturday. Will you come? Di and Steven, your grandchildren want to meet you. We have a grandchild too. It's a garden wedding at the Botanical Gardens. You always loved it there."

"Oh, how touching, I would love to. But . . ."

I knew it was coming. I knew it, dammit.

"I am so sorry; it's hard for me to shop these days living in this hotel. How will I get you a wedding gift?"

"Your presence is your gift," I said, recovering. I'd stolen the expression she'd said a thousand times to her birthday guests who had flown in from foreign countries and come directly to the party.

"What a lovely thing to say. Wonderful. Thank you for your graciousness, my dear Juliette."

I turned to Angela and discussed the timing and the plans. She agreed she would come along since she knew my mother's routine and wants.

We said goodbye. My mother hugged me and thanked me profusely for coming and for such a pleasant, long-overdue visit. "I'm so pleased we've connected."

I fell into the front seat of my car and wept. I'd never felt the warmth that I'd seen her employ that so easily charmed everyone who knew her. Why hadn't I visited sooner? I was overwhelmed with a flow of emotions—relief, regret, guilt, anger, forgiveness, love.

I pulled the handle to slide open the scissor gate to our service elevator door. I loved our modern loft. Still, I hated to think some-one had to die for us to get it, but that was how it was. Too many jokes about it, but when it came to apartments in New York City, macabre humor reigned.

Each time I arrived at our apartment and the massive doors spread open like an awakening giant's eye, I would breath and smile. The blink revealed a stunning wall of glass displaying what-ever drama mother nature was painting for our pleasure. Like an impossible, boundless gallery, the art changed every day. Sun today with thick streaks of clouds and a fading contrail with a hint of pink in an arc across a graying sky.

Our white brick walls held up oversized artwork splashed with color—simple, nothing to invade your mind, no expertise required to enjoy it—not making you a stranger or a guest. Collector's items, I admit. I laughed when our unpretentious taste was described as "Modern Welcome," in Architectural Digest; "It says, relax, come in, we're happy you're here."

The photographer had especially admired the two works that hung over our fireplace and in the dining area. He inquired as to who the artists were. "Extraordinary," he'd said.

I had to repress a laugh watching his face when I pointed to the two easels that stood mid-works in front of the far window, and revealed my children's names. We'd blown up Steven and Di's kindergarten masterpieces for the places of honor in our home.

No suffocating in this uncluttered space. My shoulders dropped. I sat on the comfy couch, put my feet up on the black glass coffee table and thought about making dinner. But no. Too much to process after my visit; I had so much to feel. I hadn't felt this peaceful in decades. I closed my eyes and let out a deep sigh.

Then Sam walked through the spreading door with Thai take-out in her arms.

The kids and my granddaughter arrived just behind Sam, and we set out bowls and chopsticks.

I was the heroine of the family when I shared my success with Sam and the kids who'd come to hear the news of my visit. "I can't even tell you how wonderful it was." I gave them all the details of my time with my mother. It boded well for the wedding. Although it seemed too easy, too strange—it was all too good. Sam told me not to be cynical, but to be grateful. Once I let myself, I felt in love and loved.

"It's something you just can't let go of, even though it feels sick," I said to Sam in bed that night.

"What's that?"

"No matter how illogical, it's biological maybe, wanting your mother's love and approval."

"Well, you have it now, Jules. You deserve it." She held me.

The wedding day was glorious as June can be in New York City after a dreary and gray winter and a questionable spring. We had a limo pick up Mother for the noon wedding, re-arranged just so the hour wasn't too late for her to attend.

Sam was beautiful in her sexy white tux cut to flatter her sensational body. Her spikey silver hair lit up in the sunlight. This wedding took months of discussion for us. Both wear dresses? Tuxes? How formal? God, we were planning and deciding on the details night and day. We had a lot of laughs. When it came to the honeymoon plans, I told Sam to surprise me.

I chose a full-length, strapless white dress gathered at the bodice. I liked that Mother would approve, as though I might have done it just for her. Some of my mother's love of clothes and dressing up had certainly rubbed off. I wanted to be beautiful for Sam. The whole wedding was a world of confusion for us. With few models or traditions to follow, we'd just did what made us feel special and beautiful in our own way.

Di and Steven walked in to "Trumpet Voluntary" and waited for us in front of the gazebo. Our granddaughter, Casey, Di's four-year-old, strewn rose petals on the ground. It was surreal for me, listening to the vows, knowing we had lived them already, a backwards kind of thing, like a memory—loyalty, love, acceptance? Yes, we'd already done that for forty years, so nothing to worry about. No fears that we couldn't live up to such commitments.

The children stood by our sides and we turned to make our vows to them. Again, we smiled knowing we had raised them up to our best ability and we had a loving family. Sam and I gave them what we wanted for ourselves—acceptance and love.

I kept peeking at my mother in the front row, knowing she would approve of such a traditional and sentimental wedding, and incredulous that she no longer seemed to disapprove of her daughter marrying a woman. Sam and I were pretty traditional by nature. So it wasn't posturing for mother, it was *us*. She was smiling.

The reception in the atrium was so perfect. One hundred favorite people, music food, and Mother holding court at her table in her blue silk dress, eating her meal, and telling stories of her worldwide adventures as a *prima ballerina*. Every eye was riveted on Mother. I had peace inside me that I can't describe.

Sam and I approached the table and I bent down and kissed my mother's cheek.

"Who are you? Angela who is this again? I'm sorry—"

Sam tried to help. "I see where your daughter, Juliette, gets her charm and beauty. Doesn't she look stunning today, my bride?"

"Excuse me?" My mother's head bobbed left, then right.

"She's talking about your daughter, Mrs. Dupont." Angela reminded her.

"I'm confused. I don't have a daughter. I only have a son, Gregory. Yes, I think it's Gregory."

Her words were like a punch to my stomach.

Gregory leaned closer. "Mother, it's me. I'm here. Juliette and Sam just got *married*."

We hadn't been close. My brother's constant travels had kept him away most of our lives, but he was supportive through the years. His wife, not so much. She'd never adjusted to having a lesbian sister-in-law.

"Your daughter Juliette and her partner, Samantha, just got married. Those are Juliette and Sam's children, your grandchildren, and your great-granddaughter," Angela explained.

I was frozen in place. Lost my ability to speak.

My mother turned to Angela. "Juliette—she's the new marvelous friend I met at my hotel last week. I thought that nice young couple got married. And why were those women standing up for them, no groomsmen?" She had that look of disapproval I knew so well that had made me shrivel up inside as a child.

"I'm confused . . . two women can't get married. It's a travesty." As though my mother hadn't even been at the ceremony, as though she hadn't seen us kiss. It was absurd and sad.

"It's legal now, Mother." Gregory added.

She pushed away from the table and nearly fell. "I won't be any part of this. I need to go home to my hotel."

I couldn't speak. Every cell in my body rocked with the disbelief. Sam stepped beside me and grabbed me by the shoulders.

Angela stood up, put my mother in her wheelchair, and touched my arm. "I'm so sorry. This happens at this stage. Ups and downs."

"Have I eaten yet? Where are we?" my mother asked.

"So sorry. Thank you for the lovely day." Angela wheeled my confused mother away.

I was falling apart on the most beautiful day of my life. My kids apologized and tried to console me; they felt they shouldn't have interfered. I needed to gather myself. No one but the people at our table noticed anything was wrong. Sam shuffled me outside and slipped me into our awaiting limousine to talk. "Give us a minute, please." I heard her say to the driver.

Sam slid in beside me and took my hand. "My God, Jules, it's so tragic."

"I want to scream and run. You've spent your entire life holding me together, Sam. I finally thought she—"

"We hold each other together. You can't change what was handed to you, hon. The only thing you can do is give something different to your own kids, and to the people you love."

"True."

"Do you see what you've done? You've made my life over the top. The kids are both happy and secure. Your gallery is a huge success and—"

"And, what else? Please keep going." I raised my head, and tried to smile.

She wiped my tears. "And most of all—you are the mother you never had. Defining, I would say."

I touched her bow tie with my finger, and her look made me blush. "How do you do that?" I felt a smile rising up. The whole reunion was surreal, such a farce. So unimaginable.

"You do have everything—she has nothing." She took my face in her hands and kissed me.

"So you think if I visit her, she won't remember any of this?"

"Maybe you should Photoshop the pictures, after all, Jules."

I couldn't think about what had happened at our wedding. I knew my mother wasn't all there. But, truthfully, if she were there she would have said the same thing. Well, no, not true—she wouldn't have come. I had to let go of the hope that my mother would accept me, my life, my family. It was too late; she was no longer there.

I looked at Sam's beautiful face. It wasn't fair to take this day away from my wife. Wife, a label we'd never used before. "So, *I* say, let's go back inside and celebrate *us*."

After the wedding ended, and we'd said our farewells and kissed our family goodbye, I slumped into the limo exhausted. "After all that, we ended on a good note didn't we, Sam?"

"Yes, I'm impressed how you salvaged the day."

"I did it for my new wife."

"Well, I did something for my new wife too." Sam nodded to the driver and we took off.

I didn't really feel like celebrating or traveling. My emotions were spent from faking my way through the ending to what should have been the sweetest day of my life. The honeymoon hadn't even been on my radar, I'd been so distracted with the whole mother thing. Heartbroken was the word, I thought. "Where are we headed?" I tried to sound upbeat.

"I'm taking you somewhere you've always dreamed of going."

"New Zealand?"

"No. Guess again. Oh you'll never guess it."

We pulled up to Pier 83 at West 42nd Street. I was confused.

Sam took out a brochure and read. "Climb aboard for a 2-hour romantic twilight cruise of New York Harbor and relax with your favorite cocktail as you enjoy the incredible sunset views of

Manhattan and listen to your expert guide's commentary about the sights of interest."

My stomach clenched. "Sweetheart, I can't . . ." My mother's voice screamed in my head, as she'd pulled the drapes closed on my childhood's treasured view. *Juliette, we are not going on a boat ride on that filthy Hudson River!* Too many painful memories were spilling out. I knew it was silly in a way, but the boat trip was symbolic of everything my mother had denied me, especially her acceptance and love. How could I celebrate our newlywed joy surrounded by such associations? But, looking in Sam's soulful brown eyes, I was softening to the idea. It was so thoughtful of her. She knew me. Sam knew what I needed to break through.

She stopped my refusal with another kiss.

The boat horn sounded.

"This is your childhood dream, and you need to let yourself have it before we can have the proper honeymoon, I've planned for the woman I love. Think of the cruise around Manhattan as the appetizer before the entrée of your life."

"Sam, I don't know what to say."

"And you know what *I* say?"

"What do you say, my love?" I was melting with her words, as always.

Sam squeezed my hand between hers. "*Relevé*, my darling, *relevé.*"

The End

The Real Me

THE BRASS BEGINS that boogie-woogie beat, and the Back-up Babes and I jump in with our vocals just in time. I can't distinguish the drummer's rhythm from the syncopation in my heart. A whiff of acrid aircraft fumes and a hint of my favorite fragrance whirl in the salty sea breeze around me. A scent I know I'll never forget. Could I be happier?

We let out our wartime warbling with those tight harmonies, and our boys in uniform spring to their feet. The thrill starts swirling inside me, lifting me up, when those hundreds of sailors' fling their white hats sky-high. Those spinning caps snowing down on us send chills down my arms. My prolonged smile at our encore hurts my face; *oh my, we're stars*, I think. Stirring applause electrifies my spine—applause like the buzzing sound of incoming Douglas BTB Bombers performing perfect two-point-landings near our temporary stage on the aircraft carrier's deck.

Turning the photo toward the sunny window, the memories flash, and I run my tremoring finger along the keepsake's deckled edge. The scents and tastes seems like yesterday, but they were memories from a lifetime ago. The insulting smell of synthetic lemon hospital cleanser blended with the greasy inedible breakfast on my nearby tray abruptly brings me back to now.

I lower myself with an audible puff into the well-worn divot in the cobalt vinyl chair. It's good to be up and out of that adjustable hospital rehab bed. That resounding applause had roared past my days like the thunder of the locomotive that used to rumble past my summer house in Rehoboth Beach. Only the pitch of the nurses' voices rises now—no sailor hats, no ovation, no audience on their feet.

The only stars I see now are the flickers of dustlets dancing in the band of sunlight through my venetian blinds. And who is that wizened widow in the dresser mirror who stares back at me? The less-than-full-step-down at my daughter's house had tripped me up. Weeks later, I sit here, my left leg in a soft cast; me cast in a new role.

The black and white photos in my hands don't begin to convey the palette of the person I was, or who I am. I'm from a long line of longevity, I want to argue; Great-grandmother Andrews pushed 104 in great health, sharp as a tack, they say, before her demise. But, sand is slipping through my hourglass, only a few specks of time left at the narrow neck of my remaining days, they seem to think.

My daughter's strident voice floats outside my room. "Do you have to take that damned electronic device everywhere, Charlie? I thought you were coming to see your grandmother?"

"Mom, I *am* here to see Grandy."

"Well, I need to get to work. And she doesn't seem too chipper today, so don't upset her."

Through the rectangular wired window in the oak door, I see Charlie nodding his head. I'm glad my daughter's off to work; I prefer the company of her son.

He cracks the door open. "Grandy. *Grandy?*"

Such a lovely moniker my grandson's chosen for me, *Grandy*. I straighten the white waffle blanket across my lap.

"Charlie, are you here for your daily story?" He's so sweet to listen. I'm such a bore with my relentless reminiscing, I think. I examine his new Comic Con 2018 T-shirt and think of the hundreds of his favorite comics I've bought for him in past years—perfect, preserved in plastic, like new. Like I wish I were.

"Yeah, I want to know all your stories, Grand." He props himself on the edge of the bed next to me, picks up the pile of photos from my nightstand, and shuffles through them, smiling. "These are so cool."

Charlie looks over his shoulder at the nurses' station across the hall. "I don't get it."

"Get what?"

"Why they talk to you like that . . ." Charlie crosses his arms in front of him.

"Like what?"

"You know, 'Oh, Mrs. Andrews, have we had our pills today?' I hate that. What's with the '*we?*' I don't see *them* ever take any of those pills."

We laugh.

"It seems my *aging* causes their vocal chords to tighten, like they're talking to a kitten, or a child. They mean well."

He gets it—my comrade, my confidant, my teenage soulmate in the clan.

"You should tell them, 'Hey I'm still *me* in here.'" He turns the old photo toward me for proof—a picture of me all dolled up.

Lately, Charlie's been constantly asking me for my memorabilia—personal letters to my husband before we were married, old wartime photos, recordings—especially of me singing. Asking what's your favorite this and that? So touching that my grandson cares. I'd thought perhaps he was making a birthday scrapbook of some sort, but he'd returned all the photos and scraps—the only remnants left of my past. Is he worried that I'm almost gone?

It's just a bruised leg; just a normal fall, I think. Well, and those numbers the doctor keeps rattling off, pursing his lips, shaking his know-it-all head that keep this princess trapped here in this tower.

Charlie kisses my cheek, and I light up as he pulls a package from behind his back. I untie the bow and pull the techno gizmo from the box.

"What have we here?" An iPad kind of thing. I don't dare say what I'm thinking; I'm too old to learn this stuff.

He grins, pushes aside his long swath of black hair that floats above the two buzzed sides of his head, like our unfinished lawn when my husband Ben stopped mid-chore to eat his lunch. Charlie flips the Do Not Disturb sign on the door.

I tilt my head at that—what's on this thing that no one else should see? I'm intrigued.

He touches the button to turn it on, and an image of me-in-miniature appears on-screen . . . Me. Well, my *used-to-be*.

"Your avatar, '*Eva Marie*.' I made her for you. Happy Birthday, Grandy Eva. Eighty-nine-years-young."

That brings my smile and an unexpected ache in my chest. "Avatar?" It's a term that's vaguely familiar, some movie, some cartoon? There on the iPad screen floats a vision of myself on an aircraft carrier stage, twittering a tune to smiling sailors. My face, my smile, my body, my hair coiffed forties-style, wearing a true-to-life sailor-girl blouse, and skirt, cinched tight, with the trio of those famous Back-up Babes behind me.

My avatar looks left, then right, tilts her head, so coy, awaiting my command. I can perfectly project the emotions I am feeling on her digitized face by a single tap; I can perfectly *feel* the way she's looking, a bit sassy, a touch coquettish. The photos bring my memories to life. She has my habit of running fingers through her hair to show confusion or flirtation. She has *me* down.

"See, I designed a replica of *you*. You can control her like this." Charlie runs through a series of touches and taps.

I practice moving my avatar self through some of the digi-places, as Charlie calls the locations he's designed for me. As though I am actually walking down the streets. Realistic replicas of life.

"Watch this." The American flags behind me blow in a westerly wind, and the setting sun is threatening the need for spotlights on the carrier. Angled beams flash off the windows of the readied fighter planes. "Boogie Woogie Bugle Boy," a recording of the hit song comes on with my voice jump-jazzing the words. It makes me laugh out loud and cover my face, peeking through my fingers. I can almost smell the faint scent of fume and fragrance. We watch my avatar's lips move to the lyrics, her body to the sound, her hand wrapped around the giant old-time microphone. My own hand is moist now with the memory.

"I gave you Paris too. He swipes a finger across the screen.

"Aw, Charlie, so sweet, darling boy." I pull his delighted head toward me and kiss him. I'm thrilled beyond. "So wonderful, Charlie, how did you—"

"Wait, that's not all. Look . . ." He clicks it alive again. He watches me practice until the visiting hours end. "See you tomorrow, Grandy. Love you."

It isn't long before I am living my life out loud again—my songs, my scenes, my dreams—moving across the screen at will, singing, my voice linked from the old records to my avatar's lips. It's as though I can feel who I am again, be who I was again, feel my future again. Like I'm alive in my past. A futuristic time warp that resurrects me.

The green walls of the rehab center that had sucked the joy from my days, fade into the background as I peruse the streets of Paris. My folds of flaccid muscles find their fortitude again on-screen. When I tire of exploring Paris and all the charming Parisian men I see—tire of all the coffee and croissants my avatar can fearlessly eat, slathered in butter; tire of sitting in a rickety wooden chair in a charming café near Montmartre; exhaust myself having my youthful sketch done by a charming man in a felt beret who gives me a double-cheeked kiss goodbye—I learn to travel home across the screen to Rehoboth Beach.

After three days of non-stop time travel into *me*, I've yet to interact with other avatars that I see. I'm too shy. Voyeur seems to be the very most I can muster. Charlie says I'll be more at ease, somewhere familiar where I feel at home.

This is the first year I can't make it to my beach house with my friends flowing in and out—a loss Charlie knows makes me ache inside. This damn leg, and something else I suspect. I've been feeling weaker by the day these past weeks. I'm grounded by a passing storm called aging that swept in without a warning and took me down.

"No need to be left out, I've created Rehoboth here," Charlie says, demonstrating how to walk the boards, negotiate the rides at Funland amusement park, sip steamy lattes at the Coffee Mill in my favorite bricked alley, flip my finger along the book titles at the Browseabout book store for something new to read, and navigate the sandy shoreline—all as my avatar, Eva Marie.

"How did you ever think of this?" I ask during one of his many reminiscing visits.

"My friend made one for his grandfather too. I thought it was so cool. You said, *cool*, back in the day, too, right, Grandy?"

Well, in one of my back-in-the-days, I'm sure I said, *cool*. I'm delighted, grinning that Charlie's created my beach town world for me. For a week I enjoy the treats of being in my digitized existence. I walk along the fantasy shoreline one morning after the nurse takes away my half-eaten breakfast, as bland as the tan tray it sits on. I'm anxious to get back to my life online. Jogging toward me is a handsome man about my avatar's age, well, maybe a bit older. He has a dog, a rusty colored solid-bodied brute, named Baron. I feel an electricity from days gone by. Am I cheating, if my husband's passed, if I'm an avatar? Ridiculous. The intersection of my past and present causes a moment of confusion. Not eighty-nine *inside*, I think. I grin and let myself have it, after all . . . it's not real. "Good morning."

"Hello." He stops.

I get a smile back. His dog decides he likes me; putting his front legs down, and with derrière in air, he wags his tail as though he knows me. "That's funny, Baron never does that with anyone else." He stands alert so the dog doesn't jump up on me. A gentleman.

There's a moment of flirtation in his eyes. My avatar, Eva Marie, I guess it's me, actually reddens, a blood-rushing blush.

I affix my glasses straighter on my aged face, shift in my chair, pause the scene on the iPad, and hobble up to open the hospital room window. I need a gulp of that fresh early summer air; I'm feeling a tad flushed. I get my composure, and quickly click back on.

"Shall we walk together . . . as long as we're both here?" the realistic avatar says.

It seems there is no point in playing hard to get, though one can be so bold and free when playing games. If it ever gets to be too much, it's so easy to just shut down the screen, I think. I want to maintain my manners and mores with the arresting stranger, but I'm out of my self here, so I say, *yes*. I'm glad not to be constrained by the times, any times, past or present. I smile down at my swollen propped-up leg that is invisible to my avatar admirer and turn away from the dresser mirror. Why ruin my own illusion?

His name is David. David Lakefield. In just a few circumspect glances, I notice his muscled shoulders, lean waist—a body I can picture swooping out of a pool, chestnut hair flipping a spiral of droplets after a deliberate fifty-two laps. A Burt Lancaster kind of guy. We share stories, have so much in common, seem to know each other from the start. Standing at Dolle's Salt Water Taffy stand, we fill our box with the same favorites.

"I bet you like licorice." He winks. "So do I. Well, now I do."

Among one hundred flavors of ice cream, we both order Jamoca Almond Fudge.

We can hold each other's avatar gaze more easily knowing it's pretend, or is it? It sends a tingle down my arms. So real, the feelings, as real as I've ever felt.

He tells me of the books he's read; I've read them too. Our favorite movies match. Our conversations are so satisfying; we're on point politically, progressive. He complains about discrimination, says his son's married and gay. David has one grandson, Jonathon, loves him, very close. I agree, and agree, and agree, as subject after subject unravels who we are.

"I fooled around a little with Shakespeare," he says.

"Really? What roles?"

"Richard the Third, Fallstaff, a few others."

"Love those parts. Where did you do theatre?"

"Oh, a little theatre in London."

I'm impressed. He's humble. When he hears that I'm a former singer, he quotes, "If music be the food of love, play on."

Romantic, like me. Good. I feel the rosie-red of my face as I remember a long-ago memory my body can't forget. When I'd first met my husband Ben, and he crossed the room to stand before me at the USO dance—the heat in my face, the allure of his smile.

I click off the screen, feeling awkward. I hesitate, feel a yearning, then turn it on again.

I huddle in my room each day, irritated by the interruptions—the nurse, meds, blood pressure. Oh, dear God that awful rehab, lifting little weights with stringy arms, walking on a treadmill when I could be back with my buff boy eating pizza with abandon and no harm. I can't wait to get back to being me, on my screen with David in my preferred life. I have a future there.

Sitting in the lounge chair by the window with my iPad, the sun on my shoulder, the breeze in my hair, makes time on the beach with David feel even more alive. On the seventh day since I've arrived in digi-Rehoboth, David spots a pod of dolphins. Such a thrill.

He puts his hand on my shoulder to point them out, squeezes, and a charge goes down my arm. "See? Eleven o'clock?" Leaning his head in next to mine, he speaks into my hair.

I tremble. "Oh yes, I see them." Two dolphins simultaneously leap into the air and splash down at twelve o'clock. We're moving forward. I feel the warmth of our friendship, the beginning of a romance. Dear Lord, I'm an old woman, for Pete's sake. I laugh, but let myself go on. I'm not dead yet. My eye follows his muscled arm as it surrounds me, pulls me in for our first real kiss. Like a replay, like it's happened a thousand times.

His shiny hair lights up in the afternoon shafts of sunlight that stripe the sand with shadow as the glowing orb drops behind the town. His blue eyes are the kind that change with the light, like the color of the ocean behind us. I stand facing him, the waves roar in a rhythm, crash in a cadence that seems to mimic the pounding of my heart. Like my music has returned. I sing a few notes out loud. An edge of rust, but not bad.

My resurrection begins to lift my vitals, lowers my blood pressure, heals all the things my blood reports can tell.

"I'm impressed . . . your EKG looks good," my doctor says.

He doesn't hear the flutters and skips on any EKG when I'm online with David, and I say nothing of my travels against his orders as my invincible avatar Eva Marie. The *real* me.

"I'm releasing you to go home, Mrs. Andrews."

Go home? I never thought I'd hear the words.

"It's a near miracle," he says.

I smile. "Yes, it is."

My daughter picks me up from rehab and drives me to my beach house for the summer. I haven't told her about my favorite pastime. I feel guilty as though I'm having an affair. And then, I'm truly in my Rehoboth Beach home, filled with sweet memories like a full candy jar, but absent of my David. I miss my privacy.

Charlie arrives that evening. I'm sitting on the porch in one of our rockers, and he joins me. The shade has taken over the painted planks on my covered porch; one of those extra salty, balmy June nights is in store.

"How's it been going?"

"My health's taken a good turn, the doctor says—"

"So glad to get you out of that place. You look great. But, uh . . . how about *online?* I mean, you had the guts to meet someone yet?"

I tell him the truth; he's the only one who deserves it. He has a funny look on his face. No one puts much over on this Grandy. "What are you up to, Charlie?"

"Nothing, it's just cool, right?" He runs his fingers though the hedge on top of his head. "Can we hit the boardwalk tomorrow really early? Like dawn, before the crowd gets there? You up to it?"

"Of course, you know I'm always up early. But a short walk, sweetheart, OK?" That's my doctor talking, I think. I've been tread-milling twice a day since the cast came off. I feel, *well*, I feel amazing.

What will it be like to be at the beach without my David? Wait, there is no, *my David*. I laugh, and for the first time I dare to think about the person on the other end of my avatar romance. Is it some pimply teenage boy? Goodness, I never thought of that before. Why didn't I think of that? A young technology nerd in Thailand? Adolescent in Africa? Lonely old man in Oklahoma? My partner's on another planet as far as I know. That thought deflates me. No matter, the emotions were real, the experience so wonderful, and now I'm well enough to be right where I want to be. My beloved beach town. Well worth it.

After lunch I send a message to David; I tell him, *TTYL*, as I sign off. *Talk to you later,* one of many short hand phrases Charlie has taught me. I add, *I'll miss you.* OMG, I'm in too deep; I have no idea what I'm doing with this techy stuff. Am I addicted, like Charlie? I hear my daughter coming into the room. I pretend to be asleep. She takes my gizmo and sets it on the table. I feel the invasion. I hold my breath, feel the loss. I pray David doesn't answer me just yet.

She leaves. I exhale.

No answer for a few minutes. I can't help curling in my shoulders, arms holding myself, grinning like a young girl when the bird-whistle signals the arrival of his return message. David answers, *Me too. Later. Missing you.* I choose to not imagine who my David really is; he's who I think he is. Really, isn't that the point? Like the imaginary friend my daughter had at three years old.

Why destroy the fantasy?

We're up at dawn, and Charlie drives to Rehoboth Avenue, drops me by the bandstand, and looks for parking. "Why did you bring your laptop?" I ask when he returns.

"Uh . . . I'm meeting a friend to play a game. Here he is now."

He introduces his friend Jay, a sweet blonde with an Oriole's baseball cap on backwards. They plop on a white bench in front of Candy Kitchen, and begin to click away.

"Grandy, you gotta feel the sand, take a walk by the water, like you always do. Need my help?"

"I'm fine." I haven't walked on sand for so long. My feet have only fast-forwarded on a treadmill these past weeks. I take my shoes off. Bending isn't easy, but I have more energy than I've had in years. I easily make it to the edge of the water. The cool wet sand's so soothing. It's almost as if the gulls remember me; they swoop down to greet me. The ocean curls just right and foam pursues me, hissing over my feet.

Only one man is on the beach wearing shorts and a Harvard hoodie. He whistles to a dog who's out of sight behind the dunes. The ruddy dog sidetracks and rushes toward me, curious, twisting left and right, bounding in a way that isn't threatening.

"Baron!" The man calls the dog.

Did I hear right? *Baron?* I'm confused. I hear my name. "Graaaandy!" I look over my shoulder and Charlie and Jay are standing on the bench pointing toward the man, cheering, hooting, high-fiving each other.

The man approaches, silver-haired, walking with the drag of feet that have marched many years, like mine.

The dog is at my feet, derrière in air, tail wagging, making little whimpering sounds.

The familiar man comes closer with his handsome head tilted. "Eva Marie?"

I can see the resemblance blurred by many years, but there he stands blue-eyed before me. "David?"

"It appears we have been had by modern-day matchmakers," he says pointing back at the boys.

It take a minute for the reality to sink in. "So that's why Charlie has been collecting my memorabilia." This is too much. "I see, the gizmo he gave me has a fast forward."

We laugh.

"And this is the project my grandson Jonathan was working on so diligently."

"Oh, I see, that's Jonathan—Jay."

David nods and shifts the leash around his leg. "Thank goodness you're mature and beautiful. I imagine that unripe lovely avatar would be quite disappointed by my current seasoned-self in the flesh."

Plucking the word *beautiful* from his sentence, my heart races. Not the kind of flutter that worries me. I distract myself by ruffling the dog's head.

"Look. One o'clock." He extends his arm with pointed finger over my shoulder, tucks in behind me, leans his cheek against mine and whispers, "See them?" The dolphins' slick and leathered backs rise up, arch, and stitch their way through the sea in shadow against the horizon.

No way to shut down the screen on this scene. No need. I'm glad not to be constrained by the times, any times, before or now. It seems there is no point in playing hard to get.

David reaches out his hand and takes mine. I am comfortable

with the enlarged veins on the back of his weathered hand, like tree roots weaving in and out of a welcoming wooded trail. The applause and howls of the boys rise behind us, and we laugh. The squeeze of his tender grip is asking me to stay.

Where is this path going? I'm too wise to ask myself, too old to care. "Are we in our future or our past?"

He laughs. "It's as though we've been together from the start. Shall we walk together, as long as we're both here?"

I, my used-to-be, my real *me* . . . we say, *yes.*

The End

First published by Salt Water Media, Inc. in *She Writes: Visions and Voices of Seaside Scribes*, 2018.

Second Place, Delaware Press Association Communications Contest, 2019.

Street Talk

HAVEN'T BEEN TO church in thirty years. Not since I watched my baby taken down that aisle in a little casket with the carved angels on the side. Not since I walked out that door and down 17th Street to Connecticut Avenue and slumped down against this wall.

The drink a down-and-out guy gave me that night was a long drink; I've hardly seen a sober day since. Not since my daddy shined shoes on this very spot—just like granddaddy did—Connecticut between L and M with a view of the park. I can still see his hands flying, buffing, shining those fine black shoes on some fancy important man wearing perfume like a lady.

So you see, this spot's like home to me.

I like thinking I live near the White House just across the park and up a bit. Makes up for some of the losses somehow. Never been beyond a few blocks of my spot.

Sleep in the park, visit the Mayflower Hotel ladies' room for a cleanup, and I go to work.

The sun's blazing on this wall today. Too close on the heels of that nasty snowstorm to be so hot. I'm freezing one day and sweating the next. I don't worry; I've got layers. Lots of them. I'm not complaining about the splatters of brown slush that dot my shoes when the bus slams by. It gets the shelter people off my case now that the storm's over.

I love that heat beating through my blue button-down sweater, and I love this long ultra-suede skirt they dropped off to me. Hides a multitude of sins. And how about my wide-brimmed hat hanging low over one eye? Makes me chuckle right here in the middle of winter looking like Easter Sunday.

It's harder to get the collections going when it's nice out, though. Easier when they're thinking you might die overnight without their few bucks. Like they're saying, "Oh you'll be OK now that it's nice out." Like my stomach only aches empty in the cold?

The wind flipped the page of my journal for me this morning. I write in it every day. Today I write, *this is gonna be my lucky day. Praise Jesus.* I know one thing—Jesus forgives, so even though I've been bad, I'm good.

You all listen to me. Today you're going to be so generous you won't know what hit you. I'm casting a spell. I got all cleaned up at the Mayflower Hotel. Ha! I rhymed—spell and hotel. A nice, high-class place. They know me. You all know me . . . though I've got these new clothes on from the shelter people.

One of you called me a *landmark*. What am I—the Washington Monument? Should be Lincoln Memorial for my slave ancestors. All my years here, never been to either of those famous spots.

Who shall I be for *you* today?

I read your faces when you pass me by and I pick out the

right costume that will make you drop that coin or buck. Thirty years, I've been reading all of you. Some of you give; most of you don't. But I know some of you like family—picking up clips of what you say when you walk to and from the Metro. Watching the clothes you're wearing, I follow your lives and I put you in my journal here.

Lots of sucking up going on along this street. There's always an upside one and a downside one. One of you uppity lawyers always walking tall with your hands moving around, talking to a down-on-his-luck man with his shoulders slumped, looking really worried. You toss out useless phrases. "Now don't answer if they ask you that . . . You have no legal obligation to . . ." Advice is always flying from you lawyers. Ideas buzzing from you corporate types too. Sometimes I get a clip of what happened with your kids or spouses. It can get juicy. Hard to catch it all sometimes with those buses blowing fumes, and you people late for work blasting horns worried you're gonna lose your fancy-ass jobs.

One good thing—I'm far enough away from that donut shop so I don't suffer *those* fumes all day while waiting for a dough-nation. Makes me laugh when I'm clever. I write it in my journal.

Some lady gives me one of these thick journals and a couple of new pens every Christmas when it's bitter and I sit here with blue showing through my black. I write small and it lasts me all year long. Had to write on the inside covers this year, real tiny. She says someday she wants to publish it. Make me some money. I've got dreams for that money. I'm gonna stop drinking and get a job—a real one. Every year she comes and collects the full one, gives me a fresh journal. Three years now. But no money. I can't imagine what I have to say is worth much anyway, so I don't ask.

You all don't know I'm educated. I wouldn't expect you to. Sitting here all unkempt. That's what my mama used to call me when I'd roll in drunk—*unkempt.* "Louise, you gotta straighten up and fly right. You're hanging around acting like a damn deadbeat."

Daddy's dead, Mama's dead, and I feel dead ever since I killed my baby girl.

Today's my anniversary of my laying claim to this spot. Everybody knows and nobody ever tries to take my place—Farragut North, exactly twenty-two steps in from the corner. Cops don't like me being at the corner, where all you pretty Washingtonian people have to turn sharp coming up out of the Metro to trot your way down Connecticut Avenue. The escalator's been delivering you to me for three decades. Special delivery. Why would I ever leave you? I've spent too much time getting to know all of you.

Yes, yes, when I look in your eyes, I know which *me* you need today. One of you might want my "crazy self," you have a brother in the booby hatch. That could be worth a good ten. Another of you might want my "everything's-hunky-dory" self. You know who you are. You can't do sad or pathetic. I say good morning, all cheerful like everything's fine and I just happened to stop here to chat with you. You show your gratitude for me not making you feel sad that I've fallen on hard times. A homeless woman, bag lady. Yes, I've got the bags to prove it. Your gratitude could be worth enough for my trip to Central Liquors. Sometimes I even take a cab.

I know which ones of you work out in that big second floor glass gym across the way. I see you pedaling, lifting, sweating, then coming out of that door onto the street all clean and fresh, carrying that fancy bag of stink. Nobody would ever know.

Here you come now. Out of all those people passing by, you're my favorite; you're always looking so nice in your suits and the crocodile briefcase and not-so-high heels. I ask, where'd you get that bag? You say, "Singapore." Now I'm really listening. That's a place I know nothing about. I'm gonna look it up. You don't treat me like some street bum. You're the only one who ever asked me my name.

Every day you say, "Hi, Louise." You're in the middle. You don't make me fake cheerfulness; you don't want me to be pathetic either. You don't always give me money; you know I'm buying booze. You say so. But you say, "You have to have dinner with those cocktails, Louise." I laugh.

I see you walking by with well-dressed men. They treat you like you're the boss. I hear you talking about setting up meetings with ambassadors and once you mentioned the prime minister of Thailand. I heard you speak what I guess was Thai to some Asian man—you say you learned Thai at the Foreign Service Institute across the river in Rosslyn. See? I'm clever. I remember everything I see and hear—not in my boozy brain, in my journal.

You don't ignore me when you're with someone important. You say, "Hello Louise. How are you?" One day you introduced me to your client. "Louise this is my client, Peter somebody, vice president of Mobil." Holy Jesus! I smiled the rest of the day. I know you want to show me you aren't some snobby white woman; you're just you. I know you want to show me you've got your priorities. And you want to see if that big shot does too. Look at you, sizing up your client's insides. Smart. You say it helps you when you're negotiating, knowing what kind of man he is.

Mostly, I like when you come by on your way to lunch and you take my order like I'm sitting in a fine restaurant. You ask me, what I'd like today. You tell me you're "doing Indian." You bring me a menu from that Bombay Club. Just put it on my account, I say like I'm some fancy executive with a tab running at a high-class place. We laugh.

Next day you ask me, "What's your pleasure, Louise?"

"I'm going American today," I say. "I'll take a burger medium rare, lettuce, onion and tomato, but don't let them put those pickles in there near the bun so it gets all soggy."

You write it down like my waitress and say, "Yes, Ma'am," and we laugh. I'm feeling like I'm somebody. I'm feeling less and less like I need to pick who to be each day to get you to drop the coin. You're not just some high-class white lady anymore; you're kind of a friend.

I mention you to some folks in the park at night and they say, don't trust that white bitch. I'm thinking they don't know you. Truth is, I don't know you either. I'm feeling strange. First time I'm seeing a rich white lady up close, like a real person.

You have those big blue eyes. I'm guessing you're size four. Haven't seen that size since kindergarten. I've been watching your hair change over these five years you've been walking by here. I like it long and shiny best. Not all business like. You're always changing; I'm always same-ing. Except lately. You aren't looking so great this year. Gaining weight. I don't want you fat like me. You say shame on me and tell me to say *full-figured*.

A long time ago, my aunt gained weight; it was her thyroid. I tell you, and you go to the doctor, and yup that's it. You say you're grateful. You're losing that weight now. I can see. I feel proud like I'm taking care of you like I should've taken care of my own baby girl. I figure you're about how old she would be—thirty-something.

I'm about twice your age. I know your birthday. Saw you going home from work with balloons on February 18 and now, you know mine, December 18. You ask the best questions.

I see you drop your little blonde daughter off to her daddy in front of Farragut Park. He's one of the guys that won't cough up a dime. Says he knows I'll always buy booze. Price of his shoes could keep me good for a couple of months. I know your custody agreement—he gets the child every Tuesday and every other weekend.

Your face is bright and smiling on the way to the park talking away with your little girl. I feel sad for me, happy for you. My girl would be a woman by now if I hadn't been drunk and stumbled her off the curb into that bus. Only two years old back then.

When I got pregnant, doctor says to quit drinking. I do; then Emma comes along; then I don't. I always see her eyes under that big bus—wide, wide eyes.

After your ex-husband-hand-off at the corner, you watch your little girl hold his hand and walk away. She turns her head and gives you that look. Sometimes those days you forget to say hello to me. I say, "It'll get better."

You turn around, like you shake it off, get yourself together, and pull out a lucky twenty-dollar bill for me. You tell me your philosophy, "when you hurt, you should give." I almost wanna give it back. Almost—I'm no fool. I need that more than you, and you need to give it to me more than I need to give it back.

How come I never ask you *your* name? I heard you say it once but I was pretty pickled. Embarrassed to ask again.

February 17, day before your birthday, I start coughing worse than usual. You've been saying I need to take care of that for a few years now. You always want to take me to the hospital. I refuse in a way that makes you not want to push. I don't want to go near that hospital. I'd lose control; the city would own me; someone would steal my spot. And it's not like they have a liquor store next to the gift shop in there.

In the early morning on February 18, the red runs out of my mouth into my hand and is making a bright pitter-patter pattern in the snow. I'm woozy trying to write my name with the red stream. I want to leave a sign for you. *L O U* . . . I try to leave my name. I've got a bad feeling. Some do-gooder calls an ambulance and it takes me to the ER. I know you'll be worried when I'm not there at my spot, and on your birthday too. I write a note in my journal so someone might read it and tell you. It hurts me to leave my only friend behind. I try to tell them when they put the oxygen mask over my face. "Wait, read my journal. OK? Tell that woman . . ." But they don't listen. Last thing I see in the ER is my journal dropped in a hamper with my pile of filthy clothes.

I am floating, hearing voices far away.

"We're losing her."

I'll miss you whoever you are . . . you were my favorite. You were the only one who ever asked my name.

I'm hearing voices and a glowing light hangs over me like a full moon. It's not heaven; sure ain't hell. I'm alive. Go figure.

"So *there* you are. Welcome back." Some nurse is smiling down at me. She's holding my journal. Says she found it in the hamper and kept it for me. I'm dopey but I can tell she's been reading it.

She's got some funny look of amazement that I wrote that stuff in there. She means well, touching my arm and squeezing it like she knows me now.

"Someone's here to see you," the nurse says. She has a confused look on her face. Then she takes a step back and *your* face appears over me. You take the journal from her hands. You know what's mine, what matters.

"Louise." You smile.

Now it's getting really strange you being so close to me. I'm feeling shy inside. I think about my breath, my body odor. But I feel fresh and clean like those workout people coming out the door across the street from my spot. Strange to think what happened while I was knocked out. Someone washed me, even brushed my teeth. Even tried to run a comb through my nappy hair. I haven't been touched in years, I think. I feel like someone else in this bed—not leaning on my wall. I don't do shy. I'm looking for my usual wisecrack, but it doesn't come to mind. You seem a little awkward too.

You tell me I've been out of it for a week. Everything's gonna be OK. Too much booze. I'm looking at you close-up. So pretty. Splash of freckles on your nose I never noticed before. Not as much make-up as usual either. Not much of you, all petite and small. You've got jeans on and a pretty blue sweater. You must see me noticing. You look down at yourself, nudge your hair in place like you're embarrassed and say, "Oh, it's Saturday," and you laugh.

The nurse calls from across the room. She tells me you've been here every day, nearly all day since right after the ambulance brought me in. "You two must be good friends," she says.

Something comes around my throat and squeezes, and tears almost roll over and drop.

Then you tell me how you found the blood by my spot, twenty-two steps in from the Metro corner. You say it wasn't the best birthday present for you. I watch your slow swallow. Your voice gets all shaky. You say you called all the hospitals nearby, found me in the one where they take *indigents.*

I know what that means. I'm educated, you know. Well, mostly from reading at the library since I graduated high school. Thought I was going somewhere, then I didn't. When a cop called me *indigent* years ago, I walked three blocks to the bookstore and peeled open a dictionary. Looked it up. Made sure it wasn't something dirty. Indigent: *poor, needy, impoverished, poverty-stricken, destitute, impecunious, deprived, penurious*—there's a lot of words for being me.

The nurse sets a tray of food in front of me. Tells me I'm released to eat soft solids now. Says it all flowery. She steps on something, and I rise up in that bed like Lazarus.

You sit in the chair beside me. I love the red leather boots you got on. I'm seeing you in a different way all casual like this. You put your hand on my shoulder. You tell me you did something for me. You're nervous, pushing your shiny hair behind your ears while I'm trying to push a shaking spoon down through the jiggling red stuff they call lunch. No booze for a week? Glad I was out cold for that, I think.

Feeling like friends one minute, known each other for years, then awkward strangers the next, getting up this close. I've never seen you when you weren't confident. Except around that ex-husband.

I say, "You've got to get me a menu from one of our favorite restaurants." We look at my tray of tasteless food. We laugh. Feels better when we laugh.

It's quiet then, and you start. You tell me you called the number in the back of my journal. Talked to that journalist lady. She's Station Manager of a radio station, you say. She's been using my journal word-for-word for three years now for some show about the streets of Washington—homeless people, things like that. You said you did something I might not like; you had no permission.

I'm listening.

You did some negotiating, you say. Did I ever think about her never paying me for my work, you ask.

I guess I thought it was coming some day and she would make good when it was time. I didn't tell you I didn't feel it was worth any money.

You tell me you have something for me. You're shifting around like some criminal in handcuffs.

I say, anything you did, I'm OK with it.

Then you drop the news. You got me back pay for the three years she's been using my stories for her radio show. "Street Talk," she called it. Only it's my words, and she's been using it; stole it from me, you say.

You heard that show on your car radio last week when you drove to the hospital to see me. Wouldn't have heard it if you'd taken the Metro as usual. It was divine intervention, you say. You recognized your own self from my journal she was reading on the broadcast.

I didn't know you were a lawyer, I say.

You laugh. No way! You leave that to your *ex*, you say. You're a contract negotiator; you make deals—international business development, you tell me.

I remember that Mobile oil guy and how all those men look at you like you got the Holy Grail. I'm feeling weak but this story's getting better.

You pull out a thick stack of papers and a check.

I've never had a checking account. Nothing's wrong with a mattress, my daddy always said. I look over and see a three and some zeroes. Still I'm a little woozy.

You tell me you got my last name from your friend at the hospital. Against some privacy rules. But you couldn't write the check to Jane Doe you told me. You laugh again but with a little edge of nervousness.

Jane Doe, that's a name we street people know well. It's what they call you in the morgue. Then I think I hear you say you got me thirty thousand to start me off. Of course I say, "Thirty thousand *what?*"

Well, then you tell me to calm down. You say you know that's not much after three years of writing but there's more—

"Not *much?* Wait a minute. What's *your* name? I can't be talking thirty thousand anything without knowing someone's name." I kept being afraid to ask your name, I say.

You tell me *Kirsten McCabe.*

"You mean we've got the same 'Mc' names?" I laugh. It's like we're related, McKenna, McCabe. Or we're some law firm. I can't get my mind to slow down. *Thirty thousand!* "Dollars?" I ask again.

You tell me yes, I heard right. It's dollars. I'm watching you. You're sitting there all proud but like a cat who's got another canary in your mouth. You tell me there's more.

More what? I'm wondering. But I'm seeing this Kirsten McCabe woman is holding back something. I'm thinking about the park folks warning me about you, calling you a *white bitch*. But I've seen nothing but kindness for five years now. Maybe, finally here it comes. My stomach's churning over.

I see *your* throat's squeezing now. You're shaking your head to get all the emotion out of the way, and you say you want to talk about what I said. You ask if I really meant it when I said I wanted to quit drinking and get myself together when my ship came in.

"Yes, get kempt," I say. I guess that's the opposite of unkempt.

You have a deal for me, you say. You negotiated with that radio lady for me. You got me a spot.

A *Spot?* I've *got* a spot, I tell you. Thirty years the same spot, Connecticut between L and M. I'm trying to joke my way past this one, but you're not laughing.

"You have no home, Louise," you say to me, "and no job. This is the chance you've been dreaming of."

Now I see. You really thought I'd be raising myself up someday like I was always saying I would. You don't know the streets. I've only known one other woman from the park who dragged herself up, got a job from her sister cleaning offices. Went to AA. Got clean. Tough lady. The others keep trying and bouncing back. I've never tried either, figuring I was a bounce-back type. I never really thought the time would come I'd be able to leave that spot. Easy to say I would when it wasn't gonna happen. Kept telling you every time you dropped a big bill in my hand—when my ship comes in. When my luck turns, I'd say; when hell freezes over, I'd think. I start to laugh.

Then I see your face get all ugly and you start crying for real. I haven't had anyone close in my life crying with me for as long as I can remember.

I reach out and put my hand on your shoulder; then I feel something deep, a long-time-ago memory. Brings *my* crying time to mind. My baby girl dead in my arms. The bus driver bending over me yelling, "You *goddam* drunk. You *killed* her!"

I pull you into my chest, patting you, holding you tighter, and my own tears—held back for thirty years—scream out of me. My baby'd just turned two when I killed her. Never thought I'd ever cry with a white woman wearing red boots, but I do.

After we stop the sobbing, I feel clean. You start talking between your sniffing. You say your daughter knows me. I need time to get myself healthy.

Hell, when's the last time I'd call myself healthy? The doctor says I need care. Care? When's the last time I had *care*?

You say I can get myself together for a few days at your house and think about what I want to do.

I've got thirty thousand dollars. You've got a Mercedes that takes me to your beautiful home up the fancy end of Connecticut Avenue. Now I've got a room with a view of another park, Rock Creek. I slept in a bed for two weeks, seven days in a hospital, seven days in your king-size pink palace with more pillows than a woman can stand, trying to find enough places for them at night without them touching the floor. What are those pillows for anyway?

The housekeeper keeps bugging me, asking can I get you this, can I get you that? I'm taking a real shower every day, trying to be polite. I stare at the bottles and jars of creams and hair stuff for a white lady in my private bathroom and laugh.

Feeling nervous in my brain, I'm out of place. I'm getting stronger in my body, more worried in my mind. Feeling like bugs crawling up there. Watching TV, with a little white girl in my lap, makes me happy and sad. A little white girl where my Emma used to be.

Your Janine calls me *Miss Louise*. Asks me to read to her. "Hand me my new glasses, sweet girl," I say. Then I hear music outside.

Your little girl screams, "Ice cream, please? Can we, Miss Louise?"

Ice cream truck? Since there's no booze, I think, *yes*. "Hand Miss Louise her bag, will you baby? Never mind. We can read later. We need to get ourselves some ice cream."

We run outside and hail him down on the street. Your baby girl's dancing to the music from that truck, and so am I. But don't worry, I'm holding her hand really tight standing on that curb.

She orders a fudgesicle; I order a vanilla cone. That makes me smile.

It tickles me when I watch my own hand sending that ten-dollar bill out in the other direction. I like the feeling of giving, not getting. I hear your words, *when you hurt, give.*

Keep the change, I say.

You tell me about that job, my radio spot. You say I'd get paid for just being me. Three times a week, fifteen minutes on air. I just do what I do. Talk. Tell my story. You have big dreams that I can help other women on the streets. Inspire them. You say, imagine you helping women get off the street.

"Imagine *me* off the streets." I say it to keep you happy. I'm not sure I can make the switch. You don't really know my life, like I don't know yours.

The next day, we take the train together. I'm missing my spot real bad. Missing my booze, worse. I come up out of the Metro like Alice in Wonderland coming up out of the rabbit hole back to real life. I've got a piece of paper says my life has changed to the tune of 30,000 bucks.

I see my spot. Someone's leaning there collecting on my people. My back goes stiff and my chest is tight. I know that woman; she sleeps next to the second bench on the far side of the park going on six years now. Young. Had purple hair when she first came. She sees me coming and scuttles away. That's right, *my* spot. I feel good. I want to hug that wall like a long lost lover. I miss leaning. Been leaning all these years. Doesn't feel right to stand up all day long without my wall. I'm home.

You leave me at my spot and go to work. You say you're coming back at lunch to take me to get my birth certificate so I can open a bank account. This is getting too complicated. Too much buzzing in my head. Can't think straight.

Then I see all of you people passing me by, looking at me like *oh you're back.*

I'm feeling like me again. But not really. I keep thinking what to do.

Getting close to lunchtime and I leave my spot. There's something pushing me, like the years of Daddy and Granddaddy right behind him are pushing on me, haunting me. "Hand the gentleman his hat, Louise," I hear Daddy say. Then I'm feeling ashamed. Daddy worked all year, all week, every day but Sunday to bring home those shoe-shining dollars. Always kept us fed. Always giving, not getting. Me hanging around like a damn lazy ass, as Mama said. Daddy didn't like her calling me that, but she was right. I wasn't ever worth anything. Now I'm worth thirty thousand dollars' worth of nothing.

Kirsten McCabe, you say I need a bank account. Daddy never had to worry about his mattress holding thirty thousand shoe-shining dollars. Daddy, you'd be sleeping on the ceiling, I say. I laugh but it doesn't feel good.

I see you coming way down the street for our bank appointment, and I start running the other way up to the park. Well, as fast as a fat—I mean—*full-figured* woman can. The usual people are hanging there, the same way they've always been hanging.

"Heard you been in the hospital. You been in what, two weeks?" they say.

"Nope, just one week. Stayed the other week at a friend's house up Connecticut Avenue with her maid taking care of me."

"*Friend's* house?" They start laughing so hard they're choking and coughing up phlegm. "What friend?" they ask, sputtering with laughter.

I wait until they quiet down so they can hear me. The spring sun shows up their red eyes and lights up the shine in their worn-out pants. I'm seeing some of them for the first time it seems. I'm seeing my life for the first time. I'm thinking about what to tell them. "The white bitch," I say. I hand them each a ten and walk away from their stunned faces.

I've got to go somewhere to think, maybe get a drink. Heading up 17th Street, I remember that man saying I was a *landmark*, panhandling on my spot for all those years. Makes me think; I've never seen that Lincoln Memorial everyone's talking about. It's not far. As I walk, I'm asking myself if I can make it stick. Can I get off the street, give up my spot?

The Washington Monument pointing to the sky leads me there. They call it the Reflecting Pool. I remember you saying you went there to figure out if you should get a divorce. Maybe I need some reflecting too. I turn and look up the long, glassy strip of water stretching from the Washington Monument to the Lincoln Memorial.

It's reflecting alright. The sky, the line of trees, the spike of the Washington monument, all shimmering back at me. Walking up to the edge, I see my face shining back at me too. How did I get so old? Did I really stand on my spot for all those years—nothing changing, everything same-ing?

Then I'm seeing my baby girl's wide eyes. Haunting, wide eyes. She's looking back at me. What does she see?

I see Daddy's old, stained, wooden shoeshine box, buffing cloths hanging out of the side—one brown, one black, one tan. Him setting it down in the hallway at home and puffing down into his beat-up corduroy chair. Telling me and Mamma that his dogs are barking, rubbing his tired feet, claiming he had a good day.

Daddy was always saying he had a good day. He'd hold that word so long till it meant something better than it was. I had a *gooood* day, he'd say. Squatting down in front of some man, rocking that cloth, snapping it till he could see himself in the customer's shoes, he said. Sizzling hot or bitter cold, Daddy had a good day.

I need to give *myself* some good days, I think. Stop punishing *me*. Do it for my baby girl's memory—and Daddy's too.

I turn from all that reflecting, looking down the long stretch of calm water, and I see Abraham Lincoln, his big stone self, sitting up proud with all those pillars around him. I'm getting the message. Digging in my long skirt pocket, I search for that radio lady's card. I think of you finding me in that hospital, getting me my pay. I earned it, you said.

Six blocks down, right next to the bookstore I find the radio station. I stop. More reflecting. I'm watching my own face in the glass door. Changed. Looking a little brighter somehow.

Then I'm pulling an imagined mic in close to my face. Wondering if anyone wants to listen to me telling my story. I guess they'd been listening for three years to *my* stories, but not *my* voice. I feel cheated. I'm thinking about walking away and getting some booze two doors down. I'm wondering how to keep myself from being a bounce-back. How to give me some *gooood* days.

Watching myself in the door's reflection, I look behind me. There's a dozen people waiting for the bus watching me too. What the hell, all you people figure I'm crazy anyway, I think. So, I talk out loud, right there on the street—trying it on for size. I've got a lot to say, don't I? I've got to speak out, use my voice. Make something different of me. Make a difference.

I step left in front of the sliding door. It opens. I take my imaginary mic and start practicing my show in *my* voice. I talk just like a real radio show. "This is Louise McKenna broadcasting live from my spot, twenty-two steps from the corner of L and M. You're listening to *Street Talk*."

I smile.

"Louise, who shall I be for *you* today?" I say.

I step inside.

The End

Molting

THE EARLY BEACH sun creeps up over my deck railing and spills liquid gold into my art space. It's quiet, except for the incessant tick-tick of the Thomas Tompion clock on the mantle and the scrape of my palette knife across the canvas. The cadence of the minutes passing echoes in my vaulted ceiling—and I paint.

I stroke, press, and drag my brush until the blue paint oozes and leaves the perfect thick and thin lines that I somehow know will read as ripples in the waves from across the room. My wrist nods and flows like a conductor directing unheard music. I step back to see how the enlivened water eerily moves, and I smile because it works—yes, it works. It's the only time I feel my life works—here, near my love, in these still moments on the other side of the bridge.

It's the only time I feel I am in command, conducting some small part of my life beyond the years of running charity events, slicing oranges for soccer games, and playing the many roles that drain my blood, my strength, my me. In those few precious fleeting hours in the meniscus between light and dark, night and day, in the "just befores"—just before bed and just before our beach house full of guests awakens—I molt. I drop my mantle of motherhood and wife to release the hidden artist inside me.

I should be grateful, Oprah and my meditations tell me. I should be grateful for the pin that holds me in place, like a rare butterfly, for everyone to admire. I'm not—I'm desperately lonely, while relentlessly surrounded.

Even though we arrived late last night after the usual frantic Friday escape into traffic, I am up before dawn. I leave my husband snoring in the darkened room to prepare to see my Oceanus as I've come to call him—Greek for the Titan God of the ocean. I have no guilt for this uncontrollable love affair with the ocean and the shore. It's an irrepressible passion. I think of Oceanus, close my eyes, and smile unashamedly—even while sitting next to my husband, Daniel, in our overloaded SUV at the top of the Bay Bridge.

I can feel the ocean comforting me, listening to the whispers of my soul. It never fails to free me, and I feel myself transform, casting off my shell of perfection—the perfect mother, the perfect wife—to walk barefoot in the sand with unkempt hair, unpolished toes, and dreams of a life free to be myself with Oceanus. He likes the raw me, the real me, the me before the messages took hold that told me how to be, the me before my life of tennis whites at country clubs and hair swept back in bows.

I think of the Old Masters, whose apprentices did all the painting while the Master took credit for the final piece. I feel like that—never holding a brush to create the details of my own life, only appearing in the end to add my name on the bottom right corner to signify this was my creation. But, it wasn't handmade by me, I confess. It was made by the hands of others: my children, my husband, even a five-pound puppy that made his paw marks on the canvas of my life.

For now, I luxuriate alone with my brushes and the acrid scent of the oils on my palette: six shades of blue, three greens, a touch of red, and some golden yellows for her hair. I mix just the right shade with an urgent tapping of my brush, with one ear listening to the lapping sounds from the open window and the other cautiously attentive for the footsteps and flushes in the ceiling above.

I take in the selfish aroma of my one-cup hazelnut Keurig, not wanting to wake family and guests with the alluring scent of a full brewed pot. Raising my shoulders, I'm not yet ready for the clarion call to relinquish my selfish time in my secret world—to take on the cloak of mother, the role of wife, the demands of host, queen of the beach house.

I'm conflicted, wanting the morning to move on so I can see my Oceanus in the new light, but I don't want my creative process to be rushed. After all, it's from the ocean that I've learned to set my boundaries, demand my space, and feel my worth. I've learned it, although I've yet to live it. He's strong, dependable, and steadfast, yet he allows his natural moods to flow freely with no apology. I need to learn to do that rather than adapt myself to suit the moods of others.

I work wherever I please on the canvas, unfettered in my rare freedom, and the painting takes shape. Surfacing from the blotches of color, my mermaid flashes the shimmering scales on her tail, and her blond hair with bits of shell and tiny fish dances on the canvas with wild abandon. The foam and bubbles push her forward in the powerful flow of the sea that surrounds her. It makes her reach out, unashamed of her nakedness, as if she could swim into your arms.

I angle the easel closer to the emerging natural light and add a final touch of glimmer to her captivating green eyes, quickly cleaning up a tiny splatter of oily evidence from my immaculate wide-plank hardwood floors. Her look comes together—tender, enticing, yet pure and full of heart. My own heart beats faster, and I inhale deeply. It's good. *No, it's very good*, I tell myself, and I push aside my usual self-doubt.

Tonight I'm throwing a party for my seventieth birthday and our forty-fifth anniversary. It's our summer's requisite hoorah. Even my birthday is overshadowed by my husband. He isn't to blame; he's just as much a victim of this life of routines and rules, this cardboard box we share. It's all he's ever known. I'll order this, arrange that, and celebrate myself and the years of birthing and bonding to this man who gave me his name. Waiting on friends, cooking, cleaning, I'll toast my seven decades living as a crustacean who has never learned to molt.

I think of the quote that inspired me to paint this seaside siren who calls desperately to me to live out loud, to find my true self, to audaciously create in broad daylight. "I must be a mermaid," Anaïs Nin wrote. "I have no fear of depths and a great fear of shallow living." Yet, I still paint in shadow, thinking my true self would not be welcomed in my daylight world.

I have lived in this fear of shallow for all of my adult years, so why did I succumb to the demands of my affluent suburban life? I was enticed by the neatness of it all, the comfort of the rules, knowing just what to say and do, with marker pen poised to slash the white space from my children's calendars. I should be grateful for this safe and perfect life with perfect shoes.

Her face has become clearer now with the final touch of my brush. She wears a look of serenity that I don't share except in these precious, guilty, stolen moments when everyone sleeps and no one asks me: "What's to eat?" "Where's my suit?" "There's a button missing; can you sew it on?" "Where'd I put my keys?" "Can I borrow the car?"

I rip off my painting shirt and store it with my mermaid in my secret place.

Someone has brought a puppy without permission. He stretches and lumbers to my side. His tiny sharp tooth lodges itself in the leg of my yoga pants, signaling it's time to go. He drags along behind me, and I pry his little jaw open and release him. The symbolism doesn't elude me. I open the sliding screen door and silently close the latch. The whine of the little dog and the first upstairs flush fade behind me, and I'm free just in time.

The salted air lures my hurried barefoot steps along the dunes to the south end of the boardwalk. With my water sandals swinging in my hands, I stop to fill my lungs with salty anticipation. For good luck, I touch the rough gray splintering railing that marks the boardwalk's end, and my fingers register the feel of its ridged and rugged texture. I save the memory for my art.

My blue, size-small "Life is Good" T-shirt is stretched tight across my middle. Some weakness this season has made me surrender too often to the long-forgotten beach food; I have returned to Thrasher's. The punishing gulls swoop down to attack my familiar oversized salted cup of fries scented with apple cider vinegar, trying to prevent my sin, screeching, "No, no, no!"

I have much to ask Oceanus today. He's always there to listen to my aching heart, and today I need his wisdom. I need his arms around me. I fear I am disappearing into a dark place.

I pick up my pace. *One mile of boardwalk exercise, then my illicit escape awaits me*, I tell myself. I slip on my shoes and hypnotize myself with the thumping sound on the boards beneath my impatient feet. A sticky glob of ice cream, a stray Funland ticket, and a Dolle's saltwater taffy wrapper connect me with my jealousy, thoughts of husbands who don't golf all weekend and dreams of mothers who don't plan their own birthdays, but then I think, *I do it so well*. My tears begin.

I stop to pick up a lost hermit crab, its natural shell decorated with the painted helmet of a Philly Eagles player. I know what it feels like to live beneath a label. His claws neatly line up, like fingers on a praying hand, and he pulls back in embarrassment as if he feels my eyes on him. The smell of dying rises up from his shell, and I reach through the boardwalk railing to place the escapee on some dune grass with hope.

I have my love in my sights in the distance beyond a rounded wall of sand that was sucked up from the ocean floor in one of his unexpected moods last night. I turn right and follow the winding fenced-in path. I'm almost there.

I run to him, my wonderful Oceanus. He thunders today at the sight of me. Unlike my husband's moods, he doesn't make me pull into my own shell. He allows me to be real, and to bravely bring to him whomever I am each day. It's a freedom I feel with no one else, except maybe Helen, my best art college girlfriend, who accepts me as I am but lives a freer life and struggles to relate. I'm alone along the early shore, empty as far as I can see, two far-off concrete towers half-wrapped in morning shadows like paper around an ice-cream cone. I feel some brief relief as my feet sink into the cool sand. I watch a horseshoe crab soothe itself in a cooling massage of foam, encrusted with dependent travelers—shells, barnacles, and tiny misled crustaceans clinging for dear life, like me. I nudge it until it catches the current of a rescuing wave.

Something is different today. I am being swallowed by all the expectations in my life. The errand-filled planning of my own party opened a wound in me that has been festering all week. The sun is pushing through the bank of gray along the horizon. It's a westerly insistent wind that lifts white wisps from the crest of each wave, and I see Oceanus is also in an agitated mood. Still, he will always listen, so constant, so deep in his understanding. He often leaves me with a feeling of resolve that melts like the secret cup of Kohr's custard that I sometimes indulge in on my walks home. The sugar high readies my lioness to leap, yet each time I enter my door, my courage to change somehow dissipates, and I keep my paintings and my feelings locked up like a secret lover in a closet where no one goes. Instead, I take out the frying pans to prepare the brunch—omelets for thirteen, me and the one dozen sets of sunburned legs and arms sprawling on white organic cotton sheets upstairs.

Today is different. No. Not anymore. Not ever. Today is different; I've reached a point. I'm done. Walking beside Oceanus and confiding in him isn't enough. I've never actually gone in the ocean in all the time I've used him as my secret confidant. I've never let go of my fussy concerns about the cold, getting my hair wet, the grit, the undertow, the excuses that prevent me from feeling him raw and real. I step lightly through a half-moon of old crushed memories, broken shards and shells left behind by the tide. Only one familiar woman and her curly-haired white dog are in the distance, too far away to see my sin.

A sudden blanket of foam swashes over my feet, draws back, and I follow. Ankles, calves, knees, and the swell of my belly chilled by his hands make me hesitate, but he entreats me. I see the watery arc above me and I give in, pulled under by his power into the churning sand. I'm tumbled in the roiling bubbles, my long graying hair dances in the restless water like my mermaid's tresses. I feel my breath needing to escape, to be replenished, yet I stay, marveling at the sound of the pounding waves, caught in the hydraulic of confusion.

I am drawn farther and farther from my contrived life, and I'm transformed into the woman I was—hopeful, youthful, creative, unfettered and alive. I see my tail growing and shimmering with blue-green scales, my youthful breasts lifted by the current, my long silky hair with bits of shell and tiny fish playing joyfully around it like an alluring coral shelf.

I feel the current taking me deeper. His desire for me pulls me farther out, and I succumb to the freedom. I watch the bubbles of my final breath rise up above me to the surface. I see my daughter's pleading eyes, my son's search along the shore, my grandchildren's tears, my husband's regretful face changing with kind promises, my friends begging me to love them enough to stay.

The sun reaches through the water surrounding me, and I rise up with a sudden understanding. I push my way through the final crushing wave that holds me, and it pulls off my mermaid tail, freeing my legs. My cheek rests safely on the sand in the gentle foam, and my rapid breath slows. My hand lies next to a set of bird footprints, and my eyes follow their silly drunken tracks that wander off in any direction at their whim. Nature is so wise, I think.

I walk along the shore for hours, gathering stares in my disheveled state, meandering where I please. I'm not concentrating, just giving myself time to absorb. I'm boldly molting in broad daylight.

The sun goes high, turns down toward the horizon again, and urges me to return. I walk up onto the deck of my oceanfront home. When had the cedar shakes turned from silver to brown? I wonder. Imperceptibly, over time, just as I had slowly weathered? Just as my husband has slowly gone bald? I am the reverse; my aging has turned my sandy brown locks to silver beneath my camouflage of blond.

I look through the sliding doors and I see them standing silent, staring—the entire gang. I imagine how I must look. I don't care. Even the caterer is frozen in place, waiting for the tap of my baton. My nervous guests are dressed so stylishly, champagne in hand, standing in my precious predawn art space that has magically turned into the family room again.

"Bridget, where *were* you?" Daniel steps out behind me and talks through teeth under his breath. "The guests are here; they're hungry," he says through a smile intended for those watching at a distance, but not for me. I laugh to think there is one hundred dollars' worth of food per person, waiting within reach just over the granite counter, to save them from starvation. My perfect husband stands tanned, tall, and trim. I smile. I am not the only one who suffers from the disease of perfection.

"Have you seen yourself? Have you looked in the mirror?" he asks.

I think the same—have you, have *we?*

"You were worried about me, weren't you?" I translate, touching his face. Without a word, I walk across the room and drag out my easel from the storage closet. I dramatically whip off the cover, which is actually my daughter's forty-year-old baby sheet.

My friends and family draw in their breaths and everyone applauds.

"Oh, it's beautiful."

"Spectacular."

"Is that your gift from Daniel?"

"Oh my, Daniel, where did you get it?"

"Who is the artist?"

"Do you mind sharing? I have to have one of his works for my collection!"

They examine my painting, step back, and then lean forward with concentrated appreciation. They're silenced by her look. My mermaid emerges from the blue and green of the windy sea with arms that promise to hold you, heal you, love you as you are. The water moves and undulates around her. Her vibrant green eyes look deep, catch the light just right, and electrify her admirers.

My friend Helen, the only one who knows my secret, walks toward the painting, which is as tall as she. "Well, let's see," she says and winks at me, an understanding gesture that makes me glad to be alive. She bends over to examine the lower right-hand corner. "Bridget King McDaniel," she reads, in three distinct words, and I feel the last of my shell peel away and clatter to the floor.

I accept a loving hug and kiss from Helen, who kindly plucks a length of seaweed from my wild hair. In my peripheral view, I see my children's faces, lit with amazement, and watch Daniel walk toward me with a look I haven't seen in many years. He studies me intensely with wonder, and his eyes flicker, searching mine.

"Danny." I smile, calling him by his college nickname to instantly rewind us in time. I so desperately need him to remember two imperfect, optimistic dreamers: he, the dedicated architect who rebuilt villages after earthquakes, and me, the promising artist who secretly painted colorful seaside murals on dreary city walls. Can he see himself tenderly plucking that dab of turquoise paint from my hair nearly half a century ago? Can he remember the deep connection and convictions we once had? He glances at the painting and then at me, and pauses for a painful minute.

Tick-tick is the only rebounding sound, and I wait. Then, he shakes his head, grinning, and I know he sees me. He looks through the mess that I've become—weathered beauty, unknown artist, shells and tiny fish in my hair—to see his mermaid. He steps forward and kisses me with lips that taste of long ago. All along it was I who had to change, to change my world around me. I am the artist of my own life now, and I step back and smile because it works, yes, it works.

The End

First Published by Cat & Mouse Press, Lewes DE 19958 in *Beach Days*, Rehoboth Beach Reads series, 2015
Winner Judge's Award

The Instigator

"JACKIE, WILL YOU be OK here?" My suntan-lotion-scented husband Eric asks.

"Yes, yes, I don't want the twins to miss out."

"I'd take you but . . . you know what it's like with a guy my size in those little boats." He forces a laugh. "I'd get decapitated again. I'm going to paddleboard out there with them. OK?"

"Honestly, I'm fine here with Josie." I don't tell him I never feel quite *fine* anymore. I don't reveal the fear beneath my smile. I don't say, I never feel like *me*. I hear Eric linger a little longer than he needs to, and I read it as his guilt. "Those boats are really meant for one, or two low-to-the-ground kids," I say.

I laugh at the memory of Eric and me sailing off on that little squirt of a sailboat when we were teens—the boom whipping across the stern of the single-sail Sunfish, blasting 6'2" Eric in one unexpected swoop into the murky waters of the Rehoboth Bay. My words returned at the memory of him drenched, dragging himself out of the waist-deep water. "I always said you had *sandy* brown hair." We'd laughed together back then, once we knew he was OK.

"Bye, Mom." "Bye." My ten-year-old twin son and daughter's voices drift away.

I hear the sailing instructor directing them into their positions on the small sailing craft. That should be me instructing them, but that's not in the realm of the possible now. It brings me back to my summers at the sailing club on the rental boats. I'd liked the two-toned one called Orange Crush.

I listen to the gentle gurgle of Eric's paddle moving through the water as he pushes off on his paddleboard to enjoy being out on the bay with the kids. How can I relate to my family now? I'd been the leader of the pack when it came to my kids' activities. *Now*, I can't see a ball to catch it, can't lead them on a hike in the Shenandoah's, certainly can't take them sailing. I was a former collegiate, gold-winning woman in tennis, former pilot, former everything—a disabled veteran now.

The VA rehab team at VISOR, the Vision Impairment Services Outpatient Rehabilitation program, told me that in time my brain would rewire itself. It's called neuroplasticity, the therapist had explained—although still blind—my other senses would open up the world to me again. After I'd been thrust into darkness in that ambush, I would find my life through my ears, my touch, the scents of the world, they'd said.

But how long before I'd find my new normal with my family? When will my children ever have their mom back again? How can I be the family *instigator,* as my husband always called me, if I can't see? How would I ever be the architect of all things exciting and unexpected—the Easter Egg hunt at our cabin in the woods, our dirt bike adventures, the hilarious zip line rides from their bedrooms to the barn?

Being my husband's wife seems an easier role. He can take care of himself. But being my kids' protector with Eric off to work each day when I can't see the world around me? And how can I be in charge of that one thing my kids counted on me for in my former sighted-life as their mom—*fun?*

I twirl my finger around a drooping curl on Josie's soaked, corkscrew coat, at the base of her neck where she loves to be massaged. I can almost hear the hissing as the penetrating morning sun evaporates the bay water from her back. Sensing my tension, as she always seems to do, she edges closer to my low-slung beach chair—my water-loving guide dog, Josie.

I'd never had a pet growing up; Mom had allergies. So I'd never quite understood the closeness my friends felt with their dogs. Now I do. When my service Labradoodle first nuzzled into my neck as I squatted to greet her at the VA rehabilitation hospital, I had no understanding that I would fall in love so hard, so fast. I had no idea I would be this *wounded warrior* sitting on my childhood beach on vacation in Delaware—in the dark, tethered to my new life by this loyal animal.

As always, my furry comrade sits so close I can feel the heat of her body, feel the rapid or slowing rhythm of her heart, smell her breath. She is my eyes, my *calm*, my new source of courage at a time when I need it. More than when I was fighting in Afghanistan, I need it now. Doing my military job was one thing; I knew how to fight and lead my team. This was about my children, my family.

I had to be told Josie was a caramel-colored pup when she first arrived by my side. The poodle part of her made her quick to learn.

Originally bred as a fisherman's helper, the Labrador in her loves the water. With her kind nature, Josie adored me instantly. That felt good, almost flattering; she liked me.

The intensive weeks at the rehabilitation center had taken down my fears a bit. I was hopeful I could function when it came to the basics. I'd learned some tricks myself—like hooking my finger over a glass as I pour my juice to prevent an overflow and navigating safely around a room filled with furnishings. I'd come a long way from that villager finding me face down in the dirt after the explosion. Why go into that now? Right *now*, I am trying to enjoy a glorious beach week with my husband, son and daughter.

I grab the scruff of Josie's neck and give it a loving tug. I could feel her dedication from the start—her affection, resting her chin across my forearm as I sat listening to music in my rehab room. Tapping her paw on my thigh when she sensed I was sad. Her protection and desire to please me—I'd *experienced* all that. She'd already kept me from several falls and mistakes negotiating my new white-cane life. We're a team—best buds. Can a dog really be a woman's best friend? This dog and this woman, yes.

She'd become my "eyes" and my unconditional friend, just as they'd told me she would. I couldn't have understood months before, just back from Afghanistan, that she would bring down the darkness of my sadness as well. Although my moods still flow with waves of gratitude and rip currents of melancholy, Josie is always the tide that can lift me.

She carefully guides me down the edge of Rehoboth Bay to play. I take off her harness. She needs some freedom; so, do I. My husband had bought me this long plastic rod, called a "Chuckit!" It has a ball cup on the end that allows me to play a game of fling and fetch with Josie. I fling the tennis ball far out into the darkness of the bay ahead of me as I stand by the lapping water. With each hurl, Josie rescues the ball, swims to shore, drops it by my feet, and barks. She knows how to talk to me.

Josie nudges me closer to the water. I become aware of every pebble and shell underfoot. My muscles tighten and I hold back, but the Rehoboth Bay that I know so well is a good place to start— no crashing waves to threaten me. The sand texture changes from packed smooth to pebbly to silky silt under my feet as I enter the edge of the chilly water. Small strips of seaweed wrap around my ankles pulling at me with the tide saying, *you can't back off now.*

My guide doesn't share my fear. Josie herds me over to the right avoiding a horseshoe crab that touches the edge of my foot. I lean over and examine the prehistoric creature with my hands, just as I'd re-discovered the faces of my two kids through my touch.

Now Josie smells of salt and that damp, musty dog scent of a canine who just can't resist retrieving grungy tennis balls from the water. Shaking the gritty sand from her thick curly coat, she nudges me again, and waits for me to replace her guide harness with the handle to lead me back to the chair. She's become such a part of how I see my new world.

Why was I reluctant weeks ago when my husband read the Wounded Warrior Project invitation to a September beach week with my family? "Seas the Day"—a vacation including my child-hood amusement park Funland on a beachside boardwalk and sailing at our old local sailing club? Honestly I wasn't sure if I really wanted to come back here in this condition—back to where I'd vacationed with my parents and sister every summer with me winning every game on the boardwalk. I was good at aiming—

shooting a water pistol into a flower, tossing miniature basketballs into a hoop, and rolling balls into holes for points—I'd go home with a pile of prizes. "Eagle Eye Jacqueline," my Dad called me.

Being at this beach town nestled between the Bay and the Atlantic ocean unable to see the water's ever-changing colors as it turns from see-through cerulean, to sapphire, to dark navy on a cloudy day—unable to do the things I used to do with my twins, who are still nervous around me—weighs on me. Yes, my blindness weighs on me—feels like the dark clouds that hang over the horizon. I pray I'll find my way.

After battling inside over my reluctance about the beach week, I decide more than anything I want to find my way to happiness again and to give the kids a reprieve from their own fears around having a blind mother. They were used to me being an athlete, the fun one in the family. Now I can't drive them to their ball games or shoot hoops in the driveway. But I'm not here at the beach now to regret, I tell myself. I'm here for The Wounded Warriors Project "Seas the Day" program.

After meeting my fellow soldiers at the opening dinner last night, bravely functioning without full-faculties, rising up from far worse challenges, I want to be grateful to be alive, and enjoy our first vacation since my blindness took us on an unexpected detour in our lives.

Yesterday, when we first entered the house that was donated for our use, I could feel the large spaces around me from the echoes of our conversations. I began to explore my surroundings with my hands. So lovely.

"Wow, Mom look how beautiful the view is! Oh, sorry, Mom." Erin stopped and said her usual apology for using the word, *look*.

"Sweetheart, I told you no apologies—we are all adjusting." At ten, she is aware enough to notice when the words slips out—words like "see" and "look." Our son seems a bit afraid of me since I'd returned from rehab, as though I am a stranger. Yes, I feel strange experiencing my entire life through a different lens. But my husband is unflappable. He'd already stepped right into my role, taking over the chores and cooking and taking care of the kids when I was deployed. He did it not knowing I'd be home only a few months later. As a former military man himself, Eric gets it. But where do *I* fit in now?

Just as I plant myself back in my beach chair, I hear someone approaching. I hear the sand sifting under dragging feet, and labored breath with a slow walk that sounds like an older person, maybe?

"Jacqueline, right?"

A man stands above me and speaks. His voice has a familiar timber with a gravelly edge. "Yes, but I go by Jackie now. And you? You sound so familiar."

"Sailor Bob. Well, they don't call me that anymore. Old Bob, I hear these days." His guttural laugh has the sound of a lifetime of smoking in it. Under the layer of smoke, the breeze carries his subtle scent of salty sweat past me.

The memory rises. Sailor Bob. "You taught me to sail, right?" I pictured the lean tall man tattooed on one shoulder with an anchor and on the other forearm the initials LSM are etched in a heart. A wife? A lover? The sailing class always tried to guess the stories behind those tattoos.

"Right there, lassie. So you're here with the Seas the Day vacation? What are you doing sitting here on the beach?"

I don't want to state the obvious, but I'm sitting on a beach chair with a guide dog next to me. "I'm . . . blind."

"And?"

"And being blind, I can't see." I laugh.

"*And?*"

Now I am getting a little confused, maybe annoyed. I can almost see his smile. But his tone is serious.

"I see your husband and kids out there. Wave to them," Bob commands.

I wave. He tells me they are waving back. That's something Josie can't do for me. I imagine my children's happiness over that small gesture. Just a mom waving at her kids having a good time. Simple. But not simple for me.

"So you don't have the sailing bug in you anymore?"

The question stings a bit. I think about that. Don't have it in me? The "I'm blind" answer hasn't seemed to work with Bob. I realize what he's up to. Wouldn't I have at least as much courage in a sailboat on a sweet sunny day as I did fighting under the flashes and booms of the artillery attack that blinded me? But truly, sightless and alone in that little boat? Seems impossible. How could I? Then an idea lights me up and I take the bait. "Do you still have the *Lightnings* for rent? The ones we used to sail when I took lessons with you?" I could picture the sailboat—a good six feet longer and much wider than that little 13-foot Sunfish my kids were sailing. There had to be room for Josie.

"Now you're talking. Sure, there are two in the slips right near us."

"Sailor Bob, want to be my sea guide? I'm blind, you know."

Bob blurts out a short laugh with a tone of surprise. "Well, I'd need a little help." He pauses, the only sounds are the gulls taunting and the wind lightly flapping a nearby flag. "Why not?"

Is it possible that I can almost hear him extend his arm to me? Can I feel his helping hand in front of my face? I reach up and grab his wrinkled dry hand and spring up out of my beach chair nearly pulling the old man over.

"Josie will have to come. She loves the water. Is it calm? No, don't tell me." I listen to the slow washing of the waves on the shore and feel the wind. "Calm enough, but I'm guessing it's barely enough wind." Maybe I have an out.

"Wind picks up just out beyond the dock. It's perfect. I'm in—let's go."

Josie sits beside me in the boat; both of us outfitted in life jackets, thanks to Bob. The sun finds its way through my jacket into my back. I feel good. My balance is different with no vision, but I'm alert to every movement as we board and the boat sways with our weight. I pull my ponytail through the back of my baseball cap and move to the starboard side.

"Hey, what are you doing over there? I'm an old man, you'll have to skipper this ship."

"Me? Bob . . . can I call you that, sir? Need I remind you . . . I'm—"

"Yeah, you may be blind, but I'm worn out, bad back, can't work the tiller. Your idea, lassie—I'm nearly ninety."

Now I remember how hard he was on us kids when he taught us to sail. And now I understand why. Mistakes have their price out on the water. I realize he must have been in his late-sixties back then, a retiree, a lifer in the navy, so if I'm thirty-three now, and I was a young girl then—yes, that would make him nearly ninety. I hadn't thought of that when I'd asked.

I move to the port side and take the tiller in my hand. Josie settles in by my feet. I rest my left hand on my dog's head. She sniffs at the air and poises to do her job. My protector. I kiss her sandy snout.

"So, let's head out southwest. Can you figure which way that is?" Bob's voice has a hint of joy behind his serious sailing instructor's words.

"I think so. I feel the morning sun on my right shoulder. The lapping water behind me. I have a picture of this bay in my mind, having navigated these waters for so many years as a child. The dock is to my right. On the shore behind me, just a bit south, I picture the old WWII concrete lookout tower on the bayside. The channel marker is ahead of me and across the channel is a strip of land near the Yacht and Country Club.

The fluttering of the sail above tells me I'm not quite on course, and I move the tiller an inch closer to me. The sail catches the wind. Full now, the flutter in the sail ceases, and the warmth of the sun moves around my cheek. I am gliding us smoothly southwest.

"Dead on, Jackie." Sailor Bob's voice is filled with pride.

I smile, feel Josie's paw tap my thigh twice, as if to say, "Good going, Jackie." Why do I want to cry?

"Ready about?" Bob calls to me like a proper captain. I anticipate our turn and push my emotions away. I know how to do that when there's work to do. I know how to soldier-through.

"Hard-alee!" I thrust the tiller hard towards the sail. We lurch; then turn to port. The sheet slips through my left hand; I feel the burn, breathe deeply and loosen my grip on the line a bit. As I'm shifting myself to the other side, the boat tilts. The sail is luffing, the rigging clanging, and Josie double-barks a warning.

For a minute I think I have lost it; I'm disoriented. This wasn't a good idea. I don't accept my failures well. Used to winning at everything. Then, I tell myself to focus. My instinct is to duck. The boom swipes safely past me overhead to port side, and the bow moves through the wind. I pull in the sheet to tighten it and pop the snaking line into the cleat, keeping the tiller under control.

The sails are full; we're moving smoothly in the perfect wind again. Two more tacks and Bob commands, "Let out the sails." I release the tiller and loose the sheets and our sail gives up a gasp, flutters, and our boat slows to a drift.

I gasp for air, thrilled with the challenge, then laugh out loud and throw my arms up, celebrating my small victory. I hear my children's voices.

"Go, Mom, Go!"

"We're over here!"

I turn toward their calls and the sound of their little sail luffing in the breeze. We glide for a while to the tune of their giggles coming closer and closer. Josie barks. I know that bark; it's one of recognition. She loves my kids. The Sunfish is close now.

"Wow! Mom, amazing," my son, Eric says.

I can imagine his smile; the warm beam shoots through me.

"Daaad. Look at Mom!" He calls out loud.

I hear my husband's voice calling from a distance. "She's amazing! Right, Bob?"

Bob mutters, "Your damn right, she is. You know she's blind, right?"

I release a laugh, a welcome stranger. "So, Bob, you finally get it."

"Woohoo!" My daughter's cheers skim through the warm September air and wrap around me.

Josie barks a hello, and her wriggling body leaps up on the bench beside me and waits at the rail for my permission, her tail slapping against my leg. *Please Jackie, can I, can I?* I imagine Josie saying.

"Go, Josie." I give her the natural freedom she craves. Am I supposed to do that? I don't care.

She launches into the air, and the backwash of my lifesaving pup plunging into the water soaks me. I sputter as the streams of brackish water rain down the bill of my "Seas the Day" baseball cap. My blonde hair hangs in damp strings on my shoulders. I imagine my too-large T-shirt sagging around me. We all begin to laugh again.

Eric's voice is close, Erin's too. Is there anything more joyful than the belly-laughs of young children, my children?

My laugh echoes so loud it covers up my deeper emotions at first. Who is this woman in the sailboat with no sight? I try to avoid the inevitable, but those repressed feelings erupt, push up against my eyes, grab me by the stomach, and shiver down my arms. My spirit sinks as fast as it had risen. This is what happens; I just begin to feel happy, and I go into a nose dive with the reality of it all. Such loss, I think. Not just my sight; the challenges have just begun.

I push past the loss and my fears. They'll always be there, I think. I need to learn to embrace the moments of joy.

Then all of my senses become electrified—I hear the sounds of my family's laughter, my dog barking, encircling my boat. I imagine the parting of the water around her furry chest, her legs pumping underneath the surface. I can hear her nails scraping against the side of the boat begging to come aboard, feel the sun embracing me, the briny water tingling on my arms. My husband's proud, loving smile emerges in my mind. I sense it all; I'm here in this moment.

"Mom, that was so much fun." Erin squeals.

There's that word I've been aching for—that word that makes my efforts all worthwhile, that elusive thing I'm seeking in my life with my family—*fun*.

And I see the drenched woman in the boat, the fumbling, wounded warrior with so much to learn, the soaking, blind sailor with the loyal dog—the family *instigator*—is me.

The End

First published by Cat & Mouse Press under the title, "Sea to Shining See" in *Beach Fun*, Rehoboth Beach Reads series, 2018.
Winner Second Place

The Time of His Life

GREAT-GRANDPA HENRY King was none of those things—
not great, not really Mother's grandpa, and definitely not a king
. . . except for once.

Mother took in the old, bent gentleman after the tragedy. The
automobile accident that had stolen the lives of his only son and
daughter-in-law had left him without care. We'd found him on
that same windy summer day, unresponsive as he'd always been,
rocking on our neighbor's porch in his handmade wicker chair
waiting for their return.

The Kings had only moved next door to us a short time before
this poor soul lost his only living relatives. We didn't know a tad
about the old man, not his age, not his history, nor his pedigree,
no clues that weren't in the outdated clothes and the leathered
wrinkles of his face and hands. We were neighborly, not nosey.

"God planted the desire in my heart," Mother had said. "I can't
call myself a Christian or a Methodist if I don't take him in." As
the daughter of a founder of the Rehoboth Beach Camp Meeting

Association of the Methodist Episcopal Church, Mother's faith was deep, and she lived her words. "Virginia, make up the bed in the guest room, please."

"Yes, mother." I thought the whole thing was an adventure. Although I confess, I was a little afraid of the silent gentleman.

"I'll help him across the yard and move an extra rocker out onto the porch." There was no argument from Father; there never was. And that was that.

Mother made the arrangements, and Great-grandpa Henry King moved to rock in his chair on our front porch, as though he had always been a part of our family.

Mother fed him; Father kept him clean, groomed his bushy handlebar mustache, and parted his hair in the middle, the comb following a stubborn, well-worn groove from another time. My brother and I competed to see who could make him talk or move, or smile. His stiff collar and bow tie style were decades behind the times. No matter how hot the summer days became, he wore his oversized suit with dignity, the excess of his shirt escaping through the missing button on his vest until mother sewed one on. We imagined he must've been a big man in his time, his body withering to frail from sitting.

It was 1928 when he'd moved in. I'm sure of that. June 17, the very day Amelia Earhart crossed the Atlantic on my twelfth birthday.

That same year, we took Great-grandpa Henry King on his one and only excursion to the main street to see the last passenger train leave our Rehoboth Railroad Station. They were closing down the line. It was a mere few blocks by foot into town to the station. He preferred his special perch on our porch or a stroll to the ocean in the other direction, but the mention of the train's fate was enough to spur him to join us.

The way that sight got Great-grandpa King's attention got *my* attention. He stared down the empty tracks waving long after the locomotive's black cloud of steam was gone. We had to drag him in the other direction home. It was the last time he would go into town. That image—the slump of his shoulders, and the gray cast that came down on his eyes as the train pulled out of the station—stayed with me for years. It was a memory I took out and brushed off every time I rode a train.

I don't remember him ever speaking back then, not once. But each day, no matter if the sun rose up or the clouds dropped rain, he hobbled down the three blocks to the beach, took in three deep breathes of the salty air, and trudged along the shore until he found a perfect, intact seashell. I never knew what it meant to him, but he buffed that shell on his shirt like shining an apple, and placed it in a wooden fruit crate he kept in his room beside the old iron bed.

Once Mother or Father planted him in his chair on the porch to enjoy the day, Great-grandpa Henry King sat there quietly, his gray hair lifting with the ocean breezes in two pieces, like wings of the complaining gulls that hovered above. He had a kindly silence about him, with a touch of sadness.

"Shall I read to you?" I asked, sitting on our porch rocker beside him. My brother had bored easily of the silent man; I couldn't stand him sitting all alone. I did the only thing I knew to do. Sometimes I read my school lessons, a few pages from our story books, or a parable from the family *Bible*. From the first time I read to him and every day after, when I finished the last word of a book, he'd push himself up with his shaking arms on the rocker, amble into the house through the creaking screen door, and return with one of his treasured shells. He held it up, kissed it goodbye, patted my head, and handed it to me with a smile.

In turn, I sneaked back into his room, and feeling the burn in my face for intruding on his privacy, I replaced it deep in his collection so he wouldn't notice. It was just that way he looked at those shells that made me know they were precious friends, or held a memory for him. Or maybe it was simply all he had to give. And thus our circle of giving went on.

He sat quietly, except three times a day at exactly the same times, when he waved his hand at some invisible crowd, and smiled. His eyes saw something I couldn't see; they lit up, showed a kind of joy, then faded right back to gray. I kept track. He was like a statue or a frozen mime, then like a coo-coo clock's bird, he came alive at exactly, 8:22 a.m., 11:22 a.m., and 5:52 p.m.

There were times when I was a child that I worried about him out there in the blazing sun, staring off across the yard somewhere, dull-eyed. But he frowned at coming inside. At the end of each day, after he took in the last bastion of angled sun, after he smelled Mother's apple pie or shrimp and grits through the screen door, but just before he came in for supper, he saluted, nodded his head, looked up at a certain spot in the distance, and smiled.

I felt sadder to leave him than I did my own parents when I went off to get my teacher training in New York. The memory of his moist eyes as I left him, inhabited me for days. As I unpacked my things at the house where I would live for my year of schooling, nestled in my satchel was a perfect conch shell, smooth and pink inside and stark white on the outside. I cried. Nothing was as steadfast as that sweet old man. He was like an anchor in my life, my silent, great-grandfather clock.

I wrote postcards to him every day; mother read them to him; I just didn't want him to feel alone. With my mind on my studies, time passed through a full cycle of seasons quickly, and it was time to return. On my way home in the train headed to Delaware, the memory from years before resurrected—his sentimental eyes and his face at the sight of the last locomotive shrinking off into the foggy distance—the tracks merging into a mere pencil line pointing into the horizon.

When I returned to town to take a teaching position at our local school, I became obsessed with the very thing that we all came to take for granted since my childhood—Great-grandpa Henry King's mysterious rhythm, the wave and smile that like clockwork after ten years, still went on and on.

I began my research though I had no idea just what I was searching for. It was a schedule. For what? Not any repetition I knew, not any local train schedule, not a factory whistle pattern. I became determined.

Our retired postmaster nearing ninety was my first stop. Smoothing my floral dress to cover my knees, I sat in a rocker beside him on his porch.

"What can I do for you, Virginia?"

"I'm looking for clues to the meaning of the pattern of Great-grandfather's habitual happiness." For it was only at those times he seemed to come alive. There was no need to explain; the entire town had witnessed it over the years. "Would the times eight-twenty-two, eleven-twenty-two, and five-fifty-two mean anything to you?"

"Not our schedule for sure," the postmaster said. "Our trains were on the half-hour every third hour precisely, in the summer season. Less frequent in the winter. Why now?"

I explained my passion to know more, but he had no idea, nor any interest. "It's just what the man does," he said. And that was that. "Why not try Widow Smyth? She's been around since day one."

She knew nothing. Great-grandpa had been a newcomer after all. And so it went with every elderly soul in Rehoboth, no answers, but quite a bit of tea. I realized I wouldn't find what I needed in our town.

When the school year was over, I took the train to New York City where I stayed with my cousin for ten days. I poured over newspapers, and consulted with historians, genealogists; I had to know. I had to solve the mystery of the man who rocked on our front porch, the curious timing of his reliable wave and smile, and his sadness at the last train departing from Rehoboth that remained fresh in my mind and still made my chest ache.

I was discouraged. Tracing the King family was impossible, such a large Irish clan they had in the US. There were lists of James Kings and Henry Kings. None fit.

On the day before I planned to return home, a librarian suggested another source—a Mr. Jonathan White at the Railroad Antiquities office. He knew trains like family members, she'd said.

"Well, I won't rest until I figure this out, Miss." Mr. White immediately began to pour through his books.

"I leave tomorrow, unfortunately, sir."

"Check back in before I close at six. I'll see what I can do."

I was impressed with how intrigued he seemed with my quest for clues to Great-grandpa's life. By the time I returned at five minutes to six, he'd found the thread I'd sought. "Eureka! Here you go, Miss." He was lit up, beaming with his success.

There it was before my eyes, a schedule of the stops on the train from New York to Philadelphia to Washington, D.C., 8:22 a.m., 11:22 a.m., and 5:52 p.m. I had to turn my back to hide my tears.

The following morning, at his request, I stopped by to thank him on my way to the train for home. There, with papers scattered over his desk and the scent of bitter coffee in the air, I found a disheveled Mr. White with a wide grin on his face. He handed me the most important discovery he'd made. The sun angled through the oversized, soot-streaked office windows onto the yellowed newspaper article—my pot of gold. My hands shook so hard the print blurred.

March 10, 1888

Engineer James Henry King ended his thirty-four years of service to the Pennsy today at sixty years old. "I've never wrecked a train, and I've never injured a passenger," he was quoted as saying on his last but prestigious run to Washington, D.C. on the Congressional Limited Express. King carried a very special passenger that day, President Grover Cleveland. "How does it feel to have a President as a passenger, Mr. King?" the reporter

asked, as a photograph was flashed. "Maybe we should ask how
the President feels about having a King for an Engineer?"

I read Great-grandpa King's answer and laughed. To finally
attribute a sense of humor and a life to the enigmatic man who
was a beloved ornament on our front porch, caused me to drop
tears again, and I hugged the article to my chest. He'd retired just
one day before the Great Blizzard of 1888, forty years before he
arrived on my porch, keeping his record of no wrecks, no injuries,
I thought. I guessed if he'd begun his railroad tenure at twenty-
years-old, that would make him about ninety-four. What had
taken his voice and mind? When had it happened? I'd never know,
but I finally had some answers to the mysterious man who was
James Henry King.

After making a purchase in the railroad antiquities gift shop
for him, I secured a copy of the photo taken of President Cleveland with Great-grandpa King in front of his locomotive from
the newspaper published on that day in 1888, and a copy of the
schedule from New York City to Washington. I traveled home
with a fluttering in my stomach all the way, knowing he'd once
beheld the very scenery passing before my eyes from his front train
window, time and again.

Great-grandpa Henry King was rocking according to schedule on
the porch when I arrived. He stood and extended his arms with
a box containing ten perfect shells, one for each day I was away
in New York. How long his quiet days must have seemed to him;
how fast the time had flown for me.

I sat beside him, strapped the souvenir Pennsylvania Railroad

Commemorative wristwatch on his arm, kissed his cheek, and showed the photo and the schedule to him at exactly 5:52 p.m. He tapped the watch with one shaking finger, engaged my eyes, rested his elbow on the chair, and waved to an invisible crowd. I could envision his shoulder leaning out the window of the locomotive; I could see the passengers on the platform waving back, through a bank of evaporating, hissing steam. I could see his lips were about to move; and they did.

His voice couldn't escape the dungeon where it had been chained for so many years. But with effort, he clearly whispered, "King," and winked at me.

Staring at his face lit by his pride, I knew his tenure with the Pennsy was the time of his life.

Something like a laugh escaped his mouth. Then he covered my hand with his, closed his eyes, rocked, and smiled. Sitting beside him rocking in rhythm, I closed my eyes and smiled too, feeling as thought I'd known him all my life.

He was not great in any usual way, nor was he my great-grandpa by blood, but he was a King, a king for a day.

The End

Dedicated to my great-grandfather, James Henry King, Engineer on the Pennsy for fifty-two years.

First published in *Rehoboth Reimagined*, an anthology by the Rehoboth Beach Writers Guild, 2017.

First Place, Delaware Press Association Communications Contest, 2018.

A Beautiful Present

TOMORROW I'LL FRAME the occupancy permit for our new home, along with the fading photo of my grandmother's mildewed cottage it replaced. I'm smiling at the tender blue paint color in the master bedroom that turns silver-gray when clouds hang over the bay. A thousand decisions and joyful interior design choices kept me afloat in the midst of a two-round push through breast cancer chemotherapy. Finally our retirement home is here.

And so am I.

I see myself perched on a ladder in the grass nine months ago, precisely positioned to see what the view from our bed would be like from the second floor we were adding. I'd held my left arm tight across my chest back then, not wanting to disturb my own reconstruction. I never thought I'd sleep in a room with that view. Tonight I will.

Forty-four years of parent-teacher conferences, thirteen hundred and thirty-five fifth grade faces, each distinctly etched in my memory. Plenty of time to imagine what I wanted during nearly five decades of vacationing with our daughters on this quiet lane in Dewey Beach.

We'd torn down every wall to capture the water view that had squeezed its way through the tiny cottage windows. With glass and more glass, we now have our own beautiful slice of Rehoboth Bay. Despite the mini-mansions that have sprung up beside us like two colossal wooden soldiers guarding a miniature dollhouse, our life feels rich.

It was always worth the four-hour drive from Western Pennsylvania to Delaware to be at the ocean. We had neither the time nor the money to rehab it until now, and we shook every coin from our pockets to make it our own.

Jonathan moves in the last few boxes we'd put in storage during construction while I sit at the linoleum table working on our budget.

"Here you go, the last of them. Once we purge through these, we'll be in good shape." My husband rubs his back. Despite his age, despite time or his blonde locks turning silver at seventy, he is still the kind, attractive guy I'd met in grad school. The man who'd been my loyal partner through it all—child-rearing for our two daughters, the deaths of our parents, my cancer, and his car accident.

I put my pencil down. "Honey, now that the house is so *us*, this old junk furniture seems like an insult to the fresh space."

He scans the room. "You're right—it does. There's no money for new furniture, though, right? You know the budget better than I do."

"From my calculations, it looks like we'll be getting a tax refund. We can splurge a little then."

The phone rings, and I tense. We've been waiting for my recent scan results. Across the room, Jonathan answers it, mumbles a short conversation, hangs up.

I've given up taking those dreaded calls. He has permission now to take the news for me. I've learned he always delivers the results so much better than my doctor would.

"Who's that?"

Even his brief pause makes me grip the edge of the table.

"Jonathan?"

"Oh, sorry. Your Doctor."

"My *Doctor?*" I stand, already feeling my knees losing strength. I knew it. Why would I ever have allowed myself to be hopeful? My hands start to tremble, then the shakes vibrate through my body. "*Well?* Are you going to torture me?"

He shakes out of his daze, replaces his cell phone in his jeans pocket, crosses the room and takes my shoulders. "Sorry, honey, I was . . . processing . . . third time's a charm, Bridget. No cancer. You're clear." His eyes fill, and I exhale, letting go of the breath I seem to have been holding for so long.

Later, we deliriously celebrate in neighboring Rehoboth Beach, wrapped arm and arm, walking down the boardwalk to get my favorite hand-made ice cream, mocha almond fudge—cup, no cone. The warm spring morning has coaxed white buds out on trees along the main street as Rehoboth comes alive again for another summer. The voice of the rolling waves makes us sigh as we sit on the white bench and eat our ice cream, counting our blessings.

During the walk home, Jonathan is quiet.

I understand that; so much to take in after all our suffering.

Before bed, we climb the stairs and stare out at our good fortune. A twinkling strip of land glows across the bay and a low full moon streaks light across the water like the zig-zag lines of a healthy EKG. Grateful tears glint in Jonathan's eyes. Mine too. For so long, we've been separated by stitches, IVs, strangers in scrubs holding vigil, and the whining sound of beds lifting and lowering my damaged body.

For hours we reminisce, whispering in the dark as though we're huddled under the dining room table-tent Jonathan always built from blankets with our girls. We share memories of our daughters riding little boats around and around in Funland; digging in sand on the beach, capturing sand crabs; the seat belt around our victorious six-year-old's life-sized teddy bear arcade prize.

"Bridg, we made it—the house we've always fantasized about. You did a great job renovating. Who would believe this is the same dank cottage?" He snuggles into the crook of my neck and kisses me.

This home is the last roll of our financial dice, I think. It feels like the culmination of decades of running out the door a million times, unfed, with only coffee in hand, to teach other people's children, sacrificing time with our own. This home is my rising up.

I hear Jonathan take a deep breath. "Yes, I'm relieved as well. Have we ever shared a more joyful night?"

It's just before dawn when Jonathan shares his lie in the safety of the dim room where I can't see his eyes. He wanted me to have just one day and one night of happiness, he says, to enjoy our new home before he shared the truth: The cancer's back.

"*What?*" I manage to open my throat enough to say it. My heart is leaping to escape my chest, and it takes a moment for the reality to settle in.

"I wanted to give you just one day to—"

I sit up and turn the bedside lamp on. "To what? Set me up to be crushed, again?" I tremble, and the sobbing begins. I see his tears dropping too, wet rivulets running through the graying hair on his chest. I swipe them with my hand as though I can erase his words, then throw back the covers and escape.

"You're no different today than last night, Bridget. You're here, alive, beautiful, and—"

"Don't." I can't talk to him. I pace in front of the windows.

"How did you feel last night?" He pleads, trying to embrace me.

I step aside. "I felt grateful. Blessed. Close to you. Unlike right now."

"But nothing's changed, except . . . our minds, our perspectives."

I feel numb, hug myself, and look out the window. A thin golden line slices toward the horizon as the day pushes light across the bay.

"The reality is you had cancer last night and you have it today. But last night you—were in the moment . . ."

"No! In my mind, I *didn't* have cancer last night, but I do this morning. Thanks for the gift." I pause. "What were the doctor's exact words, Jonathan?" I grit my teeth, jaw set.

"*The test was positive. Bring Bridget in. Yes, I suppose you can wait one day.*" He watches my face, his words hanging heavy in the dim light.

Any remaining sense of hope escapes me like the last bit of air that keeps a child's balloon afloat. I can't calm down. Jonathan's pre-dawn admission of the truth is a cruel ending to my lovely, peaceful night.

He sits back down on the edge of the bed helpless.

There's a buzzing in my head that won't stop. I feel scorched as though a meteor has landed in my life. I can't process, can't talk to him. I need air.

A spider's nighttime spin stretches across the doorway. How can she keep on weaving as though nothing has changed? Everything should stop. Take a moment of silence for my agony. I dip below the web, and leave the house.

Outside, my eyes trace the shoreline of the bay. The protective piled rocks are drizzled with white streaks from the comings and goings of blue herons, snowy egrets, and ospreys. I hear the taunts of the ubiquitous Laughing Gulls—the ones that look like they've been dipped in black ink—white body, black heads, black tail tips, black legs. How fortunate to have only one emotion, one expression—laughter, a sound too foreign and impossible for me right now.

I still hear Jonathan's words in my mind. He wanted to give me one day, he says, a good start to life in our new home—to inspire me to fight for it. I think hard about that. Did the trick work? Can I forgive him for breaking our long bond of trust?

I review my oblivious yesterday. In that one day, I'd imagined years of standing at my kitchen window while gazing at silver sunsets. I'd imagined listening to the gulls and the lapping, sighing, bay sounds, as I sat in the screened-in porch watching filtered sun through slats along the deck. I'd fantasized holding my unborn grandchild in my lap, smelling her sweet skin, snuggling, breathing her in. I dreamed someday I'd look up at those dark ink-dipped birds, point and say, "See the birdies?"

I'm split in half now. I'm grateful for that joyous day, and I'm devastated, hating him for withholding the brutal truth. How did he keep his secret from exploding out of his mouth? His face never showed his agony while the hands of the clock insufferably pushed their way around the course of his day-long loving lie.

The quarter moon is still visible, and I walk on the shore, taking in the soft sunlit dawn, searching for a way to start again, to find my strength.

It's that time of year, the horseshoe crabs scatter in my path. I find one on her back, upside down in the wet sand, spindly legs beckoning. I slip my foot under the brown leathered edge to right her. There is no longer any shell visible for the crowded party being celebrated on her ornate top like Grandma's gaudy, antique jewelry box—twisted cones, bi-valves and tiny mollusks that were smart enough to avoid the crab's hungry wrath by riding on her baroque encrusted back. They'll take another free ride to another shore now that her eggs are laid. She's alive; and she'll return. The symbolism isn't lost on me. I'm seeking meaning, seeking solace, hoping my fate is like hers with the haunting sound of those words in my ears, "The cancer's back."

Ironic I should find a horseshoe crab this morning. Their blood is used in cancer therapy research, and in IVs to detect impurities, and I imagine the crab's blue blood flowing through a tubular tether into mine. Will I be seeing you soon? I say to the creature who has survived on earth for thirty million years. Was I asking too much for another ten, or two, or one?

I look back at the house; the bay water is reflected blue in its massive glass eyes. Jonathan stands staring out the bedroom window. Trying to squeeze love for him from beneath an overwhelming swell of gloom, I'm still angry at his cruel and tender fabrication. Will I be here to love him and our home into old age?

Walking away from the bay, I spy an osprey pair nesting. The female perches high atop old wharf pilings twenty feet above me with talons dug in. Her yellow eyes focus on me, the intruder. The red-eyed male arrives clutching more branches and dried grasses and a forgotten, shredded T-shirt from the shore to add to the ever-growing nest. Its circumference is like the fat black inner tubes we'd used to slide down the snowy golf course hills with our kids.

I've watched these powerful winged beauties return year after year, rebuilding their home stick by stick after the winter wind and storms, sometimes from a meager branch or two that held on until spring. It won't be long before last year's perch is ready for this year's hopeful eggs. Thoughts of my diagnosis momentarily fade beneath the shadow of the wingspan of the imposing bird overhead.

I tell myself I too can live, flip myself over like the ancient crab— so many hitch-hikers on my back in need of a ride. I can rebuild and take flight like the osprey. Still so many dreams to unfold, and nothing sadder than a woman's empty nest without her.

He gave me one day, a day *he* never had.

I return home to find Jonathan staring out through a circle he'd cleared on the foggy window on the second floor.

I climb the stairs and stand at a distance behind him. "We can do this, whatever *this* is," I say. "But promise me we'll stay in the moment. We'll talk about the weather, a bird outside the window, our new home plans, *not* cancer."

He turns his head sharply, as though the real me has reappeared like magic. "I promise . . . come here."

"I'm still angry." My arms are folded but they want to reach for him.

"I know you are."

The emotion is peeling away with his pleading eyes. I see our half-century together in his face, and the gift of one day softens me, mellows me. Still, I don't let him hold me.

Until I do, and do, and do.

The End

First Published as "A Beautiful Present: The Gift of Living in the Moment" in *Delaware Beach Life* magazine, Rehoboth Beach, DE, May 2017.

Third Place, Delaware Press Association Communications Contest, 2018.

Unplugged

WHEN BOB DYLAN'S voice came on the radio singing "Maggie's Farm," Billy lowered the limo window between us and turned up the volume. Ad-libbing Dylan's lyrics, Billy sang, "...ain't gonna work on Mitch's farm no more." He started chicken-necking his chin back and forth, biting his lip, purposely uncool, just to make me laugh.

I didn't. The last person I wanted to think about was Mitch, my slave-driving manager; the last song I wanted to hear was Bob Dylan's song that had torn apart my life five years before. Billy couldn't have known. That was before my best buddy from high school reconnected with me and became my driver and bodyguard. That was before the Farrell Sisters had split.

My leather pants stuck to the seat as I shifted in the back of my limo. Leather on leather never works; I'd learned that with Mitch. How had the guy seemed so cool and thrilling when we'd met? He was using me, making millions, taking advantage of my heartache; I could see that now.

Billy turned and glimpsed at me over his shoulder. "You're quiet tonight, Franny."

"Just rehearsing lyrics in my head." Not true. As we crept our way through the Jakarta traffic on my way to rehearsal, I was sucked back to the day I'd first heard Dylan sing that song live. Truly live.

"Do you believe we've been on the road since we were twelve years old?" Jan had nudged me as we sat in the back seat of our traveling transport on the trip from Boston to Newport.

"Yes! But *this* is the coolest, Jan. Unreal! Thanks, Mom," I called out to our mother, who was driving the old converted school bus. "How'd you ever do it?" It would be our big break, performing at the 1965 Newport Folk Festival.

"Fran and Jan rhymin' and timin'—the Farrell Sisters," my twin and I both said at the same time.

Folk singing had been our family's bread and butter since our dad had died. Snagging the gig at the famed Rhode Island venue on our eighteenth birthday was the pinnacle of Mother's efforts as our manager, she'd said. "Girls, this will put you on the map. Now just relax and do everything just like you always do. Doesn't matter if there are a dozen or ten thousand people. Sing to each heart. You'll be stellar—better than stellar."

Mom was our loving manager, looking out for her folk-singing girls. From the time we were kids, music was in us. We *thought* in lyrics and spooked everyone back then, singing those words at exactly the same time out of nowhere. Without a word between us, we'd break out in the same song. The lyrics just came to us.

We thought alike, looked alike—wavy platinum hair, blue eyes, petite bodies—well, sure, being identical twins. Still uncanny.

The outdoor Newport venue was perched high, overlooking the ocean. What a mind-blowing experience—being on that stage on that summer night, stars under the stars with hundreds of eyes on us. In beach chairs, sprawled out on the lawn, the steamy summer audience fanned themselves, sipping, and toking, and applauding like thunder. The two songs we wrote and performed were well-received. How had we made it among the greats?

I would never forget July 25; it broke me in two.

When our performance was over, my mother was high on the joy of our success. After a hundred hugs, she went off to celebrate and talk with the few managers she knew.

I sat down on the grass next to my sister, feeling grateful we could enjoy the singers we admired—Joan Baez, Peter, Paul and Mary, and Pete Seeger. "I can't wait to hear Dylan's new song. Have you heard it, Jan?"

"No, I haven't. What's it called? And why are they moving all that equipment on stage?" My sister's excitement was palpable.

"So he can play 'Like a Rolling Stone.' And it's not acoustic, it's—"

"Oh, shh, shh, Franny, he's coming." Jan clapped along with the crowd.

Dylan lunged onto the stage with his backup guys, tuned up for a few seconds, and began to rock out "Maggie's Farm," playing an electric guitar, the speakers blaring.

There was a lull, a silence, then a rumble, and the incredulous crowd booed, hissed, and cursed. Folk Dylan had gone rock 'n' roll.

Jan screamed in rebellion along with the angered folk crowd; I was electrified.

"Boooo! Unplug yourself, Dylan!" Jan got to her feet and joined the frenzied mob.

I was fired up by the sound. "Jan, it's so cool. Come on." I grabbed her arm.

"It's evil—drugs and sex, don't you know that's where the name comes from—*rock* and *roll*, it means having sex, Franny. It's not music with space for us girls either! It's gonna ruin everything."

In that instant, we were no longer, the Farrell Sisters. When the music split—folk and rock—so did we. It ripped me in half.

As Billy turned into the parking garage of the Jakarta concert venue, I thought about the first night I sang without Jan: Me—a gig with an unknown rock band in the Midwest; she—on tour with our mother in the South.

Folk seemed passé to me. Trying to talk Jan into switching singing styles was useless, not even the new folk-rock worked. There was no compromise.

If we were one egg split in two, then was I half the person I used to be without her? Or if I was already a half, was I a quarter now? Because I certainly haven't felt whole since she left.

Mitch was so supportive back then, charming me into singing for the group he was putting together. Well, what other choice did I have? Alone, at eighteen.

"Folk's for old folks," he'd said. "You're cooler than that Fran."

Billy broke the spell. He turned off the car, hopped around, and opened my door. "You were really off somewhere. You still here with me, Franny?"

Jakarta was the last stop on my Southeast Asia tour; I realized my life had gone so far off track. When I arrived at the rehearsal, Mitch gripped my shoulders. "Where were you? You're late."

I broke the hold of his grasp. This didn't feel like a lover's embrace. "Mitch, I need a break. And you need a break, don't you think?" I'd been touring non-stop for five years. I'd felt hollow ever since my mother died suddenly of a heart attack while I was on my first tour in Asia—only a year after that July night at Newport in 1965. Did I really break Mom's heart? Jan blamed me; *I* blamed *me*. When my remorse took over, hiding in the blur of screaming rock touring, drugs and drinking had become my escape.

"*Hello? Fran? Are you crazy?* I've already booked your next tour. Look, let me give you something to calm you down." Reaching in his pocket, Mitch pulled out the pills he used to keep me under his control. "You always get this way, baby. It's normal—a touch of stage fright."

Why hadn't I seen through him? He ran his hand down my waist-length blonde hair, like he was petting a pony. I made the decision through the blur. No more, "baby," no more petting, and no more falling for his temptations again. No blue eyes, no alluring smile, no racy man, no fame, no high; no one would stop me. I needed out. "I didn't agree to another tour, Mitch. And that's always your answer—keeping me high."

Fingering the velvet curtain while standing off-stage, my escape plan came into focus. The first focus I'd felt in years.

"Baby, come on, we're in this together. It's your dream." He kissed me and shoved me on stage as my band played the intro to the first song.

At the end of the last tune, I escaped through the ladies' room window with the screams of the hotwired fans fading behind me, and maniac Mitch waiting in the wings for my encore. I could hardly breathe. Panic. Shakes. Petrified of him. What was I thinking? Skipping out on the final night of the tour after the final note of the last song, no less. No encore. *I'm sorry fans.* There would never be a good time to escape. I couldn't face the usual post-concert screaming, program-signing, after-party, booze and drugs scene one more time. I jumped to the ground.

"Selfish bitch. Drama queen," Mitch yelled through the window as I fled the concert hall and ran into the parking garage stairwell.

Holy Shit. I was so scared to be so bold. Two flights down I burst through the door and spotted Billy waiting in the limo at the appointed spot. I jumped in the back seat.

"What's going on? Concert let out early? You OK?"

Last year's hit album invaded my thoughts, the Beatles, *Abbey Road*. "She came in through the bathroom window." My laugh broke through my fear. "Let's get out of here, Billy."

He burned rubber out of the venue parking garage. "You don't look so good, girl."

"Billy, I need a little break." I saw his worried blue eyes in the rear view mirror. "*What*, Billy?"

"You know *what*. When are you gonna stop? You need more than a little break from that psycho, slave-driving, pill-pushing idiot."

"I take it you don't like him."

"Funny, Franny. The dude may not beat you, but there are still lots of bruises . . . here." He punched his heart.

"Seriously. Maybe now, Billy, maybe now I'll stop."

"Heard that before."

"You know what? Billy, take me to the airport. I'm going to Bali, for a rest, to think."

"Bali? Why Bali? I mean I hear it's sweet but . . ."

"Remember my nanny when I was little and my mom and dad toured?"

"Oh yeah, Marisi."

"She was from Bali. She always talked about how beautiful and peaceful it was."

He turned around and stared at me. "Peace? It's about time. You're in a tailspin sweetheart. And that jerk is eating you alive with his schedule and the booze and . . ."

Didn't anybody tell her?—as the lyrics go, I thought. Yes, *she* did; my sister, Jan, told me, warned me, I thought . . . and my mother did too. *Mamma told me not to come.* Three Dog Night lit up my circuits. I couldn't get a grasp on my feelings or complete my thoughts these days with so many intruding lyrics. Focus interruptus.

Billy turned around before he ran the darkened window up that separated us, so he could listen to tunes and I could sleep. "Here you go, this year's new top 100 tunes out today, Sweetie." He handed me the list. "You done good for a *rock chick*, got two this year—both above the top fifty mark. Just notches below Simon and Garfunkel and the Jackson Five, sister! You earned this break."

"Tell that to Mitch."

"Rock's day is coming, baby! I feel it. You're building the bridge for Rock chicks, Franny. But you don't want to burn your own bridges doing it."

The sound of my childhood nickname made me sentimental. Brought me back to happier times. The person I'd become was sorely lacking in direction and confidence. Those aspects of me lurked somewhere in the recesses, but too far away to reach, still blurred by last night's dope and Southern Comfort. A gift from Janis—Joplin—not my sister Jan. Night and day, those two. The only southern comfort my sister knew was a rocker on the porch of an old Inn in Georgia after one of her folk gigs for fifty old loyal fans of ours.

"Rock's too hard, too fast, too sleazy. Drugs and alcohol, Franny," she'd said. "It won't last. Immoral. It's not *us*, not for girls."

I *rock*-rose up; she *folk*-fizzled out.

Jan was wrong about rock. OK, true about the booze, drugs and sleazy part. But not about it lasting . . . and right about the girl part—I'm an exception they say. And, true I could've used some time on that mellow rocking chair on a Georgia porch.

The sweltering Jakarta heat dripped a stream down the back of my T-shirt that already stunk of fake fog. Our limo blended into the teaming traffic. Horns blasting, going nowhere fast. I was almost free. "Which way you goin' Billy," I sang. "Leave the window down, will you Billy? I need to see you. It calms me."

"You got it." He turned and gave me that gaze, that sweet smile of his. "Think about that while you're on the beach, OK? That Mitch—he's sucking you dry, using you up, killing your music. Man, I don't know how you can—"

"I'm over that soul-sucking jerk."

"Over him, really?" Billy's head whipped around but he didn't say anything else. He just gave me this blue-eyed look I couldn't quite read.

"Walk a mile in my shoes," I sang. "Billy, seriously, I want out but there's some contract I'd signed in a haze. We can regroup and figure the whole career thing when I come back—and I won't be high every day where I'm going. That scares me, actually. And *don't* call my sister! *Please.*"

Billy turned. "But this is killing you, Franny. You and Jan really need to—"

"*Billy. She's* the one who left *me.*"

"Franny . . ."

"What? *Say* it." He didn't need to say it . . . I knew the words that stuck in his throat . . . *you missed your Mom's funeral.* Mitch and his damn possessiveness . . . did I ever have a brain when it came to that guy? Yes, I was touring on the other side of the world. Yes, I had commitments—no, I should never have listened to him.

"Your Mom would have wanted the show to go on," Mitch had said. "She was a true professional."

And I *bought* that? What did Mitch know about what my mother would have wanted? I never forgave myself and Jan never forgave me either.

I flipped my prescription sunglasses on to read the Top 100 List. "Billy this reads like my life story. Listen—

"Reflections of my Life."

"Evil Ways."

"Travelin' Band."

"Spill the Wine."

"Psychedelic Shack."

"Everybody is a Star."

"It's Only Make Believe."

"Tighter, Tighter."

"The Thrill is Gone, is that my life, or what, Billy?" My eyes scanned more titles and I hummed the tunes. "They Long to Be, Close to You." "Didn't I Blow Your Mind This Time"—that would be my fans. "War" and "I Want to Take You Higher"—that would be Mitch. My head buzzed with lyrics, never quiet, a song always running behind everything I did. I needed peace. It had to be the mind-altering stuff's fault. Six channels on at once. "Mama Told Me Not to Come." "Without Love Where Would You Be Right Now?" I couldn't think about my twin now; I missed her so much. "Look What They've Done to My Song, Ma."

I needed quiet. No rush hours with sweaty, packed, fuming buses; no shouting, waving fans; no Mercedes and pedicabs fighting my stretch limo for road-rights, scurrying like rats in and out of a maze of towering buildings; no green rooms with exotic foods I never indulge in for fear of nature calling in the middle of my rocking set; no rehearsals till all hours; no concerts to be late for; no band members' egos competing.

"God, Billy, Mitch's gonna be so pissed."

"This rest is about *you, Fran*." Billy handed me my guilty pleasure—tuna on rye, a bag of pretzel rods—not twists—and a root beer.

"Oh, Billy, you're the best." No wonder I loved this guy, my high school buddy who kept me together all these years. "A Bridge Over Troubled Water" and "I'll be There," came to mind. That was Billy. I hadn't eaten, as usual, the dope and booze from the night's concert was still flowing through me. If my mother were alive she would have done the same—fed me, warned me. Well, if my mother were alive . . . "If I Could Turn Back the Hands of Time" ran through my head.

I could tell something was wrong. Billy turned up the radio. "Janis is dead. It all finally took her down." He must have seen my face drop. "No, babe, Joplin, not your *sister*!"

October 4, 1970. I would never forget it. I had chills. Oh, Janis.

Billy kept flicking his eyes at me through the rearview mirror. "Sure you're OK, Franny?"

"I can't get my head around it. She was just here. . . we'd partied hard together. Even sang her song, 'What Good Can Drinkin' Do?' and laughed, while sucking down that Southern Comfort poison."

I knew I was seeing myself two years from now. Or one? I felt a familiar ache. It started somewhere inside in a place I didn't have a name for—*soul*, maybe? I missed my twin.

"Yeah, sorry, Franny." Billy reached his hand back through the window and held mine. A traffic cop told him to move on as we entered the airport terminal road.

I got out of the limo, slammed the door, turned around, took the bottle of Southern Comfort that Janis had given me from my bag, and tapped on the window. Billy rolled it down. I tossed the bottle on the front seat, blew him a kiss, tied my scarf over my head and headed into the airport incognito.

"Call me," Billy yelled behind me.

"Aretha Franklin," I shouted back. "'Call Me,' number one hundred on the top hundred list." I played our little name-the-song-and-singer game to avoid the emotion of leaving my best friend. "I'll call you . . . I promise, Billy." I turned around to wave goodbye, then ran around to the driver's side and kissed his cheek.

He touched the spot on his cheek where my kiss had landed and hesitated. "I'm serious, Franny. Are you sure you're OK? I worry about you."

I couldn't burden him with the way I felt.

"Get some rest." He pulled away.

The truth is . . . I was scared shitless. I needed more than rest.

No autographs on palms and programs; no running cables to connect me to the screaming, teeming crowds of Jakarta—or am I in Prague, or Miami, or London. No song selection decisions to make; no vocal cords to vibrate, slack and tight, lalalalalalala. No driven, maniac, manager Mitch. No searing lights—just sunlight, just me, and a beach, and a sunset, and a non-stop string of syrupy low-test drinks. Or as Gilbert O'Sullivan sang, "Alone again, naturally. No twin."

The truth is . . . I didn't know who I was without her.

The first day of the month I escaped to Bali, I just needed to get some sleep. I arrived in the tiny outdoor Bali airport in the late afternoon anticipating the sunset like a child. I'd dreamed of Bali since my childhood nanny Marisi had filled my head with fantasies about the beautiful island in her home country.

The driver took my ten-dollar, gray backpack I bought in the gift shop. I imagined my Hermes crocodile tote bag in the hands of the stunned ladies' room attendant in the Jakarta airport, and I smiled. I'd told her how much it had cost. "Don't sell it cheap," I'd said. It was worth the $99,000 Mitch paid for that couture thing in Paris for that one look on her face. I couldn't even imagined how it would change her struggling life. That fancy purse wasn't *me*, anyway. What *was*?

A big old 1957 rattletrap, two-tone India Ivory and Tropical Turquoise Chevy Bel Air sedan with glorious long fins took me to the hotel. How did that *sweet, smooth, sassy car,* as the old radio ad had called it, get here to this remote island on the other side of the world? I was redefining luxury—a delicious twenty-year-old beat up ride with no champagne in the back seat, no privacy window that rose with a hum at the sound of Mitch's irate voice, no welcome cards, no overwhelming scent of wilted flowers, no fan mail stacks—just cracked ivory leather seats exposing yellowed, pocked foam to support my aching derriere. And a cocoa-skinned man who understood my attempts at rusty Bahasa Indonesia I learned in our Boston apartment from Marisi, too many years ago.

"It's All Right Now." The song by the English rock band Free danced in my mind.

I was riding in one of only a dozen old American cars on the entire island, the driver said. Even a parade wouldn't cause a traffic jam. Relief. Less stimulation. Less to look at, less to hear. All that *less* felt like a guilty pleasure.

The truth is, I was more than just tired; I was a total mess.

When I arrived, my hotel reservation was lost. No one swept in for the interception, no manager, no publicist. I begged, "Isn't there anything available?"

"*Tidah,* No."

I refused to use my name to get a favor; I bit it back. I tried my Indonesian. "*Selamat Sore, Bapah. Saya dari America,*" which meant *Good evening sir, I am from America.* (Hit number three, "American Woman".) I told him I was so very tired, but I used the word for "lonely" by mistake. *Sendiri.* (Hit number forty-four, "Hey There Lonely Girl.") I couldn't stop the songs from coming; the more exhausted I was, the more they invaded my mind. Vocabulary is always lost first in an unused language. I read that *lonely* was a serious thing in a communal culture. From birth on, one is rarely alone—and *alone* and *lonely* are often not distinguished.

The front desk clerk's eyes saddened. He whispered to a sympathetic higher-up, and the golf cart swept me off to a stone walled compound—President Suharto's private digs, I'd later learned. Lonely was a powerful thing.

I climbed the elevated dining pavilion, and looked out on the floating candle-strewn pool in the middle of the exquisite private space. My eyes ate up the view. Oscillating young lime green rice fields on one side and the beautiful blue waves of the ocean framed the other, as though Mother Earth was orchestrating their movements in concert with a soothing song in her heart.

My thoughts went out to sea, and then drew back to me. I couldn't imagine being in Jakarta with Mitch. Who was he screaming at right now? Which of my lyrics were the government censoring? Anything political, peace, love? I confess, I had to giggle like a kid let out of school for a snow day.

Relieved to be alone, I watched from my perch in the compound. Liquid women swayed along the beach against the burnt orange sunset that turned them into floating shadows with vibrating auras of gold. They pulsed rhythmically with impossible piles of cloth, Jenga-balanced on their heads like a month's worth of folded laundry. I imagined they were headed home to become themselves again after a long hot day selling batik sarongs to tourists on the beach, simple.

Being myself? Not so simple. Surreal. At twenty-three, I felt like I was fifty, a ghost of my real self.

I entered the cottage, climbed the steps beside the king-sized bed and plopped there to admire the intricate carvings that climbed up the ten-foot-high bedposts. The ever-present geckos, the green lizards that stayed suctioned to the ceiling, chastised me, *tsk, tsk,*

tsk—tsk, tsk, tsk, tsk. I counted them. Seven castigating lizard sounds for good luck, the natives say.

The bathroom was open to the sky. Despite the privacy of the four high walls, I felt exposed. Stripping, I slipped into the over-sized bath that had already been drawn and submerged myself. I took time to notice my body. Reed thin. Breasts deflated. Pale. How long since it had seen the sun? Miami 1968. Sinking down I held my breath underwater.

Looking up through the crystal water, I pushed aside the lotus blossoms suspended on the surface to see the vibrant sky above. My hair danced in the water around my chest like sunlit, waving sea grass. How long since I'd felt at peace?

Night stars one by one illuminated the sky like the altar boy lighting the candles before Mass. How long had it been since I'd had faith?

The truth is, it wasn't only my hotel reservation that was lost.

I just wanted to be alone. Wrapping myself in a batik sarong the next morning, I wandered to the beach through twisted walkways. Stone-carved Hindu statue guards were posted at every intersection wearing black and white checkered sarongs, preventing evil spirits from passing through, according to the Balinese belief.

I lay on the hotel towel on Kuta Beach. A boy thrust an unre-quested umbrella in the sand to shade my pasty self, and a string of females sat peacefully beside me for hours. Small but tender gestures. So strange—no booze, no pills, no Mitch, only my banging headache and trembling hands. When one of the woman moved on to sell something to a nearby hotel guest, another would appear by my side. No lonely here, never *alone.* The word had spread about the unaccompanied American woman.

Young women my age, already with several children, sold me batik sarongs to make my wardrobe obsolete. Old women with gnarled hands massaged me with coconut oil from the fresh fruit that dangled precariously overhead on palm trees that edged the beach. Young boys shimmied up to retrieve the precious orbs with agility—that made me smile.

Fascinated with my long fair hair, little village girls ask to touch it. The zig-zag waves were like a child's finger painting, my Mom had once said. Their request was delivered in such a shy and humble way, so unlike the fan girls who'd screamed at me when I left my dressing room door.

Several gracious, village women sliced and fed me exotic fruits named *rambutti*, *mannga* and *manggis*. The soft kindness of the village women made me want my mother, but she was long gone. Dad, too. Only my sister and me now. No, even that duet was long gone. From eighteen to twenty-three years old, no Farrell sisters.

No burgers, no pizza, no donuts, no booze, no sex, no drugs, no rock 'n' roll seemed necessary in my new paradise—just noodles slipping off of polished chopsticks with chicken and vegetables, or bits of fresh fish cooked in pots of boiling hot oil with an array of luscious dipping sauces of coconut, peanuts, hot peppers and fresh herbs—my new menu.

The truth is . . . having no stimulants was a first in a long time.

The second week of the month I stayed in Bali, I needed to belong. I had no more ache to be alone. The cluster of Balinese women and children around me invited me to their village religious ceremony.

That was my best translation, anyway. I put myself in the hands of a Pedi-cab driver, and shared the name of the village.

We rode through the darkness with flashlights bobbing up and down to the rhythm of men and women walking in sarongs with only the sounds of the wheels rolling on the smooth dirt-packed road. Soft voices, called *"Selamat Malam,"* "Good evening," as I passed. I translated other mumblings, "There's an American woman coming tonight. Welcome, welcome." Not because I was a famous star, just because I was a rare and welcome foreign guest who'd come to see their dance.

The villagers gathered around an open area in the middle of a clearing under the trees with torches flashing. The Hindu Ramayana dance began. Exquisite hands expressed emotion, bending in ways I couldn't. White flowers and golden crowns covered their heads, paper fans fluttered in front of their glowing faces, beautiful fabrics tightly coiled around their chests, and wrap-around sarong skirts nearly brushed the ground around their bare feet.

A fragrance that smelled like love wafted from their floral head pieces. Small children dressed like golden deer moved so gracefully with delicate, flowing hands, it made me cry. There in that simple place with no spotlights, no tickets, just torches and our eyes, the performances came alive. The costumes they wore had threads of pure gold. How had the villagers raised the funds for these exquisite things? Priorities, I thought.

Beautiful princesses and the monkey king named Hanuman told an ancient tale. I remembered in my parents absence when my nanny Marisi told me Indonesian bedtime stories, back when I used to feel safe and loved.

When the dance performance ended, I was the lone clapper. The performance wasn't for tourists, I realized. It was their offering to the gods, not some form of entertainment. I stopped my applause and bowed my head. Their art was alive in their daily lives; mine was contrived, postured, played to the crowd. Their art was played to Hindu gods.

I thought about the line between my fans and me. The lights, the stage, and the screaming. I'd never thought about it before. My ego. What were those fans screaming about? And why did they keep on shrieking when the music had ended and they saw me exit the stage door? I'm not my music; it made *me* disappear.

When the performance was over, the Balinese players gathered around me, their faces lit with bliss—the sarong-selling women, the fruit ladies, and the girl who touched my hair. They were my humble beach friends young and old, transformed. They'd left their modest jobs along the beach at night and *became*. They'd never seemed to question their ability to change from a simple village girl to an elegant, enchanted dancer wrapped in gold. Moving exquisitely to the rhythmic gongs, they transformed as though raised to dance in a palace all their lives. Unlike me when I stood on a stage, I became less than me with drugs and Southern Comfort flowing through my veins. They became more, connecting to a hundred fellow souls. I became less, separated from two thousand screaming fans. I became a misled, disconnected goddess.

The strange truth is, in Bali, a place so foreign to me, for the first time in forever, I felt that I belonged.

The third week of the month I immersed myself in Bali, I became addicted to roasted pork from an underground pit that was luscious beyond compare, and shadow puppets, and smiling. No band, no fancy stage, no mic, no Mitch. Unplugged.

A goat skin was stretched between two trees with ropes. My gang of gals and me were seated on the ground as the night came down on us. A small shy girl twisted braids in my hair.

Dozens of puppets cut from leather with holes hammered out to cast just the right shadows from a constant torch, acted out battles with heroes and princes, buffoons and princesses. Thousands of lines of Hindu tales memorized through a lifetime by the village story teller were presented in a trance. Groomed from childhood, the puppeteer was highly honored in the community, I'd learned. I was a puppet of a different kind that cast a shadow on the backdrop of my stage, with Mitch manipulating my strings, I thought.

A German artist who'd moved to Bali to follow his painting and carving art in the mountain village of Ubud, whispered translations in my ear at the puppet show until the light of dawn blew out the show.

"Ibu Fran." My Pedi-cab driver knew my name and waited for me each night outside the hotel. *Ibu* was a polite way to address a woman; it also meant mother. That touched me and made me ache inside for my own mother. Night after night, he brought me village to village to experience traditional dances.

The Fire Trance dance blew my mind. Night was the time for men to show faith, too. The bond fire raged a dozen feet high. The dancer swayed and nodded like my crew after a good smoke. But this was his faith at work.

I stepped back, pushed by the wave of heat. He jumped and moved his head from side to side, riding a crude wooden stick horse with a mane made of straw. The music escalated—pace and intensity. He leapt into the fire, taking my breath away. Stamping and spinning he trampled the embers until the last of them were out, leaving a sizzling pile of ash. The villagers closed in around him, supporting him, holding him up as he came out of his spell— weak legged, slick with sweat, unburned, unbelievable. The wooden horse he rode, however, had disappeared into ash.

On another night I saw a similar sight. Swords this time, stabbed into the muscled stomachs of young men. I felt the tip, its razor edge. It was the real thing. The music drove them into a frenzy, they fell on their swords, pulled them into their abdomens. And in the end they lived, no cuts, exiting the trance in the arms of their friends. I was moved by their connection, enthralled by their powerful beliefs—the trances, the transformations, women in sunshine, men in moonlight.

The truth is . . . I realized I was completely lost without my sister.

The fourth week of the month that I embraced Bali, I knew I needed to change my life.

I sat on the beach thinking about the Balinese music, the mesmerizing music, the gongs, repetitive and haunting rhythms— a background to lure you into moods, make you meditate, pull inside yourself, ward off fire, fall on swords. No lyrics to crowd your brain. Wait. I hadn't had "focus interruptus" for many days,

I realized. My mind was washed clean by the waves on the shore, the hearts of the people.

A scruffy tourist walked by and stopped to buy a drink—chilled coconut water savored through a straw right from the coconut. He had a guitar slung over his back.

I hadn't played or sung a note in weeks, almost as though I had forgotten that I could.

"You play?"

Why he asked that, I don't know. Some kind of "meant to be" in this strange and spiritual place. Or maybe simply a look on my face.

"A little." The first English words I'd exchanged in weeks, and somehow those words led to me cradling the Gibson acoustic. I started plucking hesitantly, and played a tune Jan and I had written together. The women and the girls smiled to hear me play.

The guy said, "Cool."

Then I stood and rocked it out. It just rose up in me, and I let it go. Like the Fire Trance dancer, the men with swords, like the women in their nightly Hindu dance—I swayed, connected with what was inside me, spun around, flung my hair loose.

The German tourist pushed a pick into my hand, maybe not wanting to break the spell.

I plucked and picked and pushed those strings until they cried, and ended with three punishing full-circle strums, begging that acoustic to behave beyond what it was meant to do.

I was aching for a cord to wire it up, my own fire trance dance, wanting to connect with my audience, give them the joy that I'd conjured up inside. I played with passion, not forced by some money-making deals—just for the pure sake of sharing what was inside me. No booze, no drugs—with the Pacific Ocean as my curtain right out there, raw in the pure sunlight.

I dropped to the ground, sweat collecting gritty sand all along my side. I laughed and brushed it off, taking rapid breaths. Coming out of my trance, my newfound friends were cradling me, surrounding me with looks far beyond surprise.

"You sing beautiful." The elder women smiled, proud of her few words of English.

"*Terimah kasih, banyak!*" I thanked them, though I knew the big bold movements of my body were shocking for a female in their world—they were in mine as well.

"They've never seen a woman play an instrument like that." The tourist took back the guitar. "Neither have I . . . but I thought I recognized you. You're Fran Farrell, right? Holy Shit. Fran Farrell playing my guitar."

"No, I get that a lot. But I'm not her." It wasn't a lie, I thought. I hadn't been myself in years. But now . . .

"Boy you look just like her. Well, I've never really seen her live. Where are you from?"

"Here. I'm from here." I was still huffing from my trance.

The eldest woman ran her hand over the smooth wood of the guitar, then looked at me. Wrinkled lines around her squinting brown eyes spoke of wisdom as she engaged mine. She wiped my forehead with a sarong from her stack and handed me a cold coconut drink. I caught the word, "*Haus?*" and remembered it meant "*thirsty?*" It was so anticlimactic and matter of fact, I had to laugh. No applause.

Smiles settled in.

They understood trance.

Everyone sat as usual without words watching the sun come down. It dropped fast, leaving a pink and purple memory in the sky.

The truth is, I was connecting with myself.

The last week of the month I was renewed by Bali; I had a quiet mind.

The front desk clerk came to get me on the beach the next day. *"Panggilan telepon dari America."*

A phone call? Please, no bad news to tear me from my happiness. I hope it's Billy, I thought. I'd tried to reach him so many times without success. Tightening my blue and white batik sarong around my bronzed body, I followed him to the hotel at the front desk. I picked up the phone.

"Are you fucking kidding me?" His first words. Mitch had found me.

I looked at the three young men and a woman who worked the desk. They stood there listening, as natural as could be with no concept of privacy. It was about everyone, if it was about me. I belonged. Communal. Connected. "No, I'm no longer fucking *or* kidding you, Mitch." My old language seemed so crass; it clashed against the gentleness of my new culture.

With his nasty phone call, Mitch had just invaded the new haven I'd created. I was as far away from him as I could ever be—a woman in sunlight, and the man in the moon. I hung up.

On the next to the last night of the month I spent in Bali, I accepted that I had to find a way to leave.

It was my birthday, always a painful day without Jan.

I followed an Asian tradition I had seen in Thailand, giving birthday gratitude gifts to people who'd made you feel alive. I distributed my belongings to all my friends around me. Art materials I had brought, my jewelry, my journal and a pen, clothing—every possession I had with me except my passport and my wallet.

That night, I sat in the village watching a musical dance called *Kecak*. The Ramayana Monkey Chant. Fifty or more village men in a trance-inducing chorus seated on the ground chanting. They followed the leader, chattering sounds in patterns, moving side to side in unison, arms waving in the air, left and right, like I was at one of my concerts. Chak, chak, chak, their voices blended so perfectly in time.

I looked across the swaying choir of men and saw a 6'2" studly man in jeans who looked like Billy standing next to a glowing torch. Was it Billy? He looked so good to me, as though I were seeing him for the first time. His kind face. That gentle smile and the way he swayed, talking among the villagers. Why, after all those years, at that moment, I don't know. I thought of Billy's loyalty to me. Always by my side. It struck me then, handsome as he was, he'd never had a woman, a girlfriend—a shack-up maybe, but nothing else. For a moment I thought it was my imagination. But no, it *was* Billy.

My former life seemed so distant and unreal. He was the one person from my past who could always make me smile. And I realized I felt something for him, something deep, safe, yet exciting—a real connection.

"Happy Birthday, Fran." He approached me, smiling.

"Billy, how could I not have seen you over there all this time?"

"You were just in a trance." He hugged me, pulled back, and placed his hands on my shoulders. "Looks like Bali's been good to you." He swept his arm across the starlit sky. "And your eyes, Franny . . . they're so clear and bright."

"Only in the moonlight." I hugged him back. "Oh, Billy." Why hadn't I seen him before? All these years.

"Hang on a minute. Got a birthday present for you." Billy signaled a young villager, who came out of the crowd holding two acoustic guitars with pink bows on them.

"I don't understand, two?"

"Two guitars . . . and—" Billy stepped aside to reveal his other gift. "One sister."

"Janny, I . . ." I held onto Jan for as long as she would let me. Billy knew what I needed. The truth is . . . I couldn't live without her. An ache shot through my chest. The words couldn't come. There were no lyrics strong enough to run crazy through my calm mind. Something happened inside me, a click, like flipping a switch, as if I'd been holding my breath since we'd parted. Now I could breathe.

Not one quarter, not half, but whole; I felt whole.

"You were right, Jan, about rock 'n' roll—you know, the drugs and sex.

"Fran, you were right too. You connected to rock and now you have two top hits. It's your thing. And rock is soaring. Folk did fizzle, but I still love it."

"It's like you, Jan—endearing."

"Something's happenin' here . . ." We both came out with the same lyrics and laughed.

"Buffalo Springfield," she blurted to get it out before me.

"Oh, Jan, one more second and we could have twinned the answer . . . We were so perfect."

"Are so perfect," she said. "I missed you Fran. I had to come."

"I'm so sorry—"

"No it's my fault—"

"It's OK." We matched apologies with perfect timing.

"I miss Mom."

"I know, me too." Jan threw her arms around me.

"Was it . . . was it *my* fault? You know, Mom's heart?"

"Franny, no! Mom had heart disease. No one blamed you."

I let out the deepest sigh. "Thank you, sister."

The last night of the month I spent in Bali, we sisters entered the clearing and wriggled up onto two carved wooden stools.

Billy stood in the back of the crowd with a grin.

Our pure tones fit naturally, like the missing pieces of my childhood puzzle, as though Jan and I had never missed a beat. Even I couldn't tell if I was singing or we both were, our voices were so tight. She was the melody to my harmony. We sang "Savin' Your Life," the song that had been our last hit, a folksy, heartfelt plea in perfect blend—no drunk drummer, no fancy licks, no whining or aching, no screeching strings, no head banging or broken instruments—no applause, no Mitch pushing my high-self onto the stage—just smiles, as the crowd drew in and huddled around us too close.

Jan got the beauty of the intimacy of the villagers right away, and we shared a wordless understanding I'd missed.

"*Terima kasih, termimah kasih,* thank you, thank you." We remembered our childhood secret language learned from our nanny. Instantly, we both broke out in Indonesian lullabies. The people were charmed and laughed to hear two female foreigners sing the simple songs, softly crooned when they'd swung in their batik cotton baby slings across their mother's chests.

"A little more of my kick-ass next time, OK?" I put my arm around her and kissed her cheek.

"OK, but *my* lyrics. Rock is fine but no sex or drugs." Jan wrapped her arm through mine. "Can't believe you made the top fifty . . . twice! So proud of you. Wow, Franny."

"Jan, I'm a mess."

My sister tilted her head like she used to when we were kids and I did something crazy. "No you're not. You're my sister."

Tears running free, faces in the flickering dim light of the torches that lit our dirt stage, we stared at each other in our own "trance." My mirrored image stared back. Her dreads, my braids and over her shoulder, Billy—always Billy.

"How 'bout *folk-rock?* The Farrell Sisters again?" We asked at exactly the same time, then we laughed. "*Nah.*" We were different and the same, separate yet together. I was two times myself again.

The last day of the month I discovered my soul in Bali, I found the strength to leave.

Trance. Dance. Transformation.

The End

Crossing the Cultural Divide

I'D LONG AGO stopped wondering how the flaming logs snuggled in our stone fireplace sounded—the crackling and the snapping of kindling others had tried to describe to me. Instead, I lose myself in the fire's penetrating heat, its dancing colors, the sweetness of the smoke swirls of applewood that scent my hair. But ever since the postcard arrived yesterday from Father's cousin George, I began to wonder again—trying to translate the sounds of the blaze into my soundless world.

Today, I sit in our parlor at teatime delighting in the fire's comfort on this chilly, New England spring day as I await my parents. Sipping Earl Grey, I'm wearing my stylish, silver-blue tea gown I just bought in Paris on our annual House of Fashion Spring Fling. It's lusciously loose at the bodice, flowing train, and without a high collar, I feel somewhat naughty, exposed. Mother had resisted the modern purchase, but fashion had won out with La Mode magazine to guide her. As my British cousin, Eliza, who'd traveled with us, had said at the *House-of-Worth-Salon-de-*

Vente, "It's nineteen-eleven, Edwardian times now. Queen Victoria's long gone."

My back is cool against the upholstered chair while I warm myself in new cream, high-button shoes, laced up like a corset, with a lovely silk bow on the toe. I'm fantasizing about the postcard, but my peace is about to be disturbed.

Mother crosses the floral Persian carpet, centers herself on a large burgundy flower, rubs her hands in front of the blaze, then turns toward me. I can predict what's coming from the defiant straight-spine stance of her body, and her glaring facial expression. "Read again please, Grace."

I sign the words of the postcard's message.

Postmark May 1, 1911. Rehoboth Beach, Delaware

Dearest Grace:
We hope this finds you well. Tragically,
Anna's fevers have now taken her hearing, permanently.
She is quite disturbed to be trapped in a silent world.
Would you take pity and summer with us to help your cousin?
You've done so well with your own situation, and as a teacher.
Good cheers to your mother and my dear brother, Charles.
Affectionately, Uncle George.

"How insulting. You *trapped* in a silent world? And your *situation?* What *situation?*" Mother's hands sign emphatically. "George is so ignorant . . . Grace, the Hearing world won't be easy. Your life here in Chilmark on The Vineyard is so perfect."

Mother's words threaten my plans. I gaze at the postcard's boardwalk photo, dozens of people strolling, women with parasols, casual long white cotton blouses and skirts cinched at the waist, their arms hooked to the arms of gentlemen in straw hats, no jackets. So free. The ocean water lifts in a suspended arc beside the strip of sand. My beloved Atlantic shore. Why can't I survive one summer in Delaware? We sign our way through Paris every year and fill our steamer chests with fashionable frocks, do we not?

"Are you listening?" Mother asks with flowing hands.

I'm *deaf*, how could I be *listening*, I want to say, but I keep my hands silent in my lap. Sarcasm is so inappropriate, but sometimes . . . I glance out the window to ignore her. I know the lecture's coming—the unique history of my island village in Massachusetts, nearly everyone Deaf like me, and even the Hearing use American Sign Language.

"Cousin Anna's newly deaf. I'm a Deaf teacher; how can I *not* go? My own blood." I spell the word *teacher*, emphatically, letter by letter in stacatto, when I could have used a one-word sign. Now I'm being outright ill-mannered.

Mother turns my chin so I have to watch what she's signing. "Fortunately for you, Grace Lambert, our Chilmark community on Martha's Vineyard has given you a life of normalcy," she says with punctuating signs. She repeats what I already know: Our oppressed ancestors came from Kent County, England with hundreds of Deaf immigrants in 1690 having been treated as disabled, marginalized, unaccepted. They sought a new community of Deaf in America. Imagine, even town meetings were conducted in Sign. Mother would always fit that in.

Does she think I have no memory as well as no hearing?

"The schools for Deaf you attended protected you." I watch Mother finish her rant. "Only here do the Deaf feel they're fully accepted as—"

"Yes, Mother, I know, accepted as *normal*. And I *am* grateful." I imagine how lost my little thirteen-year-old cousin must feel— joining our soundless world, adapting to her own Hearing world where she no longer fits in, where they no longer see *her* as *normal*, even though she will still be able to speak. Mother means well, but my heart is tender right now, and I'm so agitated of late.

I want it; I want the adventure and to get away after my unfortunate affair with James. His disloyalty still stings. A Deaf fiancé doesn't guarantee your heart won't break. At nearly twenty-five-years old, the word *spinster* is shadowing me in the gossiping hands of neighbors every day. Mother's hoping for a new match for me this summer, before I shrivel up and it's too late, I saw her tell Father.

With empty tea cup, I stare out the window at the lone oak tree perched on Chilmark Pond. A wavering vee of Canada Geese passes over the marshy grasses, and shards of afternoon light flash through clouds on the ocean beyond. My one brief childhood visit to Rehoboth still lingers in my memories, the same Atlantic Ocean from Uncle George's wrap-around porch, gulls scattering. My heart flutters with trepidation and excitement at the thought of living an entire summer in the foreign culture of the Hearing world. Wouldn't that discomfort make me a better teacher? It's a rare opportunity, to help a cousin, to see what fiber I am made of, perhaps.

Mother fears I'm vulnerable, having been "cast aside" by James, as she calls our break-up, and I might become entangled with a Hearing man. I have no such desire; I stand firm on that. We've seen too many intercultural matches go wrong.

Father's in favor, secures permission from the school board

and makes the arrangements with Uncle George. Cousin Eliza's willing to accompany me. Mother's out-voted.

We leave in the end of May. I make peace with Mother before my departure.

"I love you dear. Travel safely." She kisses my cheek.

I dream of perambulating along the boardwalk, teaching young Anna to communicate in new ways.

It will be an arduous task. In the Pullman car on the Pennsy to Philadelphia with Cousin Eliza, I have my first taste of anxiety. Can I convince my uncle and aunt they too need to learn American Sign Language?

Reading lips is so ineffective. Anna will need all modes of communication. But unlike me, Cousin Anna has spent her entire young life speaking. They will want her to pass as Hearing, obscure her *tragic disability*. I embrace my culture, my deafness. Will they understand I don't feel I have a *tragic situation*. I'm educated, respected, and respectably attractive, some have said.

Cousin Eliza sits beside me. So opposite, so different. She's Hearing; I'm Deaf. She's tall; I'm petite. Eliza's unfashionably thin, like a plank; I'm classically hourglass shaped. She's demure; I tend to speak my mind. She's British; I'm American. What does it matter? Here we are traveling and laughing together, communicating quite well. It makes us even dearer, our secret world of half-silent sisterhood.

How to teach Anna? I think not only lip reading. It took me years. Though I'm quite adept when talking about common things in common circumstances, I grasp only the gist in less ordinary circumstances with Hearing strangers, or when searching for lips through the jungle of facial hair on some men.

Unlike Father and some Deaf friends, I've chosen not to speak aloud, although I've tediously learned how. If you sound like you're deaf in your pronunciation, you risk being treated like you're a lunatic, ignorant or disabled, Mother insists. Especially in modulating a lady-like volume, loud voices are unseemly to a man, she'd always added. Better for the Hearing to know I'm Deaf. I can write in my journal for them or use creative signs they understand. We can be clever, collaborate, and I have a sense of humor about our mistakes. Shouldn't we all not take ourselves so seriously?

The train lurches and stops. Eliza disembarks to visit a suitor in Philadelphia, our secret little plan. She'd met the gentleman through her American cousin when he'd traveled to London for business. Audaciously, I travel on alone.

A delicious sun-filled day greets me for the final leg on the Queen Anne's Railroad. Charming towns pass by like Greenwood, Ellendale, Milton, and finally, Lewes on the Delaware Bay. The lovely sailing town has the flavor of The Vineyard—historic, beautiful skippers bobbing in the harbor—so picturesque with its sandy beach.

The horn blows, I stand and button up my tan, full-length, silk motoring duster I wore to protect my clothes. I don't tie the mesh veil around my sweeping hat just yet so I can search for Mr. Daniel Spencer who is to meet my train. I'm trembling. My usual confidence wanes. What was I thinking? But allowing Mother to be right is not an option. I open my coach compartment window.

As we slow, I spot a young gentleman on the platform flicking his eyes from a photograph to each passenger.

He reaches my gaze, smiles, and waves. "Miss Lambert? Miss Grace Lambert? Daniel Spencer." Taking off his hat, he exposes shiny locks of thick chestnut hair.

We smile, he bows, and shakes my gloved hand through the open window.

I step down off the train onto the platform. Still swaying, I try to get my land legs. Daniel replaces his hat and turns his head forward to negotiate the crowd. I skitter a few steps ahead to catch what he is saying. He towers over me, making lip reading a stress to my neck, but he's minimally mustachioed, thank goodness.

Newly arrived from Philadelphia, the son of my uncle's dear deceased business partner, Daniel is also visiting for the summer, he says. I'd never heard my uncle mention Daniel in his letters. His energy is charming, his frame handsome, and his azure eyes don't seem to take notice of my deafness.

The porter loads my luggage into Daniel's Austro-Daimler Prince Henry, and the powerful and elegant car takes us at a frightening speed to the lovely beach town.

I arrive in Rehoboth Beach, and find Uncle George, Aunt Julia and several guests, all in a worrisome state. Daniel stands off to the side observing, as the guests are over-solicitous of me. Unaccustomed to being viewed as the unfortunate Deaf woman, their overly solicitous treatment causes a clenching in my stomach and embarrassment in front of the dashing gentleman.

"Please, Grace, perhaps it's best if you meet with Anna in her room, privately." Aunt Julia leads me up the stairs to Anna's bedroom door. I enter.

Her room is darkened, drapes closed; one slice of late sunlight cuts the room in two. I turn on the light. Anna scowls at me and rearranges her gangly teenage limbs on the lone, upholstered chair in the corner with no regard for her lovely yellow dress.

Anna, you don't remember me. Cousin Grace. I visited when you were a child. I write in my journal and hand it to her.

She scans the page. No reaction.

Her new sudden silence must be frightening. I put my hand on her knee.

You are angry aren't you? I write, but receive no answer. *I'm angry sometimes too.* I kneel down next to Anna's chair and put my hand on her cheek. She lowers her eyes again and presses her lips together tightly to prevent her tears.

I was like you when I was a little girl too. Deaf, my whole life. I have secrets to share. A slight flicker of interest lights Anna's eyes at the word *secrets*—a word a teenage girl can't resist. *I have tricks to show you so you'll know what everyone is saying. Did they tell you I'm a teacher?*

Anna rubs her eyes, then scribbles in my journal. *I'm deaf, so now I'll be dumb too, like you, Mommy says.*

I'm stunned at my aunt's ignorance. *I went to school with other Deaf children, some already speak, some learn to talk, some don't,* I write. *I had Hearing and Deaf friends, published a book on teaching Deaf children. I play the piano, do you?*

She nods. Her eyes go big with questions, but Anna holds on to her silence.

Sometimes our angry or scared thoughts inside us get so loud we can't hear the happy ones, right?

Anna reads my words and nods her admission.

My grandmother taught me to unlace my heart.

"Unlace? That's silly." Anna takes my bait. "What are you angry about? You're so pretty, and you're used to it," she says.

I have no way of knowing if her sounds succeed, but I'm pleased she finally speaks. *Want to know what angry voices are in me, Anna?*

She shrugs, feigns disinterest yet watches, reading my jottings with suspicious eyes.

I gesture and mime an unlacing of my heart, like releasing a corset, and I sigh and begin writing. *I was betrothed but my fiancé chose another woman; neighbors call me a spinster.*

Anna reads my script. *Why? You're still young and elegant,* Anna instinctively writes and fingers the gold band on my fountain pen.

I take the pen and answer. *It feels better to tell you my angry thoughts. We'll be special friends. You'll learn to have fun without sounds, I promise you. You can speak if you wish, and see, and touch, and write, and learn to read lips, feel the vibrations of music, be anything you dream of. And I will teach you and your parents American Sign Language, so you can talk well with other Deaf people. I'll teach you your first sign.*

I sign "I love you" with index finger and thumb stretched out and pinkie raised, knowing it isn't an easy sign for her to understand.

She squints and scowls.

I sign again, then point to my chest, cross my hands over my heart, then point to Anna.

She understands, and a smile fights its way onto her face.

I write the words, *I love you* in my journal. *You will find your way, Anna. We'll do it together.*

"You truly promise?" Sobbing, she lets me take her into my arms, and we begin.

The weeks press on, and May turns into June. Anna and I spend hours in lessons and walking the boardwalk signing. She is quick to learn and has given up her moodiness. Often we accidentally run into Daniel—and often not so accidentally.

After Daniel's parents perished in one of Uncle George's ships at sea, he'd become the son my Uncle never had, now heir to the family shipping business, Anna tells me. She is very close to him and he helps her to modulate her speech, so solicitous of her, like a brother. He spends more and more time with her.

Anna's relationship with him seems to spill over into ours. I feel a warmth between us that makes me nervous, but he is never forward.

On a lovely summer day, Daniel steps in front of us on the boardwalk, juggling three cups. "Ice cream, ladies?" He remembers our favorites, vanilla and strawberry. He's seems more than curious about me. I'm threatened by his apparent feelings, and my own growing fantasies about this handsome young Hearing man.

He catches me alone late one afternoon in front of the post office. "I don't know how to compliment you without insulting every other woman on earth, but I quite adore your silence," he says, rotating his straw hat in his hands.

I laugh, trying to avoid an unladylike vocalization. *Mr. Spencer,*

I intend to tell the world you see all women as chattering nuisances, Dodo birds, I write.

Daniel laughs so hard his eyes sparkle and drop a tear. "It's just that so much of what's being said these days isn't worth hearing, don't you think?" He's quiet for a moment, pensive. "Since my parents' passing, you are the first to make me laugh." He moves closer. "You're so . . ." His eyes are speaking now.

I raise my guard, write my tedious speech, and turn it toward him. *Mr. Spencer—*

It's Daniel, please, he writes.

I cross out Mr. Spencer. *Daniel, we come from two quite different cultures, won't you concede?*

He reads it. "Why yes, I suppose, you from that rebellious, liberal Massachusetts culture, me from Philadelphia, a veritable jungle of hooligans." His grin jumps across, spreads on my own face against my will, and I turn red, like an ingénue. He charms me.

I read his lips easily because he graciously slows, tilts his head down to assist me, and I'm so attentive. I squeeze my eyes at him. *I am referring to you being a Hearing person and me, Deaf,* I write. My ink runs dry; I fumble for my spare fountain pen. This is why I have always avoided any closeness with a Hearing man. I imagine a life of scribbling on paper, scrambling for a bottle of ink, and missing what his lips have shared or misunderstanding. I can see Daniel standing, palms up, shoulders shrugged for years to come. So impossible. And there's Mother . . . and her prejudice.

"As for our hearing or not . . . I see nothing but a second language, like you speaking French, perhaps without the snobbery, and me, some unpolished version of the King's English." He stretches out his arm and leans his hand against the lamppost. "What if I were to learn to move my own hands so you would understand me?" His fingers barely brush my temple to replace a stray strand of my hair. So intimate, I shouldn't allow it, but I do. "A secret world to live in," he says. "Two silent luh . . ." —he stumbles, and corrects himself— ". . . friends."

I know his lips were forming the word *lovers*. My breath catches.

He goes on. "I'm quite over all the chattering in public places anyway. And in private, how wonderful to be soundless with you. Forgive me, your face and cleverness alone are worth the journey."

I watch his expressive lips, read his eyes, his smile, the lean of his body. His quick gaze down my summer white cotton blouse and skirt burns me; my temperature rises from his flirtation. I know this is charming and thrilling for now, but there is no destination to this adventure except heartbreak for both of us, I think.

Then he tells me he's leaving immediately for Washington, D.C. Some business, maybe life-changing.

I'm wordless, and I work to keep my face emotionless and come to my senses. *Mr. Spencer, it's getting late, don't you agree?* His disappointment reaches across and clenches my heart. If only—but our futile intercultural fate is certain. I can never live in his world, nor he in mine. For once Mother's right, and in any case, he's leaving in the morning. So that's that.

"I'll write. Postcards. Will you write, as well?" He spins his straw hat, drops his head. "My time in Washington is . . . imperative, vital. Someday, I'll explain." His gaze suspends for an uncomfortable yet alluring time.

No need, I write. My words are barely legible.

His lips want to speak, but he turns away, thinks better of it, turns back, and kisses me boldly in public, engaging my eyes with a message I can't help but hear. He takes vital parts of me with his departure—my ability to breathe, think straight. I walk as if my shoes are weighed down by a full bucket of sand. But it's over. I'm relieved that his departure so simply solves my dilemma, but not the ache in my heart, doubly broken in such a short time.

Anna is doing so well. She has practiced speaking at her father's request and he says her words are growing free of *Deaf awkwardness*. That stings me, even though I know his comment has no negative intent. Ignorance about my world is the norm among the Hearing.

My young cousin is learning to be expressive with her Sign language. I'm amazed at her skill in so few months. Her relieved parents have found a school for the Deaf in Washington for the fall. Meanwhile, they've agreed to learn Sign language.

I receive a delightful postcard from Daniel. A sweet surprise. Then another and another, daily. I dutifully return the favor. We turn to letters for privacy as we become more intimate in our exchanges: Dear Miss Lambert, Dear Grace, My Dear Grace, Darling Grace, My Only One. I gasp and respond, Dear Mr. Spencer, cross it out, Dear Daniel.

I find a new hobby, secretly lingering in the heat with the crowd outside the Rehoboth Beach Post Office to await each day's delivery. Pathetic, for a self-possessed woman, still I succumb.

The summer's end is imminent, and I walk from the Post Office empty handed, again and again. No word of his plan to return. I want to go home where I can breathe and begin to accept the loss. Foolish to have let it go this far. Why does he keep me close with his drawer full of postage stamps?

The week before I'm to leave, while dressing, I see his automobile from my window. Thrilled and fearful, I primp in the mirror, press my lilac dress with shaking hands, and rush downstairs.

"Julia, may I see you in my office?" My uncle's smile is suspicious as he calls his wife away.

"Of course, dear. You will excuse us, won't you, Grace?" She shares his grin, as curiously, my aunt and uncle allow us time alone.

I'm propped against the fireplace mantle for support when Daniel enters and greets me.

"Grace, how are you . . . you look . . ." He stops his signing, steps forward and gazes into my eyes. Then straightening his back and tugging at his suit jacket lapels, he argues his case in near flawless American Sign Language. Clean shaven now, his lips are fully available to me.

"I've been to Gallaudet University—a private tutor. Very intensive studying eight-hour days. I spent nights in silent Deaf conversation groups for nearly three months. For you. For us."

I nearly slip to the floor—his *life-changing* work in Washington was . . . for *me!*

"I intend to dedicate myself to your happiness." Daniel signs.

I'm duly impressed. Quivering, I sign, no. I just can't see how it can work, yet he has put his soul into it. We spend hours on the boardwalk arguing the issues. I'm less afraid of losing him now rather than later, when reality sets in. Too painful.

I can't live in a Hearing world, expatriated from my Deaf culture.

He chisels away at my arguments. "We'll live in Chilmark and summer here."

I'll surely confuse what your lips are saying, you'll get frustrated, leave me. It feels good to sign with him instead of the delay of writing.

He smiles, signs, *Does the sun leave the sky?* then adds, *then speak aloud to me, if I'm unclear.*

No, never! Those aren't sounds you'd want to hear. My shaking hands expose my fear so clearly.

His signing vocabulary inadequate, Daniel writes in my journal, *You're beyond your sounds, my love. I'm deaf to anything but our loving bond. Your silence, your sounds, awkward or not, no matter, your choice. More likely you'll tire of me.*

Impossible, I think. My tears threaten. I question my sanity, chastise my heart. *Alright then, contingent upon my parents' blessings.* Cowardly of me. Consent is customary, not required, but to survive my Chilmark world, Daniel must survive Mother's scrutiny and fixed opinions.

I have little hope he'll want to carry out his intentions once he meets my mother. It's only fair he has the chance to reconsider his future.

While in transit home I coach him—how to hold his body, facial expressions, use his silence—so much more than simply signing and finger spelling. Our hands touch often; I scream for joy in my silence. His sign language is open and expressive. I teach him to ask Father for my hand in marriage.

Let's practice the kiss again. Not sure I have it down. He winks.

He's audacious. I smile, still questioning my wisdom, not my feelings. Was I setting myself up for another disaster with a suitor? What would I do if my parents disapproved and caused an embarrassment? I was more concerned that Daniel would find the realities of the situation to be untenable. Had his romantic heart really thought things through? There would be no running away with him. I could never live permanently in a Hearing community, could I?

But could I live without him?

We take a breath and enter my parents' home. Daniel's signing hesitations make him simply seem like a nervous suitor. Fewer words seem manly. I never say he's Hearing; I never say he's Deaf; he's Daniel.

We share cocktails and hors d'oeuvres, uneventfully. Daniel does well, signing through the entire meal.

Father takes Daniel into his library after dinner, and delighted with my new fiancé, he emerges, joins Mother and me in the parlor and gives his consent.

Mother takes me aside, her hands flow like a symphonic conductor, beautiful words of congratulations. "Handsome, bright, and mannerly, and your father has spoken to him about his financial status, and he approves. I've always said my daughter had wisdom."

"Did you, Mother?" I smile. "So I'll not shrivel up after all?"

The telephone rings. Our maid is preparing dinner; Daniel instinctively answers. It's Uncle George.

Mother's eyes are riveted on Daniel's lips.

Daniel keeps repeating, thank you, sir; yes, we're elated. Mr. and Mrs. Lambert? Yes, they approve. Certainly, sir, I'll be sure to call you after we depart, yes, sir. Yes, we'll summer with you, winters, Grace will teach. I'll work from here with your approval, George."

Mother's face goes ashen. Her signs are deliberate. "So you purposely tricked me? He's *Hearing?*"

"No Mother, I let Daniel have a chance to communicate, so you couldn't discriminate. You quite loved him only seconds ago. How quickly my wisdom escapes me, Mother. The doors of prejudice swing both ways."

"I can't believe it, Charles, he's *Hearing!*" Mother signs.

"Yes, and he can understand your impolite words," Father says, and grins at me.

Daniel signs to bridge our *situation.* "I love your daughter. I love her silence. I hear her voice without her speaking. I love how we understand each other. She's beautiful, funny, brilliant, actually— taking after her mother in many ways, I might assume."

My mother draws back and lifts her chin, taken in by his unexpected compliment.

I'm smiling inside but don't dare let it reach my lips.

Pausing, Daniel looks at me with such love in his eyes. "Grace is *Grace* . . . by written word, voice, silent signs, no matter—some things are beyond any language, I've learned." His signs are impeccable, expressive, touching.

I cross the room on weak legs and take his flattering hands in mine. Could my chest swell any larger? I find my courage to speak aloud with no fear of sounding awkward, like I'm a "lunatic, ignorant, or disabled," as my mother had always warned me.

"Daniel isn't *Hearing,* Mother. He is *Daniel,* and I see Daniel, and he *hears* me."

And for the first time he truly does.

The End

First published under the title, "Hearing is Believing" in *Rehoboth Reimagined*, an anthology by the Rehoboth Beach Writers Guild, 2017.

A Treasure Returned

ESCAPING FROM MY home in New York City post-divorce, I needed to be alone to think. I was no longer the wife of a Wall Street executive whose interest in female clients went far beyond managing their money. Devastated, I promised myself not to look back. I was in search of my lost *kepemilikan*—my sense of belonging.

Leaving my hectic, hollow life behind, I followed the guiding voice of the rental car's GPS and found my destination—Rehoboth Beach. I'd never assumed my husband's adventures would be my adventures; I was wrong. Hosting and arranging the best for the best, left little time for my own interests. Uppermost, my love of photography was sorely missed in my new demanding life as my husband's events hostess. A camera lens was a threat to the personal privacy of Jeffery's world of high-end clients, he'd said. And I'd acquiesced.

My first American friend, Mariah Murphy, had always spoken fondly of her charming hometown in Delaware. I just needed a destination, somewhere to find the lost part of me. Driving down Rehoboth Avenue, I thought of her and wondered where in the world my adventuresome friend was now. Mariah was a passionate itinerant portrait artist who'd come to spend a two-year post-graduate internship at my family's artists' colony in Ubud, my Balinese village.

I could hear her vibrant voice. "I just followed an impulse after I took a college class in indigenous art." Spontaneously, Mariah had written a letter to my parents and booked her flight. I was modeling her fearlessness now, leaving everything behind.

Ubud, in the uplands of Bali, Indonesia, is known as a center for traditional painting, crafts and dance. The surrounding Ubud rainforest and terraced rice paddies, dotted with Hindu temples and shrines, are among Bali's most famous landscapes. I was proud of my heritage. Intricately carved, ancient holy sites like Goa Gajah, the "Elephant Cave," and the temple grounds of Gunung Kawi, with its rock-cut shrines, were the playgrounds of my childhood.

Art was in my blood, my father and mother being traditional Balinese painters of great renown. People came from around the world to study my parents' energetic, yet refined, intricate art that resembled baroque folk art with tropical themes. They captured the scenes of daily Balinese island life and the drama of the Hindu tales of goddesses and gods in the finest details.

In awe of their genius, I'd wanted something of my own.

Mariah's boldness first opened my mind to the world beyond my remote lush mountainside village. She was twenty-two; I was in high school. I smiled remembering how I'd followed her around like a starry-eyed puppy. She'd made me realize how fortunate

I was to live in a communal society with such a deep sense of belonging, a family of artists exchanging ideas, working daily to teach traditions and techniques. I'd always felt I was a part of something—the daily energy and passion of fellow artists sharing their visions, my parents determined hands coaxing such beauty from the strokes of their brushes on the canvas.

As I approached the ocean block in Rehoboth to find a place to stay, I imagined Mariah and I dressed identically in our traditional blouses, cummerbunds, and batik sarongs yet in striking contrast to each other—my cascades of black hair and dark brown eyes, her thick blonde hair and blue eyes. She'd been incredibly kind to me during her stay with us. I taught her to speak Indonesian; she helped me to polish my classroom English and let me borrow her Nikon camera to explore my creative urge.

"Ida, you have the eye," she'd said examining my first photographs. With her words, Mariah had awakened my creative dreams. If not for her encouragement, I wouldn't have been bold enough to follow in her footsteps at the NYU Tish School of the Arts. How could I not follow when she'd written me such an affirming letter of recommendation?

We'd lost contact over the years since I'd left Bali to study photography in the U.S. I wanted to be like Mariah—bold, adventuresome in a foreign land. My family was shocked when I didn't return to my legacy; I'd married and changed my surname, succumbing to the lure of the unknown.

Mariah was nowhere to be found online; she must have changed her name too. Where had Mariah gone after she'd left Bali? What exotic foreign land had lured her where she would create her signature, award-winning portraits of village folk? I would love to see her again someday to hear the stories of her life, I thought. I'd hoped to have something rewarding in my own art to share with her. The child in me still wanted to make Mariah proud.

"It will be like unweaving the fabric of my soul when I leave your close-knit colony," Mariah had said on the day I'd left for school.

I understand that all too well now. I admit I was too ashamed to return home at nearly thirty with the warp and weft of my life torn apart—divorce, no direction, no children, no art. The collaboration and the love of a community was sorely absent since I'd left graduate school and married Jeffery.

Now I looked for the good. I was thrilled to be by the sea again—a sweet reminder of my childhood island halfway around the world. In my communal culture, the same word, *sendiri* is often used for both "alone" and "lonely." American culture was different. I'd learned that seeking independence is highly valued. But, in my current, independent quest to find my future, I felt painfully alone. My isolation snaked around me and squeezed the breath from my chest.

I found an old pink Victorian hotel on the boardwalk that overlooked the ocean. It was my fortune they had a room, and I checked-in. Sweeping back the curtains in my room, I took in the stunning late June evening. The exquisite, third-story view comforted me—oscillating, blue gray waves of the Atlantic that finished in foamy-white flourishes on the sandy shore. People walked along the beach as the burnt-orange sky melted back to blue. The horizon was adorned with puffs of stark-white clouds drifting toward an unknown destination, just like me.

I envied the families of sun-worshippers gathering up their

piles of beach towels and toys, with tots on shoulders. Jeffery, my former husband, had been too busy working, traveling, collecting, and consuming to start a family with me. He had no interest in domestic distractions, he'd said. I wish he'd told me that before we were married. Ensconced in his self-centered, possessive world, he'd smothered me. I was simply a symbol of his liberal bent, I realized. An exotic trophy for his mantle. True friends were few, and I'd lost touch with my own desires. If not for my own naïve mistake—leaving school to follow the illusion of a man who promised a life of travel, family, and a chance to capture my photographs in alluring exotic places—I wouldn't feel so lost today. Hadn't he sworn his passionate love for me? He had lust only for possessions and pursuing money and position in a society that had no communal connection.

At nearly thirty, I wished to be one of the women I saw below on the boardwalk surrounded by loved ones, heading to their seaside homes or hotels.

The next morning, I ate breakfast on the hotel's outdoor porch along the boardwalk while watching the beach town come alive. Two gulls landed on the white fence next to my table as though they felt my grief. They were my first company on my journey to solve the mystery of my new path. Tilting their heads, eyeing my toast and home fries, they made me smile. Then the ocean birds cooed and marched back and forth like prosecutors interrogating me about all the foolish decisions of my past. I had few answers. The truth and nothing but the truth, I promised myself. Tying my long dark hair into a pony tail, I paid the bill and set out to explore.

Wandering down the boardwalk, I saw a couple posing for a

selfie in front of the blue vastness of the ocean. My grandmother's voice was in my head. *When you are hurting, do something for someone else, my child.*

"May I take your photo for you?" I reached out with a smile.

"Oh, that's so nice, thank you."

Catching them with just the right light, at the right angle, evoked a sentimental ache for my photography. When I'd arrived for the first time in America, I'd clicked the shutter of the Nikon camera Mariah had given me a dozen times while flying over that welcoming statue in the New York harbor. The statue's words had called to me, offering solace from the shore. *Give me your tired your poor*, she'd said. It struck me that even though I was not poor now, I was tired; although only momentarily homeless in this beach town, I was truly tempest-tossed.

I passed a salt-water taffy store and a window that sold French fries in a cup. My airborne acquaintances from the outdoor seating at the restaurant gathered, making cawing commentaries from above. Wings spread, sun glinting through the fanned feathers, one gull's voice was silenced by a wilting fry in its beak. Click, click, click. My camera caught each scene.

A woman held up a salty treat to the sapphire sky, and one of my flying friends swooped down to intercept the beach delicacy. Click. A child's delighted laugh split my sadness for a moment. Click.

I'd left home on New York's Upper East Side suddenly, still wearing my all-black linen city outfit. I traded it for shorts and a hot pink T-shirt, bought comfortable shoes at a store called *In2Soles*, and left my high heels at a nearby thrift shop to be recycled into someone else's life.

Along the main street, I found a shop that took old-fashioned photographs of tourists. Each couple dressed up in turn-of-the-century costumes and stood against a mural background of an old saloon with the required serious expressions. The camera flash froze them in time. I envisioned the first-prize ribbon for my cityscape photograph on the NYU Art gallery wall. How had I let my passion go?

Images of my friends and I performing nighttime traditional Balinese dances came to mind. Inspired by our culture, we would magically change from simple village girls into enchanted Ramayana dancers in bedazzled costumes, moving divinely to rhythmic gongs. These memories of our symbolic, nightly transformations gave me hope. Couldn't I evolve too? I smiled and nodded. Like the contrast of the blank white canvas, I longed for the colorful splashes of paint to take form—to create a picture of my new life.

Hadn't I done that once before? If I could adapt and recreate my life with Jeffery, couldn't I resurrect my former self. Didn't she still live within me?

Every person, every shell, every ride at Funland, filled with smiling children, every little girl on her father's shoulders holding a prized teddy bear, attracted my lens. The town was sweet enough to make me want to linger longer. I decided I would stay for a while. Where else would I go? Somehow being in the town where Mariah had grown up, thrived in, and launched from, was both comforting and ironic. Perhaps there was hope for my launch too.

Each night I sat on my bed, propped up on my pillows, and reviewed the photos I'd taken that day. I had to admit they were good. I picked up *Delaware Beach Life* magazine that was left for me on my dresser. A photography contest. The winning nature shots from last year were stunning in the glossy magazine—prehistoric-looking blue herons in flight, a mother robin feeding wide-open baby beaks in her nest, cormorants drying their wings, dramatic storms over the sea, osprey flying over a local canal while carrying a fish nearly as big as she. Sorting through my photos, I found a few I might submit to this year's contest.

During my first few weeks in the beach town, I perused galleries, enjoyed jazz at a local Indian restaurant, ate pizza and beach fries, explored shops, and walked by the sea.

There was a particular pull to this delightful village. Yes, the town was sweet but then the tourists that came and went made me feel lonelier. Could I find *kepemilikan* in a seaside town that washed a tide of strangers in and out, week after week all summer long. And what about when the season gave way to frost and empty streets greeted me each chilly morning? Wouldn't that only intensify the aching emptiness that lurched inside me?

On a white bench beyond the busy part of the boardwalk near Funland, an irregular mountain-shaped stone captured my attention. I picked it up; it fit perfectly in my fist. Painted in blues and greens, it was inscribed on one side with the words *Trust yourself!* The message was so appropriate, something my grandmother had said as I left home; I had to laugh.

It was quite artistic with a tiny ocean scene of dolphins' arching backs along the horizon. After taking a portrait shot of the find, blurring the background, I picked up the rock again and rotated it in my hand. In tiny font, a typed sticker on the rock's flat bottom read, *Please post a pic of this rock on the Facebook group, M.M.W. Painted Rocks. Then re-hide.*

I slipped down onto the bench, clutched the rock in my hands, and turned it, revealing a final urging on the opposite side; *Be the reason someone smiles today.* As though my grandmother were again sharing her sage advice.

Heading back to the hotel, I read the messages on the rock, over and over. At a booth in front of the boardwalk amusements at Funland, I spontaneously purchased $50 worth of tickets and handed the strips to children waiting in line for games and rides. I chatted with each family and introduced myself with my grandmother's spirit working through me. I collected their surprised looks and smiles, and my loneliness began to dissipate a bit. They loved hearing the story of my art colony in Ubud and posed with me for photos—not my photographs but photos of me in a communal group once again.

A brick alley with a coffee shop was inviting. I bought a Cappuccino and sat in the alleyway at one of the wrought iron tables, placing the rock in front of me. Who did this?

A woman in a colorful blouse holding a miniature white curly-haired dog sat across from me, sipping coffee from a paper cup. "Oh, you found one, too?"

"There are *more?* I found this one on a bench near Funland."

"They've been popping up all over town this summer." She ruffled her dogs curly head.

"Really?" I pondered the motivation of the anonymous artist again.

"Mine was pink and blue. It said, 'Breathe,' and 'Share the bliss.' I left it on my neighbor's doorstep. She's having a hard time these days. Did you post yours on Facebook?"

"Not yet." I felt a blush pass over my face.

"I'm Christy, and you are?" The woman's silver jewelry jangled as she extended her hand.

"Ida Ayu, from New York. Actually, I'm from Bali."

"Bali? How fascinating. I spent some time there years ago buying batik garments for my boutique clothing store here in town."

"Really?" The coincidence warmed me. We chatted for nearly an hour, and I learned more about the groups of artists, writers, and musicians that flourished in the community. Christy belonged to a writers guild. Like indulging in a luscious parfait, I was discovering the layers of the town that were unseen to a newcomer like me. The more I'd learned, the less I wanted to leave the enchanting town.

"Ida, I think you would enjoy a monthly evening event called, *Night of Songs and Stories*. It's put on by our local writers guild at a restaurant in town each month. Readings and music and community," she said. "Would you be my guest?"

"Community? Of course." I accepted.

Although haunted by the sticker on the rock's bottom requesting me to post the photo and re-hide it, I couldn't let it go that week. Wasn't the rock my good luck charm? Wasn't it a sign that maybe I would find my way?

One night, I had an insight. I no longer needed to keep the rock, I thought. Its messages were in my heart. It was time to pass it on. I would carry it with me until I found just the right place to leave the inspirational stone.

I smiled, picked up my phone, and posted the photo of my serendipitous rock on the designated Facebook page. I understood the anonymous artist's intention by scrolling through the dozens of posted rock photos on benches, dunes, and splintered wood railings along the boardwalk. It touched me to think about how the gesture of painting a simple rock could spread life-changing ripples through a community. How many people like me had been inspired by the mysterious artist? How many strangers connected over coffee in an alley café sharing their precious finds? How many people like me, followed the command to "make someone smile" that day.

A week later, I received the invitation from Christy to attend the event hosted by the Rehoboth Beach Writers Guild at a local restaurant. As I entered the room, the engaging conversation bubbled around me, and my spirits lifted. The energy of the group of one hundred writers sharing creativity gave me a welcome feeling of home. "Who would have guessed this was here in this beach town? Thank you, Christy." I sat at her table of eight. She introduced me to her writer friends, including a charming woman named Maribeth, who led the organization and hosted the evening.

"I suspected this is just what you needed as a newcomer, Ida—the theme tonight is *home*." Christy smiled.

"Saraswati, the Hindu goddesses of learning, arts, and music, must be at work." I laughed.

At the mic on the corner stage in the restaurant, one writer after another read charming and intimate stories on the theme—*home*. Sarah told a touching account of her mother and growing up in Brooklyn. A yoga teacher, Ellen, expressed how the ocean view from her home had inspired her poetry and art. Three Judy's in a row read—one shared the saga of her Jewish grandmother escaping the war to settle in America; another, her escapades as a talented, youthful showgirl in Las Vegas; the third Judy captured her adventures assigned to the American embassy in Sweden. The readings continued; the applause was enthusiastic; and I was inspired. Jane detailed the spontaneous uprooting from her life-long career to open a shoe store in Rehoboth Beach. Sherri read a touching piece about lessons learned from growing up on a Midwest farm. Margaret shared feelings about commuting between two homes. Kim made her intimate story of creating a new life in Italy come alive. Irene put us in the scene and left us laughing over the antics of her Italian family; and Ginny captured her closeness with her father and their deep connections to Washington, D.C. Finally, a woman named Mimi read about her adventures moving to Upstate New York for her first job.

With each story, I was more inspired by the bravery, determination, and humor these women revealed. This small beach town had attracted an impressive group of creative and talented people. I could taste their *kepemilikan* as they shared their experiences. I related to their searches for that elusive sense of belonging that I'd ached for since leaving my family's art colony in Bali.

In between the readings, musicians Stuart and Amy played carefully chosen songs to match the writing prompt of the night. "Take me home country roads." It couldn't have been more apt, and my heart couldn't take much more. Although enchanted and welcomed by all, an ache of homesickness ran through me. At the intermission, I thanked Christy, told her I wasn't feeling well, excused myself, and left the table.

Why did I feel even more *sendiri* than ever, having experienced such a promising and communal evening? I realized, just like watching the loving families on the beach, I was *apart* from it, not a *part* of it. I paid the waiter who stood by the bar and slipped out the door, feeling ashamed after accepting Christy's kindness. I would call her in the morning to apologize again.

I carried the weight of my loneliness as I headed to the hotel. I'd come to know the art galleries and shops along the main street or tucked-in little alleyways. On my walk back, I stopped dead in front of a shop I hadn't noticed before—Art for Hearts Gallery. Something called to me.

Two plain rocks peeked out from under a cloth on a paint-splattered table in the front corner of the room. Next to them was a glass that held three paintbrushes. I gasped at the discovery—the secret rock artist. A *closed* sign hung in the glass door.

Through the glass wall, an oil portrait on the far wall stunned me. *Neneh!* My *grandmother*. I covered my gaping mouth, collapsed into the window, and wept. Impossible. Judging from her face and the background, I guessed it was a painting done about the time I'd left for the States. Her familiar look that always said *everything would be OK* was so perfectly captured by the artist. Grandmother's loving eyes followed me.

I gathered myself, put my hands together at my chest, and sent her our traditional bow.

Glancing down, I saw the gallery owner's name etched in the corner of the window—Mariah Murphy Warner. Why, after all her exotic travels, had she return to her childhood beach town?

Mariah Murphy! There couldn't be more than one artist with that name here in her own hometown; could there? I held the rock to my chest and let the joy flow through me. She'd always been so creative and kind—an old soul. Her words spoken upon our departure, years before, clearly came to mind. "We're meant to meet again, my friend."

I giggled like a child as I took my found rock from my purse and left it on the step of Mariah's gallery. Taking a photo of the gallery front step with the colorful stone, I posted it on the rock art's Facebook page and added a note. "A treasure returned. Love, Ida Ayu—now staying at the pink hotel." I hit *post*.

Crossing the street, I cut over two blocks to my hotel. How long before she would check the posts? Back at the hotel, the proprietor greeted me. "Ida, did you have fun? I have a message for you."

I unfolded the note, recognizing the handwriting. *Call me when you return. So excited! Mariah.* Immediately, I called her number and held my breath. On the first ring, she picked up.

"*Ida Ayu!* This is crazy! You and I together again?" Her familiar laugh was a welcome comfort for me.

"Oh, Mariah, how are you, my dear friend? My heart was pounding when I saw my *neneh* in your window." The words squeaked from my throat.

"Yes, I did that just after you left for NYU. I'd always intended to give it to you when I next saw you."

"I'm curious. How did you end up back here, Mariah? I thought you said you wanted to 'whirlwind around the world.'"

"I'd learned something from living with your family. *Kepemilikan.* Remember?"

"Ironic, no? Full circle?" I laughed out loud.

"Yes. Listen, Ida, I had to take your call I was so excited . . . but I'm hosting a dinner with artist friends now, and it's late, but I'm so excited. Let's do this in person. We have so much to share. How about tomorrow morning?"

"I can't wait. Coffee Mill alleyway at nine?" I squeezed my phone so hard I nearly dropped it.

"Perfect. See you then. I'm so thrilled to connect with you again."

I left the hotel and walked to the ocean to ponder the grand coincidence. The way Mariah's rock creation had found its way back to her shop steps and connected us again was miraculous. I could see myself in the future standing on the stage in that restaurant, telling the story of my journey to my new home to the writers guild.

I was alone, but not lonely. The circle of life, I thought and smiled, listening to the rhythm of the waves. Closing my eyes, I heard my grandmother's words of wisdom. *A circle represents the Divine life force that keeps our reality in motion,* she'd said. *It's both an ending and a beginning, a choice you make, my child.*

I chose *kepemilikan*—a belonging, a beginning. Mariah's life's journey had begun in my home village; mine would begin in hers.

The End

Near-Life Experience

I FELT LIKE a high-strung horse at a rattling gate, the bell about to ring. Our marriage was at near-death, and I wanted to run. Brad's idea of being an outdoor guy was coming out from behind his laptop for dinner; I was a nature girl under house arrest.

In Brad's world, communicating was talking about his latest work project, tearing up pristine nature preserves for pipelines and rigs. I worked for World Wildlife Fund. "No, it's not a punchline to a joke," I said to my new therapist. "Needless to say, it's become safer for Brad and me not to talk."

"Lynn, tell me how you two ever got together."

The therapist was attentive; it felt good to have someone listen for a change. "Raging hormones, in our twenties, his platinum hair, and the way he looked at me. Oh, and the pressure of everyone else getting married. I'm sure that was part of the reason—it was the intensity of the times."

As I looked out the window at the white flowers fluttering down from the trees outside the doctor's office, vivid memories of May 6, 1970 came back to me. I could see the beautiful festival of flowers and blooming cherry blossoms by my dorm at our Georgetown University campus. The doctor was certainly too young to have experienced those profound events, so I shared them—U.S. military action in Cambodia and Vietnam, the massacre of student protesters at Kent State University by the National Guard, the campus riots—a terrifying time.

That Wednesday in May, undergraduate students at Georgetown had begun a strike that would last for just over a week, I told her. "Brad and I were both among the student senators who'd called for the strike and a two-day boycott of classes. Following those two days, faculty representatives voted to suspend classes for an additional week. Then classes for that semester were canceled. Students never sat for finals—a threatening time for me as I needed the grades to get into grad school."

Was that it? I wondered. "Maybe we'd simply run from the chaos into the safe harbor of each other's arms. The campus riots had made us feel powerfully bonded. I guess we didn't really know each other at all," I told my therapist. "Sounds so shallow, I know. When we'd risen up out of our cloud of marijuana, we were married, and both headed to grad school."

"So he never talked to you about taking the job with the oil company?"

"No, he went to a campus job fair and came back a victim of his financial fears. We were newlyweds." I remembered Brad's glowing face. "*He* thought I'd be surprised and excited about the salary and the benefits. Neither of us came from affluent families. He was on scholarship. We had a start on our lives together, he'd said. To support his decision, I talked myself into thinking he really wasn't directly involved in the decisions made by the oil executives—he was an engineer."

I shook my head and sighed. "Dr. Noonan, I have to admit the income and benefits were attractive to someone headed into non-profit work." I averted her gaze and twisted my wedding ring. "We never spend any time together. It's not that he does anything wrong; it's that he doesn't do anything. *We* don't do anything. It's not entirely his fault. I'm often out at evening fundraisers to save the precious polar bears—while he's planning pipelines for their demise. But I want to have a family. Not at the total expense of our individual desires, but . . . there are compromises in life, right?"

"Have you talked honestly about it?"

"Constantly. I've made attempts. Brad's always working on some equipment designs. He thinks we need to be fully established before we think of children. I understand . . . his family struggled financially, and as he says, his dad was a deadbeat. His mother struggled to put food on the table. But we are both doing well. It seems to be an unfounded fear to me."

"Maybe you two need to plan some time away to talk."

"I think you're right. I'm forty next month—maybe we can arrange a birthday getaway." I thanked the doctor and left her office.

On my drive home, I decided I would talk to Brad about my therapist's suggestion. Well, first, I should tell him I *went* to a therapist. I would ask for a fortieth birthday celebration trip we would never forget.

When I arrived at our Rosslyn, Virginia condo, I stood at the tinted glass wall in our living room and looked out over the snaking Potomac River. I reviewed the reasons I'd married Brad, and wished my mother was still alive so I could talk to her. None of my friends could see beyond his job choice. Brad had been loyal, funny, thoughtful, and passionate about justice when I'd made the decision to marry him.

Where had we gone wrong in our nearly twenty years together? How had we ended up on opposite sides of the spectrum; me an environmentalist, Brad working for the enemy, destroying natural habitats. Hadn't we protested for peace together? Maybe that's what he wanted—peace in a marriage—but not a real partnership or a family.

At first, he'd argued he was contributing to our world by helping to develop the fuel we needed. Now, supporting his work was untenable—as sweet as he was, as much as I loved him. It wasn't as if he were off excavating and exploding mountains himself; his work wasn't in the field. But he was working for the company, wasn't he? Don't you have to believe in what you're doing? I thought.

"Hey, Lynn, why so serious?" Brad came up beside me and shared the view.

"We really need to talk, Brad." I felt like we were characters out of an old soap opera. I explained my concerns, the lack of fun in our lives, the disconnect being on opposing sides. No family at forty.

You would have thought I'd told him I was from Mars.

"Honey, I thought . . . well I thought we were pretty happy. We never fight. You know how my parents were always bickering. We're so peaceful—on the same page. Well, on most subjects, we're on the same page. We never have to worry about paying the bills. I know working in the energy field bothers you but we keep it on the sidelines, right?"

"Exactly how I feel, Brad—like we're on the sidelines. If we're going to use sports analogies, then I'd say I want to be *in the game*." I touched his cheek to soften the sting, I guess. Or was it a beam of emotion from the past resurrecting from deep inside me?

"This *is* the game, Lynn. It's just been a busy time. We're building a future."

"But, Brad, is just paying the bills and having savings a future worth building?" I tried to explain the loss of passion, the loss of *us*, and how painful it was that he was *working for the enemy*, as everyone would say at my office. I told him my biological clock was running out. "The things I'm fighting for are the things your company wants to destroy. We're still protesting but now against each other." I just had to bring up the elephant in the room, so to speak. Maybe that was the wrong analogy.

"Lynny, it's not like I'm off shooting endangered species myself. It's a great job. I'm not going to end up like my deadbeat dad having kids I can't support. Come on, honey."

"It's not the only job in the world, Brad. And if we wait much longer, you won't be a dad at all. You're not your father." I said it with a soft edge, placing a comforting hand on his arm. We were back to the same discussions we'd had when he'd first taken the job, except now we had the *children* issue to argue over as well. I looked out over the view and studied the bank of graying clouds moving over the city rooftops waiting for his response.

"There's nothing wrong with us, Lynn. We're just busy—in the peak of our careers," he said when I'd brought up our problems and my unhappiness again. "I . . . had no idea you weren't happy.

I know it's getting late to start a family, but my mother was forty-four when she had my youngest brother."

I didn't know what to say to that; didn't he remember our doctor's discussions of the risks of later-in-life pregnancies? Maybe Brad wasn't the only one not communicating. Or was he too busy to really hear? I thought of the old TV commercial where the man is sitting at the breakfast table holding a newspaper in front of his face. His wife is drinking her coffee across from him. She sighs and calls his name twice. On her second try, he puts the paper down. "Oh! When did you go bald?" she says. I never wanted a marriage like that. I use to think that commercial was so funny; it's no joke to me now that my desire to start a family was so timely.

"Brad, we need some time to talk, get away from everything to see who we are together now, and my fortieth birthday is coming up." We hadn't taken a vacation in two years, although I'd pleaded for a getaway. We had to stop postponing decisions or at least discussions about having a child, as well. A family would soon be mission impossible. Would his workaholic personality make change impossible?

Brad pushed his hands in his pockets and paced in front of the expansive view of the river and the bridge into Georgetown. Then he stopped in front of me. "I had no idea. I don't want you unhappy, Lynn. You're right. I'll take some time off. We'll take a birthday trip. You decide where, OK? The most important thing is *us*, right?"

I was stunned even moved by his straight-to-the-point communication. Unlike anything he'd ever said. And seemingly the first time he'd heard what I was saying.

I lay awake in bed still thinking, unable to sleep. Was there still a spark of hope somewhere buried deep under my disappointments? I hoped so. The idea of having the marriage end as my big Catholic family's first divorce was not my dream. The thought of a long, kind, but passionless, childless, static marriage wasn't either. Our roots together had been based on *passion*; how did *his* passion turn into paperwork, meetings, and plans to destroy prairies and mountain tops for a paycheck? Where did his fearlessness go when it came to having a child?

I'd tried for two decades, but I couldn't get past it. Whenever there was a slideshow at one of my fundraisers for an endangered species, I pulled my shoulders in and thought of my own husband working against everything I was working toward. I knew it sounded hippie-dippy to care about the last remaining wild, black-footed ferret, California condor, or red wolf. Still, our efforts to capture the final survivors in the '80s for intensive captive breeding programs had been so rewarding. Those last-ditch efforts to save those species from extinction had worked. I was doing something meaningful for the Earth. I would make my last ditch effort for our marriage too.

The next morning I called the travel agent. "We're looking for unspoiled, remote, and full of natural beauty." I wanted no traffic, no corporate headquarters, no fancy fundraisers, just nature and us. We could take long walks, reconnect, maybe find a way through this, I thought. If not, I'd at least have the privacy to tell Brad that *we* didn't work for me anymore. The last gasp, I booked the flights.

We sat on the plane, I opened my phone, and read more about our destination. The charming place was nestled on the eastern edge of the Cascade Mountains along the Deschutes River, where the Ponderosa Pine forest meets the high desert. Bend, Oregon. That name almost made me smile; we were going to *Bend*.

Being a crossword addict, at heart, I searched the word on my phone—*Bend, verb: to shape or force something straight into a curve or angle.* That would be Brad. *Bend—noun: a curve, especially a sharp one, in a road, river, racecourse, or path.* That would be me about to do a U-Turn at forty into the unknown. A *bend* in a river—exactly the vacation activity I'd planned. Ironic.

The lodge was nearly as far away as we could get from Washington D.C., where we'd spent our entire lives since high school. The travel agent had taken me seriously.

I watched Brad open the brochure to read about the gentle whitewater float trip on the placid river that I'd booked. The photos were breathtaking. He looked at me and smiled. "Looks like fun."

I'd wanted him to see the kinds of places his company's pipeline plans would impact. We had lift-off. *Fun*—it wasn't a word I'd heard Brad use in years. The only activities he'd indulged in were his workouts at the gym, and he'd described them as his *weekly punishment*. A spark of hope—could I excavate the man I once knew? Well, the man I thought I knew.

The mountain scenery on the way to the lodge by rental car was spectacular. I hadn't had time to think about why the mountain range was called the Cascades. The morning sun was glinting off the many waterfalls that washed their way down the rugged, crumpled peaks that rose up out of the carved valleys below.

"Man, this is incredible, Lynn. Good choice."

The scenery wasn't the only stunning thing. I began to relax.

The next morning, we had a hardy breakfast and left the lodge to explore before the whitewater rafting trip. We took a short tour along the river by car. From the road we watched the tributary drifting placidly, carving its way through the colossal Cascades.

I had crazy thoughts at first. Was Brad mapping out how to harness the tumbling water for some power plant in his mind while I was thinking about preserving the marine life? Could this partnership ever work?

"Breathtaking," Brad said. "This was such a good idea. I never think to get out in nature. I get why you're always out biking and walking by the river at home."

We headed to the tour center. After an orientation we were each given a paddle and led to the edge of a pier to the synthetic, eight-man inflatable rubber raft that would take us down the serene river. At the end of our one-hour float we'd be picked up by a van and returned to our car. Even the van ride back would be impressive, the guide told us. "We have a float trip here today, folks." The river guide insisted. "No need for helmets."

It was so calm and sunny—a good time for our new guide to get his feet wet, I overheard the manager say.

New guide? "Wouldn't it be better to be safe rather than sorry? I mean, in terms of helmets? Especially with kids on board." I had great respect for the power of mother nature. I wasn't thrilled with the way the men looked at me like I was a scaredy-cat woman. Or the way they bonded over it with rolling eyes that said, *well, you know women, afraid of everything.*

"I thought you wanted adventure, Lynn? You saw the water yesterday—it's like a bath. We'll be fine. These men know what they're doing."

One breath of fresh air and Brad had graduated to expert outdoorsman, I thought. Now I was beginning not to recognize myself. I was holding a lot of anger inside, I realized.

We shared our raft with a woman and her two nieces, ages ten and twelve.

"Have you ever done this before?" I asked.

"No, we're so excited. My mom wouldn't ever do anything like this with us. Right, Auntie Kirsten?"

The aunt smiled. "Well, your mother isn't comfortable in nature."

We stepped into the raft and took our places to balance the weight. The guide was positioned in the rear; Brad and I were in the middle seat, and the woman and two children took the front.

We were doing it; Brad and I were on vacation, being ourselves for the first time in so long. We would talk about our issues at dinner; right now I wanted to enjoy the day and *us.*

Floating down the sweet river, soft round banks covered in wildflowers on one side and pine and deciduous trees clinging to the other, the little girls were thrilled, and so were we.

Our guide called the instructions, paddle left, then paddle right. The ripples under our raft were just enough to make the girls giggle. "Thousand-foot drop on the left a mile upstream, we'll keep along the right bank. No worries." The guide seemed confident. "We'll float right by the waterfall, then we enjoy the scenery and reach the pick-up point."

I was so happy to see Brad enjoying himself. It melted some of the frost that had solidified around me over the past months. My breathing eased, a familiar peace took over my concerns. My eyes drank it all in: the colors of the wildflowers along the banks, the vibrant sapphire sky, every shade of green in the plants and trees. Yes, this is where I belonged—in the arms of mother nature.

Just around the bend, the world changed. The banks got higher and higher, changing to craggy, carved volcanic rock walls on the side where we were navigating the quiet river.

The sound came before the sight—like the roar of a train rumbling toward us.

Rounding a bend, we were sucked into the agitated water, where a tributary fed the river. Swirls and eddies took over our rubber raft, and the rush of water was threatening.

We were on a treacherous Class IV ride for pros only, my guess was. Whitewater rafting wasn't new to me. I'd gone on many trips with my cousins and my forest ranger uncle when I was a teen. But Class IV, never. That level was for advanced rafters, he'd told us.

The rapids in front of us were intense and powerful. Navigating them would require precise boat handling in the turbulent water. A large swell loomed ahead of us. Two swirling holes were in our path. We were headed through a constricted channel of jagged rocks.

The gushing rapids twisted and spun our raft, sending my heart racing. This was serious. I wanted to grab Brad's arm, and pull him close, but we were commanded to paddle as hard as possible to move through the chaotic waters to reach the calm river ahead. I could barely hear the guide's instructions through the crashing of the rapids against the rocks.

The little girls screamed, shifted, and hugged each other, losing their paddles and throwing the raft even more off balance. The fear was contagious.

"Why didn't we insist on safety equipment?" Brad yelled over the roar to me.

I couldn't deal with the irony of his question.

Glancing across to the other bank, I spotted the official tour photographer running along the opposite bank, snapping the startling pictures of us struggling to paddle. For a second, I pictured our families shuffling the photos in their hands. Were they the last images they would ever see of us?

We needed to focus, paddle, and follow the guide's instructions. No time to think. We plunged over perilous rocks into the crevice of a granite outcropping. The boat bent in half and popped us out like a slingshot into the cold, raging water.

I saw glances of flailing arms and legs before the water engulfed me. A vortex of white foam sucked me down to the silty bottom and crashed the back of my skull onto a rock. The water was only ten feet deep but it was treacherous. As a trained lifeguard, I went on a kind of autopilot, and everything slowed down around me.

I calmed myself, preserved my breath. Submerged, I was tumbled around and around in a vortex. I knew I had only one more chance. Watching for the sunlight above, on my next spin, I thrust off the bottom just as my final breath let go. Surfacing, I pointed my feet downstream while trying to control my sputtering breath.

I couldn't see anyone in our party. Dear God, don't let anyone—no, I wouldn't let myself think of losing anyone. Not Brad, when we had no closure, no time to be together. I hadn't the breath to call out his name. Concentrating on my breathing, like meditating—in, out, in, out—I engaged my right arm as a paddle. With repeated sweeping motions, I was able to get close to the rocky bank of the river.

My eyes searched up the wall formed 500 million years ago from volcanic eruptions. Only a few desperate saplings had taken root in the black rock wall's fractures. I grabbed one; it ripped from its roots and released. In my swift run down the edge of the wall, I was being drawn toward the sound of the drop-off. Grasping and clawing at anything I could along the rock wall, again, and again, my hands streamed red, as the roots shredded through my fingers and gave way.

I tried to call out to Brad, nothing came out of my throat. I had barely enough air to keep me going. No one was in sight, no husband, no children, no guide. The thunder of the drop off ahead caused me to panic. *Oh my God, I can't die like this, alone, dropping a thousand feet over a waterfall and down to the rocky river below. Please, God, no.*

Just before the river took its fatal turn, I seized a small tree that seemed to reach out to me from a crack in the rocks. The force of the rushing river ripped at me, pulling me along the surface parallel to the shore. I held on with everything I had left in me. *Please don't let go. Please!*

I got a foothold under the water on the edge of the sheer bank, wriggled up, and collapsed onto a narrow ledge of craggy rock, still holding the young tree's skinny trunk as it released. It had given its life for me. I actually thought that, as its roots gave way in my grip. I cried and held it to my chest. Still, nothing came out when I screamed for help. I lay there exhausted.

From the cliff above, Brad called out, "Lynn, *Lynny!* Help! Has anyone seen my wife?"

He was alive. My tears exploded with the relief. Still, I lay panting, unable to answer. The girls, the aunt—did they survive? The guide? My shivers calmed, my voice returned, weak at first, then stronger. "I'm down here! Brad!"

His scream echoed down the river. "Lyyyyn! Oh, my God, are you OK?"

Between sobs, I answered. "I think so . . . I hit my head . . . but I can move my neck."

"The rescue boat has the others," Brad yelled down to me. I could hear him, but I couldn't see him. "Hang in there. There was an unexpected ice meltdown above us in the mountains that caused the river to flood."

The second rescue boat came alongside the cliff and pulled me aboard.

Shivering despite the warm day, I experienced a clashing of emotions, waves of simultaneous laughter and sobbing, as I kissed the boat captain and held onto him like a long-lost friend. I was alive; Brad was alive, and the guide, and the kids, and their aunt. It took the entire ride back to the rafting orientation center for my body to relinquish control back to me.

Watching the magnificent scenery on the return trip, I could still hear Brad's voice calling for me from up on the cliff. The desperation in his tone as he called out, Has anyone seen my wife? The ache when he screamed my name made me feel such love for him, such compassion. With me down below without the breath to call to him, I couldn't imagine how he must have felt during those terrifying minutes, thinking I'd fallen over the massive falls.

Standing shoulder to shoulder with the captain, I kept repeating, Dear God, we're alive, we're OK. He'd actually put his arm around me and teared up.

As we came around the bend in the river, I saw Brad waving his arms over his head, yelling my name, Lyyyn! Had I ever felt this grateful, for him, for us? I thought he was going to jump into the water and swim out to us.

"Looks like someone has an admirer." The captain winked as he pulled up to the slip. The rail of the boat barely touched the dock, when I leaped onto the pier.

Brad and I were reunited onshore as if we were starring in a passionate scene from a movie—him limping, me with an injured neck. We were so grateful to have survived.

"Oh my God, Brad, where are you hurt?"

"I hit my tailbone on the rocks, but the guide thinks it's a bruise. And even a coccyx fracture will heal on its own," he said. "Is your neck alright?"

"I heard a crack when it hit the rocks. I'll see. I'm in pain but not too bad."

Back at the Rafting Center, I didn't have to complain about their policy regarding helmets. The aunt was threatening to sue. My body was screaming for food. I just wanted to get out of there and have Brad hold me.

We gathered our things from the lockers they'd provided. I hugged Brad; we couldn't let go. "I can't believe we're alive." I looked into his eyes.

"Hang on a minute, honey." He plucked his cell phone from the locker shelf and made a call.

"Are you kidding?" I waited, incredulous that he would actually make a phone call at that moment—our most poignant moment ever. That was *it*, truly! I turned to walk away.

He took my arm. "Wait honey, I need to call my office. It's critical."

I need to call my divorce lawyer; it's critical, I thought. Brad's action was devastating. Who *was* he? "*A phone* call? *Critical? God, Brad.* Do you see why—"

He wasn't listening. This was the absolute, perfect example. I was too exhausted to even cry. We'd barely caught our breaths or processed what had happened. I rubbed my neck and heard a popping sound. "Are you kidding me?"

He held up his hand, warding off my words. Putting his hand on my shoulder, he kissed my forehead, as if to say give me a minute. "Is Mr. Franklin in?"

Brad was actually smiling. It smothered any hope I'd had. This was what I needed, a definitive answer. His gesture and his conversation with his boss said it all. I was stunned that he would make that call that ended everything between us as it had been.

It's been a year since that disastrous experience changed everything between us. The framed photos sit on my dresser now. From my bed, I scan them each morning—Brad's arms splayed, his head wrenched as he exploded from the raft; my body in mid-flip, mid-air over the raging river, a paddle suspended beside me; a shot of us struggling in the swift, rumbling waters; the aunt and her nieces huddled on a small silty beach around the bend from the massive waterfall; Brad climbing the side of the high bank; my head bobbing alongside the opposite bank, reaching for the sapling that had saved my life. I'd kept the photos there as a reminder of what was important.

I never fail to relive the shock of that phone call; I never fail to shake my head in disbelief. Neither of us ever expected things to end that way.

Brad's bravery had amazed me. Our near-death experience had changed him like a strike of lightning, he'd said. I was speechless he'd quit his job on that call, just like that.

No more compromising his values for any amount of money. No more fear of being like his parents. No more fear of *being* a parent.

Ironic, months later, Brad had been offered a job as an environmental engineer that paid even more. We're on the same team now.

I smiled at Brad's sleeping face beside me and wrapped the receiving blanket tighter around our infant daughter, Canyon. Can you fall in love again from a near-death experience?

We did.

The End

Revision

OUTSIDE, THE GLARING late fall sun lit the bluest of skies. Not a hint of haze. Vibrant amber and russet leaves trapped in a few inches of unexpected snow littered the parking lot below. Stunning scenery my patient would soon no longer see.

I stood by the window across from my examining room, slipped the chart from the rack on the door, and read the results again as though staring at them might change the diagnosis. In my tenure as an eye surgeon, I'd regretted the times I had to say these words, *I'm sorry; there is nothing we can do for you.*

My legs lost strength, and I leaned against the door frame. Straightening my skirt, I grasped the chart to my chest, took a deep breath, and opened the door. "Mrs. Sorenson? I'm Dr. Hernandez." Shutting the door, I didn't miss the metaphor as the latch clicked. A closed door.

I set her chart on the shelf beside her and shook Mrs. Sorenson's hand, aware that mine was moist; hers was not.

"So, nice to meet you, Doctor."

When I'd received her electronic records, a referral from my former professor and mentor, I was stunned. Patient's Name: *Sorenson, Samantha*. Occupation: *Author*. Except for the silver strands that highlighted Mrs. Sorenson's shoulder-length brown hair, and the deepened laugh lines around her eyes, she was so familiar. The petite woman sitting in my examination chair looked the same to me as she had when I'd first met her in my childhood. But she would never recognize me after all these years, especially in her visually impaired state.

She still had the confident calm that had inspired me when I was young. Her captivating children's books had made me passionate about reading. The day she read to my first-grade class at our school library was the day my world opened. My favorite in the *Gloria Becomes* series that sparked my dreams; *Gloria Becomes a Doctor*.

"Can you lean forward and place your forehead against the headrest, please? Good."

She shifted forward and leaned into her destiny. Deep in her eyes, I found the expected disease and, from her condition, confirmed again that she was not a candidate for my corrective surgery.

Four years of college, med school, internships, residencies, a two-year fellowship, a groundbreaking surgical advancement—fourteen years to position me to say that there's nothing we can do. And why do we doctors say *we* when at a loss? Was it to share the responsibility for our helplessness when we had to say those words—nothing *we* can do?

"Mrs. Sorenson, we'll be more comfortable in my office." I guided her across the hall by her elbow, feeling as though I'd personally failed her. I could hear a tremor in her deep breath.

From my leather office chair across from her, I prepared to tell this vital woman in her seventies, my favorite childhood author, that she would soon lose her vision. Samantha Sorenson had inspired my vision into a future that I could never have imagined without hearing the words from the pretty illustrated pages of her books and seeing the young characters she'd created with the same skin color as mine.

As she settled into her chair, I remembered meeting her at my medical school graduation ceremony years after that first-grade reading. The story had made the newspapers, but I had a different last name back then, before my marriage, María Elena Espinoza. Now, sitting across from her, could I acknowledge that I was that scholarship student? I should. I couldn't.

Her hands remained folded in her lap, fingers fidgeting. I could picture her turning the pages when she'd read to us so long ago, her long elegant fingernails, perfectly filed and painted pink. The lilt of her soft, expressive voice still resonated in my memory. She wore the same floral scent that had perfumed the library as she'd read her stories. Stories so real, I believed I could be like Gloria, the immigrant girl from Guatemala. I could be that doctor. And now I am.

As the daughter of Guatemalan parents who cleaned the ocean-front houses lining the shore of Rehoboth Beach, if not for the woman in front of me, I wouldn't be the surgeon whose hands give sight to patients. I wouldn't be the woman who was about to change Samantha Sorenson's world. I could almost taste the painful irony.

"I've reviewed your new test results and examined you, and I'm afraid there is nothing we can do. Surgically, that is."

I shared strategies for compensating for her loss of vision and getting a guide dog for navigating her sightless world. I stood and came around the desk. "I'm so sorry. Please schedule your rehabilitation as soon as possible. The professional staff is excellent here."

"Thank you for your time, Doctor Hernandez. You were so kind to fit me in." Her graciousness in accepting the news drove my own disappointment deeper.

"I'm recently widowed, and alone now, so I'll stay locally with my sister for my rehabilitation at your center."

Dear God, how much loss can one woman take? I didn't know what to say. "I'm . . . so sorry for your loss." I hesitated. I wanted to share my hopeful words about how she could enlist technology, use her laptop with screen reader software, learn Braille, use her other senses, find new channels to create her stories again. But it wasn't my place to talk about her writing career, was it? "I'm sure when you're ready, in time you will find the path to write again." I hadn't meant to overstep.

"It's hard to explain, doctor, but honestly, I tried dictating at my sister's suggestion, you know talk-to-text, but the stories just won't come. I guess I'm not a very auditory person. I edit my books on paper. An old-fashioned process. Deeply ingrained. I'm not sure what technology could draw out my stories after all these years. I'm afraid . . . my writing career has ended."

I observed the change in her countenance as the truth settled in. That dark look, her face clouded by the reality of her fate. The edges of her liquid green eyes closed for several seconds as though she were imagining her future state.

"I don't look forward to dealing with my publicist and the press—

blind author and all." She gazed toward the light from the window and went quiet. "I've heard this diagnosis before. I guess I was hoping for a miracle, Dr. Hernandez."

"Yes, I understand." I dismissed my nurse's offer to walk Mrs. Sorenson to the waiting room to her sister. It was the least I could do.

"Mrs. Sorenson—" I stood straighter. I wanted to tell her my maiden name. Why did I hesitate? Because wasn't this about her right now, not me? Wasn't it too poignant a moment to reminisce? Or was it just too sad to have failed her after all she'd done for me?

"Please call me, Samantha."

How could I call her by her first name? I still remembered her from my childhood perspective as the famous author, and me the Guatemalan girl with few English words. The name, Samantha came clumsily from my mouth. "Samantha, here is my card. If there is anything I can do for you . . . I live right here in town. Please be in touch and let me know how your rehabilitation is progressing."

"Thank you, Doctor." Samantha touched my arm and introduced her sister Alison who stood with her shoulders down, hands clasped in front of her—a slightly younger, carbon copy of Samantha. They both stood in silence. I could almost see the hope drain from their faces. Alison took her sister's arm and squeezed.

I was at a loss; I had to say something to fill the dead space that surrounded us. "By the way, my daughter loves your books; she's read them all until the pages were worn." The image of the author reading to my class flashed again. "You've inspired her, as such a prolific author. She's always scribbling stories in her journal . . ."

I tried to delay their departure. Why? Did I think I would find some way to change the finality of my diagnosis? It was hard for me, as well, to accept that I couldn't save her vision.

"So kind of you to share that, Doctor. It's why I write . . . or used to write."

With matching looks of disappointment, the sisters turned and walked arm-in-arm down the hallway.

My regret weighed down my feet as I walked away. A waft of Samantha's perfume followed me down the hallway to my office where I took off my white cotton coat and fingered the navy embroidered name on the pocket. Stripped of my identity, I left for home in my car.

With everything I did that afternoon, I imagined how I would accomplish the same task in a non-visual way as Samantha. She would need a driver—her sister. I glanced at the clock; she'd need a clock that could speak the time.

I turned down the main street of town, and the ocean drew me, as always. Parking beside the bandstand at the boardwalk, I got out for my daily walk. The intense sun had melted the snow from the surface of the splintered planks. I loosened my scarf and continued to imagine—how do stories come to fiction writers? It was a magical process I didn't understand. I was not a creative free spirit like my husband, a musician, and my daughter, a budding artist and writer.

In my hurry to leave, I'd forgotten my gym bag with my walking shoes. My heels clicked on the boardwalk like the white cane she would use, I thought. Like the sound of the pointing stick against the blackboard tapped to draw my attention in my childhood classroom. Every sound brought me back to school and that day Mrs. Sorenson had first come into my young life. I'd done all I could for her, hadn't I?

The beach was bright with late-day slanted sunshine. Streaks of orange and pink clouds began to block the light over the buildings of the main street turning the plowed piles of snow in the shadows an eerie blue. This emotional state was new to me. I'd always been able to keep my professional and personal lives separate when I'd left work—a skill that allowed me to leave my research and responsibilities behind and bring my *best self* home to my family. But today, I was still drowning in my sadness for Mrs. Sorenson. I stared down at my empty surgeon's hands. My inability to support the woman responsible for my happy life sat like a heavy weight on my chest.

Still needing to think, I drove toward the bay, randomly chose a street that led to the water's edge, and parked. The sun was pressing down on the line of trees across the bay and beams of gold and orange rode the ripples toward me, vibrating along the quiet water. What was this change happening inside me? Such an unfamiliar vulnerability.

My angled view through my car window framed a woman with her head down, sitting in an Adirondack chair facing the muted sunset on a deck behind her house. A second woman stood behind the chair with her hands on the seated woman's shoulders. She leaned down to kiss the top of the woman's head. The scene had a palpable sadness I could feel from across the yard. I had no doubt it was Mrs. Sorenson and her sister. I recognized the color of their clothes and the tenderness of their intimacy.

Had I been subconsciously drawn to the street address I'd seen on her chart? I slumped down and waited in the car, watching.

Wanting to what? Do something? Say something? No, it was wrong to get personally involved with your patients. Or was it a sign? My mother always believed coincidences like this were messages. Was I supposed to help somehow? But what about the patient's privacy? No, I couldn't invade their private moment. The pressure in my chest and the blur of tears threatened my ability to drive. Still, I found myself leaving to see my husband thirty minutes away in Georgetown.

His windowless brick recording studio sat on the outskirts of town. When I pulled open the heavy green door, the melodious music wrapped around me. The glass window to the sound booth gave me a place to observe and listen to the sound of José's band.

José's fingers flickered over the brass buttons of his saxophone. Head down, shoulders folded in, eyes closed, his lithe body moved with his customary cobra allure. His bandmate Juan, head hidden in a hoodie, sent his drum sticks rippling over the snare, his foot working the bass pedal. Red-headed Daren's dark hands hovered above the keyboards, and tall Kenny, with his back to me, swayed his clarinet side to side, then angled the instrument toward the soundproof ceiling, releasing a high note.

I couldn't place the song. They were riffing, playing off one another, spontaneous, signaling one another—let's go this way, or how about this? Yet the song hung together and captivated me—playing my emotions. Just when the ache inside grew to the edge of pain, the song switched up, lifting me with it.

Could I ever forget the first time I saw José in a night club after a class in med school in Philly? His long dark hair swaying with his fluid movements, the hypnotic sounds of his sax; I was sold on the spot.

The recording engineer caught sight of me and called a break. José placed the sax in its stand and came out of the sound booth. "*Mi cielo*, to what do I owe the pleasure? It's been so long since you visited my studio."

The way he dropped everything, tilted toward me, smiled, pulled me close, kissed me and used those formal words—*do I owe the pleasure*. His funny, sweet ways, calling me, *mi cielo*—his heaven, his sky—it's what I needed. I could almost feel his easygoing energy drawing the tension from my body.

"Can we talk?"

"Of course, Lena."

Lena, his special name for me. So informal, so short and to the point, two syllables, a short cut he used to reach me—not my six-beat formal name, *Ma-rí-a E-le-na*. I felt my composure unraveling.

"Something wrong?" He placed his hand on my knee.

"Yes, I guess there is."

We sat on folding chairs in the green room, amid *Rolling Stone* magazines and stained, half-full, white coffee mugs as we talked. The aroma of spicy pizza from a nearby box tempted me—maybe to eat the entire pie, the way I felt. I hadn't eaten since breakfast. Too nervous. A second earthy fragrance lured me even more, José's mother's corn tortillas and frijoles. Such a different palette of color and aromas in contrast to my own workplace scented with cleansers or scentless sterility.

"José. I had a referral today."

"And?"

"A second opinion for a patient to determine if she was a candidate for my new surgery."

"So why the look, my serious one? This is something you often do, no?" He put his hand on my shoulder.

So tender, this musician man of mine. "There's nothing I can do for her. She'll be completely sightless very soon." I stared into José's eyes.

"So, you are sad? Your inability to help?"

"Privacy. Ethics. It's not my place to get personally involved. Well, beyond my diagnosis or anything surgically I can do."

"And so?"

"Is it so wrong to break the protocols? I want to do more, be involved in her recovery, help her to . . . I don't know what I want." I blurted the question that had haunted me all day. "I mean, is it such a terrible breach to support her in some way? To help her find hope—a way to write again?"

"*Mi amor*, you are asking the wrong person. My *job* is to break the rules. That's jazz." He laughed. "My only restrictions are those five lines." He pointed to the sheet music beside him in a chair. "Throwing little black notes against those lines in unexpected ways. My forte is outside the box—yours is staying in the lines, Lena. That's why we're so good together." His broad smile made me relax a bit.

"Makes my work sound so rigid, José."

"Not rigid. Dedicated. Your precision gives sight. Not a bad gig."

"Yes, but *this* woman."

"And who is this woman?

"Samantha Sorenson. You remember?"

"Your scholarship? *That* Sorenson? Baby, now I see." He put his arm around me.

"And she *can't* see. She says she can never write again." I was quiet. There was nothing left I wanted to say. I stood to leave, bent over and kissed his shiny black hair. "Thank you, darling. See you at home."

"Wait." José blocked my exit. "So, your principles say you can't cross the boundary into her private life, right?"

"Yes, it would be unprofessional. I've already encroached, watching her today like some spy. Some strange pull inside drew me to park on that street, two streets over from my usual spot. Her address from her chart must have registered in my mind somehow. I went to watch the sunset and there she was on the deck of her sister's house, her sister consoling her. I feel so helpless. I don't know what's happening to me."

"You're being *you*—caring."

"Our life is our life because of her. I have *you* because of her, and the name of our daughter too because of the character she wrote. I would never have been at the university, never walked into that club on the night when I met you if it wasn't for her. You see? Everything leads back to her and her voice on that day in the school library."

"But, Lena, you made good on that scholarship."

"I was never in touch after graduation, beyond my thank you. How could it be Samantha Sorenson ends up in my office, and me unable to return the favor? You know what my mother would say if she were alive, José."

"A message—follow." I watched José's eyes cast a far-off look. "Everything leads back to that voice . . . that's what you said, Lena. So, who says I can't do something for her?" He stood and paced with his hands locked behind him.

"*You?*"

"When you were first inspired, it was not through reading her stories in a book, it was through her *voice*, right? Imagine thousands of children hearing that voice reading her dozens and dozens of stories."

José shared an idea about audiobook recordings. It made me want to cry—it was so simple, yet brilliant, it lit my smile—my first of the day. "But she says she's not auditory, new stories won't come through speaking. She still uses pen and paper. She says her career has ended."

"Yes, but what about the books she has already written? Perhaps she has not lost her vision in a manner of speaking. It works this way."

José positioned me on a stool in the recording room and put headphones on me. "Someone in the studio reads her story into the mic, 'Once upon a time . . .' Mrs. Sorenson then speaks the same words on a delay, and we record and edit the story in her voice."

Audiobooks. José's idea inhabited my mind for the entire week. How many children out there were unable to read her books, but Samantha could still captivate them with her words, as she had me, couldn't she? Isn't that the point for a writer—to reach, to inspire, to charm?

On Friday, as I left the hospital, I checked Samantha's record to see if she had begun her rehabilitation. She had not yet made contact. I could justify making my usual follow-up call. Samantha's sister answered. "Alison, this is Dr. Hernandez calling to check in on Samantha."

"Doctor, so strange, I was just about to call you. You did encourage us to be in touch. Am I overstepping to be the one to call?

Actually, if my sister knew I was talking to you, she'd be upset. Behind her back and all . . ."

"How can I help?"

"I've never seen her so hopeless. She won't leave the house. She's usually so vibrant, upbeat. Anyway, I just wanted your advice. Is this common, is there something I can do for her?"

"Alison, I do have an idea that might be of interest to her." There, it was out.

"I'd be so grateful. My sister seemed comfortable with you. Would you be willing to break the rules and make a house call? Encourage her in some way? I know it's not the way things are done, but . . ."

The thunder in my chest nearly blocked out her words. I managed to squeeze my response through my tight throat. "Of course." My mother's words invaded. *You see? A message.* I couldn't breathe. There are no coincidences, my mother had always insisted.

"Does eleven tomorrow morning work? I can grocery shop and give you the privacy to talk with my sister."

"Of course, I will see you then."

"Oh, and I don't want her to know I was behind your visit. Perhaps we can, I don't know, make it seem coincidental. How about you bring your daughter to get her books signed? Samantha did promise that. I'll just say I invited you. We happened to meet in town."

"That would be lovely. Gloria will be so excited."

I couldn't believe I had the opening to present José's idea. Stopping off at his studio to share the news and get more details about the recording process, I could feel my mother smiling down on me. Still, my professional self was tapping her foot and scolding me. Wasn't it a kind of deception? But then, Alison had asked *me*.

When I arrived home, I found my twelve-year-old daughter Gloria in her bedroom, sketching in her art journal at her desk, headphones on, wearing shredded jeans. I swear if one more thread broke the pant legs would fall off.

"I know, Mama, you worked so hard to give me a proper life, and I wear the clothes of a homeless girl."

Our daughter. Like looking in the mirror—my long black hair, my brown eyes, my petite body—but definitely José's "be-your-own-free-self" spunk. She laughed, jumped up and hugged me. "Did I read your mind correctly?"

"As always." I wish I were as expansive and spontaneous as my daughter and husband.

"Were you working late?"

"No, I went to see your Papá to talk about my new patient I had earlier this week."

"Papá? Why Papá?" Gloria came to attention.

"I have a very special patient. She is going blind. There's nothing I can do for her." I slumped down on Gloria's bed.

"Sorry, Mamá."

Glancing at the dog-eared book that was propped in the center of the bookcase, I picked it up. "Remember this—*Gloria Becomes a Doctor?*"

"Of course. That's how you named me."

"My patient is Samantha Sorenson."

"The *author?*"

I'd never confided in my child before about a patient. I justified it; articles were already in the newspapers. "She says she can never write again."

"Why not? She's the best storyteller. I've read all her books a thousand times."

I explained her father's idea to Gloria. "I'm going to visit her tomorrow to see how she feels about the idea of audiobooks for her *Gloria Becomes* series."

"What a cool idea. Can I come and meet her, please, Mamá? Please?"

Alison was right, having Gloria along might just ease the conversation, I thought. "Yes, you can come. Bring a few books, maybe. She offered to sign them."

"Yes, that will cheer her up, Mamá."

Was it right to get my daughter involved? I didn't know but it seemed I was meant to break the rules, like José and his jazz, going with the flow. Not something I did easily. But this was a different me. I was discovering a whole new side of myself, and I wanted to reveal who I was to Samantha. I wanted to stop feeling so responsible for being unable to reverse her tragic situation. It felt so odd calling her by her first name without her knowing mine. I couldn't believe I'd agreed with Alison's pretense to say how I'd come to visit. I was sinking in deeper.

On Saturday morning, Gloria and I set out to visit Samantha. I was quiet; Gloria was chattering with excitement. When we arrived, Samantha was sitting alone on the sunny deck snuggled in a cream-colored blanket. I parked and went to the front door. Alison was waiting.

"Thank you so much for coming. I'll just say I ran into you and invited you to visit."

"I hope Samantha doesn't mind that Gloria came along."

"Of course not, so nice to meet you, Gloria. I think it might help my sister to meet a loyal fan. So, let's go."

We walked through the house and exited onto the deck overlooking the water.

"Sam, you won't believe who I saw in town. Dr. Hernandez and her daughter."

I cringed at Alison's lie.

Samantha turned her head and smiled. "What a surprise. How lovely of you to come."

What had I expected? This was no line of demarcation, no warzone I was entering. Just a brilliant author who deserved my honesty. "Samantha, I'm with my daughter Gloria. She's twelve and a big fan of yours for years now."

"Gloria?"

"Mom named me for your character from your *Gloria Becomes* series." As always, Gloria dove right in. "The book you signed for my mom. We keep it on my bookcase."

"I signed a book for your mother? I'm confused."

"Yes. I've read all of your stories, a hundred times. Maybe a thousand. They're all dog-eared."

My fearless daughter.

I was touched by the passion in her voice. I turned away not bearing to see Samantha's tears stream from her darkened eyes, then turned back. "Samantha, I am María Elena Espinoza . . . my married name is Hernandez."

"Espinoza? My scholarship? What a surprise." She wiped her

eyes and gathered herself. "How lovely to see you again, well, at least in shadow. Why didn't you tell me?"

"To be honest, I didn't want to be the one to deliver such news to the woman who'd made my career possible." My voice cracked.

"Oh, María Elena, you didn't cause my blindness. You did your best. And I'm ever so proud of your accomplishments." The cloudy dark look descended on Samantha's face, again.

I paced along the railing of the deck and watched the sun flashing on the bay. Gloria's voice became a mere whisper behind me.

"I love to make up stories. I want to be a writer like you. I can't wait for your next book."

"I'm not sure I'll be writing any more stories, dear."

"But why not? Oh, how about a story about a girl who became blind and wanted to be a writer? Kind of like you and me mixed. Please, can you write that story?"

I gave Gloria a look of warning; it was too soon to bring up the future and writing new books. Samantha had barely had time to adjust to her fate. I shouldn't have shared Samantha's belief that she couldn't write again with Gloria. But, as always, my daughter's thoughts erupted from her mouth unfiltered.

"Think how many kids can't read your books!"

"What do you mean, Gloria?"

"Like blind kids. Oh, and kids who have learned to speak English but haven't learned to read yet. Like, my mom was—just new from Guatemala. Your stories made her want to be a doctor."

I found my opportunity. "Samantha, if you hadn't read to me that day, truly I might never have fallen in love with books, become a doctor, given children sight, met my husband, had Gloria. My entire life inspired from one reading. Sounds dramatic, I know.

But it's true. Your voice to my ears. I couldn't have read your story myself back then with my limited English."

Samantha stared out over the bay at something I couldn't see.

"I hope you don't mind, but my husband, José, has an idea you might be interested in. You met him at my med school graduation . . . his quartet played."

"An idea?" She straightened in her chair.

"I went to see him after I gave you the diagnosis. I was . . . deeply disappointed that I had to say those dreadful words to you—there's nothing we can do."

"I'm not sure I understand."

"José has a recording studio. He offered to record your stories. We could start with the *Gloria Becomes* series."

"You mean audiobooks? I don't think I'm a very audio author, and it's all so complicated now."

"I understand."

"And how would I read them?" She leaned forward in her chair, and put her face in her hands, gazing down at the rough, splintered planks through her splayed fingers.

Why did I intrude? I feared the response that was about to come. What was she feeling? An invasion of her privacy? The pressure to perform? Offended by my daughter's unbridled enthusiasm? Oh, I hoped not. I had so wanted to help, not to upset her; my daughter had meant well too.

"Gloria, maybe you could let Mrs. Sorenson and I chat a bit."

Samantha turned toward Gloria. "Thank you, dear. If you bring me your books later, I'll autograph them for you."

"Really? I'm so excited." Gloria skipped down the steps and walked out onto the dock.

I sat next to Samantha. "I know you can't imagine your life without writing, Samantha, and you are mourning for the loss of your gift. That's natural." I hesitated, then it spilled out. "Maybe your voice can take over for your eyes—a kind of re-*vision* of your career."

The pain in her long pause was palpable. I pushed on. "You'll wear headphones in the studio. Someone can read your books to you, line by line—I will. You'll repeat with your wonderful voice and inflection. And José will record, edit and produce them for you. He says he will compose new music for the background, too."

"Oh, I don't know . . ."

He's quite a talented composer." As I tried to convince her, I convinced myself. I was as passionate as my daughter. "Imagine children everywhere listening to your stories. Being inspired by your voice, like I was."

Samantha sighed and went silent, still folded over in her chair.

I waited. The only sound was the bay water, marking time, rolling and sizzling onto the shore. Then, I spoke, "Samantha."

No answer. She wasn't ready to hear my words. "Such losses, first my husband and now . . . I'm sorry, I can't seem to shake this solitary feeling." Samantha kept her head in her hands. "Like a detachment I've never felt before. Is that common with your patients who lose their sight?"

Before I could answer, she turned and looked up at me. "You understand, I've always found myself in my writing, found my joy in my stories. So now, where do I go to find . . . *me?*"

As the winter passed, I also experienced a detachment like I'd never felt. Each time I gave sight to a patient and witnessed their amazement and shared the emotions of their families, I lamented that I would never unwrap the post-surgical bandages to see that light in Samantha's eyes or the joy in her sister's face. That was a fantasy that would never happen. I tried to accept that. But I couldn't let go of the memory of that day at Samantha's house and José's idea to record her stories. The hopeless look on the face of the woman who'd given me the chance to live this fulfilling life still haunted me.

Each time I saw an article about her in the papers, I held my breath mourning her tragic story, her career ended. I visualized the change in the newspaper headlines—"Blind Author Revives Career with Audiobooks." I imagined Samantha sitting in the studio, her warm voice sharing her stories to inspire yet another wide-eyed child. I fantasized Samantha playing her recordings at the local library with her guide dog by her side.

Each time I looked out the window at the dreary winter clouds and the brown slush in the parking lot and grasped a patient's chart before entering my examining room, a heaviness descended. I had to breathe and search for that satisfaction I used to feel, gather up my gratitude for the skills I had to help my patients.

The few times I checked Samantha's records, she hadn't scheduled any rehabilitation. But I'd had my chance; I had to respect her wishes. At home, there was an unspoken agreement not to bring the subject up. We all shared in the disappointment.

On the first mild spring day, I took to the boardwalk for my daily visit to the soothing ocean. The warm welcome of spring sun had drawn dozens of locals out of hibernation. With happy, lilting voices, they passed me with ice cream cones and beach fries in hand, resuming their annual rituals as the bitter season unfolded into summer.

There on a white wooden bench sat Samantha and her sister. Not surprising in a small beach town.

I cast my eyes aside.

"Dr. Hernandez, so good to see you. Please, can you sit for a minute?" Alison waved me over, shifted, patted the bench beside her, and nodded toward her sister with a pleading look. "Would you believe we were just talking about you?"

"Hello, Alison, Samantha." I settled in between them.

"How is Gloria? Dr. Hernandez, I apologize—I never did sign her books for her."

"I think you can call me María Elena now, Samantha. She's doing very well, getting ready to publish her school newspaper."

Samantha took a slow deep breath and released it. "I'd like to try out your idea. I've made contractual arrangements with my publisher. She sees the benefit in it for all parties concerned. Well, those were her words."

Was this my mother's handiwork? I smiled and closed my eyes with gratitude.

Samantha touched my arm. "I don't know if I can, but honestly, it can't be that hard to repeat the lines. Maybe I can get some press that doesn't portray me as the author who'd *slipped into her darkness and hasn't written since*, as they wrote in the *New York Times*. Does the offer still stand?"

I smiled at Gloria through the glass window in the studio as I sat next to Samantha and read the first line of the *Gloria Becomes* Series. Samantha's voice echoed my words into her mic. Had anything in my career been more gratifying?

On the second line, she stammered.

"Let's record that line again," José called through the speaker from the sound booth.

Again, Samantha stumbled.

"And again, please." José's voice was patient.

I reread the line and touched Samantha's shoulder in support.

She repeated smoothly, then missed the next line.

The studio door opened.

Gloria entered and sat cross-legged in front of Samantha, stroked her alert guide dog, and silently mouthed, "Sorry."

"Who's that, please?"

"Mrs. Sorenson, it's me, Gloria. I thought maybe you needed a kid to tell the story to. That's how you do it. Right, Mrs. Sorenson? Like when you read to my mom when she was little?"

Samantha paused, turned her head in the direction of Gloria's voice, reached down, searched with her hand for my daughter's head, and touched her. "Thank you, sweetheart. What a good idea."

I could hear the tension leave Samantha's voice, as she flawlessly repeated line after line. We worked for hours, ate, and worked more, and the readings went well.

Repeating the process for the entire weekend, Gloria's loyal guide dog lay beside us as we worked. When the last line of the last book of the *Gloria Becomes* series ended, we both put our heads back, sighed together, and laughed.

"So, it comes full circle, María Elena." She turned and smiled in my direction.

"Full circle?"

"*Your* voice to *my* ears. Isn't that what you said to me about the first time I read to you in that little library?"

I released the breath I was holding and freed my tears. "My pleasure, Samantha, truly."

She squeezed my hand.

José began editing the final recording while Samantha sat, wearing her headphones around her neck, chatting with Gloria.

I remained on the stool next to Samantha, enjoying her success and pondering my mother's belief in following your intuition—the *messages*.

Samantha put her headphone on and waved. "José, I have a story I'd like to add."

"Of course, do you have the script?" He spoke through the mic.

"No." Samantha laughed. "For this one, I don't think I need a script." She kicked off her shoes, and buried her feet under her guide dog's thick fur. "Gloria, I sense you're still here?"

"Yup, I'm right here petting your pup."

"From my voice to your ears." Samantha smiled and took my hand. Leaning into the mic, Samantha started to tell a story I'd never heard.

"My name is Gloria. I live in a poor hillside village called San José Calderas in Guatemala . . . and I'm blind. And this is my story."

The End

Printed in the USA
CPSIA information can be obtained
at www.ICGtesting.com
JSHW020342180923
48380JS00004B/156